The Sword of Tecumseh

coffeetownpress

For more information go to: www.coffeetownpress.com
www.mcarrollauthor.com

Cover design by Aubrey White

The Sword of Tecumseh
Copyright © 2019 by M.D. Carroll

ISBN: 978-1-60381-731-8 (Trade Paper)
ISBN: 978-1-60381-732-5 (eBook)

Library of Congress Control Number: 2018958012

Printed in the United States of America

The Sword of Tecumseh

A Logan Wells Mystery

M.D. Carroll

coffeetownpress

Kenmore, WA

Chapter 1

I was drinking coffee and leaning on the bar in the Lincoln Tavern, waiting for Buzz to show up. Buzz being James Buster Wildrick, attorney at law and my best friend for coming on forty years. He would introduce himself to strangers as Jim; at the courthouse, right across the street, many of the staff referred to him as JB. To most who had known him since childhood, he was known only as Buzz, a family nickname derived from a shortening of his middle name. Buzz was late, the coffee was bad, and I was starting to get a headache. Plus, it was a dreary November evening, with sleet off and on since morning. Looked like it was going to be another bleak winter. Consequently, I wasn't in an upbeat mood. There was an old John Wayne western on the small black and white TV behind the bar, so that was something.

Local history had Abraham Lincoln, in the late fall of 1859, traveling to Northwest Indiana to meet with the principals of the Chicago Cincinnati Railroad Company. The purpose of said meeting was to discuss legal matters pertaining to the extension of rail service from Prairie Stop, Indiana, to Chicago. The story was that Lincoln also secretly met with a group of prominent civic and business leaders concerning the future of slavery, as well as his political prospects, the two issues turning out to be inextricably linked. According to the tale, the second meeting took place on the spot where the tavern now stood, hence the name. On the back wall, in one of the booths, there was a small engraved brass plaque, which proudly proclaimed "Abraham Lincoln dined here, November 20, 1859", below which someone had written, "and there still aren't any towels in the men's room." The date on my watch read November 20, 1989, so assuming the plaque and my math was accurate, in five days we would hit the 130th anniversary of men leaving the bathroom with damp hands.

The accuracy of the Lincoln story had been debated, sometimes animatedly, but there was no purpose served getting upset because Buzz was late. It was his way. Having spent most of his life in the same small town, being one of its most prominent citizens, a high school football star who continued on to greater heights, Buzz couldn't walk down the street without being recognized and greeted by, well, just about everybody. And, being who he was, he couldn't let go with just a quick howdy and handshake. He had to ask about Aunt Bertha, and Cousin Earl, and whatever happened with that bypass surgery, or I heard your son was going to Purdue. He had an amazing memory for people; names, faces, sons, daughters, and the places and events connected with those people. Peculiar, because he was lousy remembering other stuff. He claimed he had left suits at the dry cleaners so long that when he got them back they had gone out of and back into style. As if on cue, my thoughts were interrupted by a forceful clap on the back, the impact of which caused me to spit a mouthful of the toxic coffee all over the bar.

"I ask you, would there be a better place to be on a beautiful fall day than Prairie Stop, Indiana?"

I turned, and Buzz reached out to shake my hand.

"The eternal optimist." I said, turning back to mop up the coffee with a napkin.

"What's to be pessimistic about? The Fighting Irish are undefeated with only one game left."

"In case you hadn't noticed, its forty degrees out and sleeting." I said, looking at him closer. "Last time I saw you, you had a beard."

"Partners didn't like it. Said it made me look cheesy, so it had to go."

Buzz looked like what he was, a former elite athlete gone slightly to seed. He was 30 pounds plus heavier than when he was a second team All-American defensive back at Notre Dame, but at 6'3" there was not much of paunch. His straw blond hair had whitened and receded over the years, but he now wore it longer in the back so that it curled around his ears and over his collar. The once chiseled face was lined and sagged a bit in places, but even at just north of forty there was still, at least occasionally, the same mischievous glint in his eyes he had at sixteen.

"You look like you got some sun," he said, looking at me.

"I've been spending a lot of time outdoors. I decided to go into the home improvement business."

"Makes sense … the original man with three thumbs. What was that thing you built in shop? Nobody knew whether it was an ashtray or birdhouse. For

I forget, thanks for coming down here. I may have something more up your alley than construction."

"Yeah? Raking leaves out at Wildrick Manor?"

"Nah, I got guys to do that. They're all illegals from Mexico, so I only pay them pocket change."

"You're a regular Rockefeller. Ok, I'll bite, what do you have for me?"

"Let's say it's an important investigative matter. I'll give you the details after I get a drink."

Buzz looked around the mainly empty room to see if anyone he knew was there. There was a group at a table in the back, who I guessed, from their dark suits, animated gestures, loud conversation and laughter, were attorneys. Due to its location, the Lincoln was a popular hangout for lawyers. Buzz raised his hand in their general direction and one of them raised his glass in a salute back. Whatever was in the glass spilled out onto the guy next to him and there was a startled "hey!" followed by more raucous laughter.

"How are the twins?" I asked. Buzz had twin teenage girls, who I seemed to recall were in college.

"Ok. They ought to be. I'm shelling out near fifty grand in tuition a year."

"Damn … I never even made that much in a year," I said.

He glanced down the bar and motioned to the bartender. She had looked up startled when I lost the mouthful of coffee.

Buzz eyed my cup. "Don't tell me that's just coffee you're drinking. Last time I had just coffee in this place, I had the runs for three days."

"Thanks for the warning. I just polished off my fourth cup. And it was an ash tray for birds. In shop, I mean."

"What kind of birds?" Buzz asked, taking the bait.

"Larks."

"I should have seen that coming. My mom used to smoke Larks."

"I remember," I said. "Your house smelled like a cigar factory for days after she had one of her card parties."

Buzz looked over at the bartender, who was now standing and smiling across from us. She was blonde, attractive, and about thirty I guessed. Large violet eyes which I hadn't noticed when I ordered the coffee. I'm surprised I didn't recognize her, since I had spent a lot of time in the Lincoln back in my drinking days.

"Pam," Buzz said, who returned her smile. "First, do you know this guy?" gesturing toward me.

"No. He came in and ordered coffee and has been quiet ever since." She said, looking at me. "Not that I mind quiet."

"This here is one of my oldest, bestest buddies, Logan Wells. We go way back, and I do mean way back. Logan, meet Pam, the finest bartender the old Lincoln has ever had. And I should know. I was here when the Great Emancipator threw the first drunk out."

I had an image of Abraham Lincoln tossing someone through a plate glass window, as I recalled how Buzz and I met thirty years ago.

My family had moved to Indiana from western New York, my father landing a job building the steel mills that were then going up like cornfields along the shores of Lake Michigan. My father, like his father, was an ironworker by trade and part Indian by blood, Mohawk of the Iroquois Nation specifically. My grandfather worked with the ironworkers who built the skyscrapers of New York City. The Mohawk workers were always at the highest point of the structures, stepping easily from girder to girder, no safety lines, where a single misstep meant sudden death. Which recalled my dad's oft quoted definition of an optimist: someone who fell off the top of a fifty-story building and cheerfully proclaimed "alright so far" as he went by each floor.

My folks built a house in Prairie Stop, a small county seat an hour east of Chicago. There wasn't a whole lot to the place back then. It was a sleepy town of about fifteen thousand, with the county courthouse and the university being the main centers of activity. The steel mills changed that. The steelworkers, engineers and managers wanted to live away from the soot, grime and noise of the mills. They made good money, and there weren't enough decent places to buy, Gary and some of the other cities along the lake were by then beginning their freefall into urban decay. The steelworkers flooded to Prairie Stop, where new subdivisions sprang up seemingly overnight. It was 1960, a new decade, a new President, and a new energy and sense of purpose.

Our house was the first one on our street, cornfields behind us and on one side. Buzz's house was the last on the existing road that connected to ours. Although I was only eight, I vividly recall standing out in the dirt that was my backyard, wondering what to make of my new home, when Buzz emerged, barefoot and shirtless, from the high corn behind our house. He walked slowly over to me, then around me, as if to size me up. Then he stuck his hand out and said,

"You must be the new kid. I'm James Buster Wildrick, but everybody calls me Buzz." Then he paused and added, "I think you and me are going to be best friends."

Buzz elbowed me in the stomach. "Say something, would you? You're scaring me."

"Nice to meet you, Pam," I said. "You been working here long?"

"About a year," she replied.

"That explains it. I haven't been in here for a while."

"Logan here has been out of commission," Buzz said. "Got hit by a bus last winter and spent six months in the hospital, three of them in a coma. Barely made it." He was exaggerating, but not by much.

"It was a Buick, two months in the hospital, and only a week in a coma." I rubbed my temple.

"How awful. What happened?"

"Line of duty accident." Buzz said, before I could answer. "Remember the Thanksgiving blizzard last year?"

"How could I forget?" Pam said, shaking her head. "I had just moved here from Florida. It was horrendous. I was thinking at the time I had made a big mistake."

"Lake effect snow. One disadvantage of living fifteen miles away from the southernmost point of Lake Michigan. Better get used to it. Anyhow, Logan was coming back from a crime scene. He stopped to help a woman who had slid off the road up near Stone Lake. Eighty-year-old guy driving home after his weekly poker game plows right into him."

He paused and looked at the bottles lined up across the bar.

"Bring the monsignor here a shot of Bushmills for that stuff you call coffee. I'll take a shot too and a draft. Hamm's if you got it."

"No Hamm's. Bud, Bud Light and Old Style on draft," Pam replied.

"I should know that. Jack Brickhouse would be shitting a brick. No pun intended. Although come to think of it, I bet he was a Cutty and water man. I'll take Old Style."

"Nothing for me." I said, raising my hand, as she was turning to get the drinks, and she paused.

Buzz waved her off.

"Bring it. I'm not drinking alone."

"Think you're better than me, or just on the wagon?" he asked after she left.

"Both, but mainly doctor's orders. He seemed to think it wouldn't aid my recovery. Imagine that."

"Good thing I go to a different doctor than you. Not sure I could make it through a day without a couple."

Pam placed the drinks on the bar. "So, how bad was it?"

"A couple of broken legs, torn up knees, assorted internal injuries, including a lacerated spleen, and a concussion," I said. "Apparently the only reason I survived was that my head landed up in the snow. The cold slowed the swelling in my brain until the ambulance showed up. Which was a while cause of the snow. Not sure if that would be ironic, or just a coincidence."

"So, you're a policeman?" Pam asked.

"No. Used to be. I am, or was, a special investigator for the Prairie County Prosecutor's office."

"And that's another thing," Buzz interjected, after draining his whiskey with one gulp. "Logan can't go back to the Prosecutor's Office because he can barely get around. Plus, he gets these bad headaches and has trouble remembering stuff. Fills his drawers when the phone rings, for all I know. But the pompous asses on the county pension board, most of them friends of mine, incidentally, say he doesn't qualify for a full disability pension on account of it wasn't a line of duty accident. They are going to stiff him for half. I threatened to sue them."

"Retrograde amnesia," I interjected.

"What was that?" Buzz asked, annoyed that I interrupted his story.

"You said I had trouble remembering stuff. That's not exactly true. For example, when you walked in here, you slapped me on the back and told me what a nice day it was. So, my short-term memory is ok. The problem I got is called retrograde amnesia. I have trouble remembering stuff that happened before the accident. It's not uncommon with concussions, even minor ones. In my case, the last couple years before the accident are hazy. Not gone, just hazy."

"How do you mean, hazy? Pam asked.

"Well, the other day I was out somewhere, and a guy comes up to me, says hello, mentions a case we apparently had worked on together, I'm guessing a couple years ago. His face looked familiar, but I couldn't come up with his name or what he was talking about. He must have thought I was nuts."

"He would have been right," Buzz said.

Pam gave him a scowl. "Other than that, how are you?"

"All things considered, not bad. The pain is less each day."

"Can I go on with my story now? Buzz asked.

We both looked at him.

"If you have to," I said.

"Ok, where was I?"

"Funny," Pam and I said at the same time. "So, anyhow, I cited so many legal precedents that their heads were spinning, but Logan here rolls over, right as I had them on ropes. Truly mind-boggling."

"I needed the money, paltry as it was," I said. "I wasn't a beat cop, and off duty besides, so technically stopping to aid and assist wasn't in my job description."

The memory of pointless meetings with smug, self-righteous bureaucrats determined to nickel and dime me to death made my head throb even more. It wasn't so much their determination to screw me over … that I could understand. I'm sure they thought it was their civic duty to guard the county coffers and that I shouldn't take it personal. It was hard not to, though. One of the board members was a steel workers union official who had worked with my dad for twenty-five years. I think they even bowled together. He called me aside before the first meeting and told me he was going to make sure I was taken care of. I found out later he was the one who didn't want to "set a bad precedent" with me and swayed the others to a lower amount.

"And the old guy's insurance company wasn't exactly helpful. You know that commercial about the good-hands people? They gave Logan one finger. I was going to sue them and the old guy along with the board, but he dropped that one too."

"I wasn't going to take his house, if that's what you mean." The pounding in my temples was getting worse.

"The man with million-dollar ethics and zero in the bank. You need to think of your future."

"A lawyer's perspective. Anyhow, I heard they're looking for stock boys over at Lujack's."

"Lujack sold out years ago. It's Foodchopper now," Buzz said.

"See, I can't even remember Lujack's changed hands."

With that, I gave in and drained the shot. The familiar heat going down my throat immediately made me feel better.

"I guess you are going to tell me, sooner or later, why you wanted to see me," I said, after the warmth subsided.

A couple had come in and Pam walked to the other end of the bar to take their order.

I thought Buzz was going to continue about my lack of prospects, but instead he reached in his jacket pocket, pulled out a newspaper clipping and handed it to me.

"You familiar with this?"

I stared hard at the article and picture for a minute, and then remembered seeing it in the Prairie Stop Messenger a week or so ago.

"The missing BHU college professor?" I asked.

"Good to see you're keeping up on with local current events. Although the biggest story I can remember growing up here was something along the lines of 'Mr. and Mrs. Smith drove up to Westville this past weekend.'"

"I remember that. It was big. They stopped in Kouts for gas."

"I tell you, my friend, the only thing worse than an ignorant populace is an illiterate one."

"Make that up yourself?" I asked. Buzz wasn't given to making profound statements.

"Either Mark Twain or Winston Churchill said it. I think between them they said just about everything."

"I take it he hasn't turned up yet."

"No. My feeling is maybe he isn't going to," Buzz replied.

I glanced at the article. I was surprised that I recalled a good part of it. Twelve days ago, Jason Matthews, a professor of American history at Benjamin Harrison University, taught his final class of the week, got into his Mercedes, drove off the campus, and was never seen again. He wasn't missed right away, because his wife, coincidentally also a university professor, of law, was out of town, and apparently not too concerned she couldn't reach him. When she came back and found him not there, she immediately contacted the police. According to the article, the authorities had made little progress in finding out what happened to Matthews, but "hadn't ruled out foul play."

I pushed the article back to Buzz. The rush of the whiskey had muffled the throbbing in my head.

"I bet they find he ran off with one of his students," I said. "Probably the one who wore the tight sweaters. Either a football player or pom-pom girl."

"Perhaps you aren't far off the mark. From what I understand, he may have been a little too friendly with one of the student bodies." As Buzz said that, he motioned for two more shots. I didn't protest this time, although I knew I would regret it later.

"Yep, sounds like mid-life crisis, I said. "Remember that gym teacher we had that ran off with the cheerleader? McMasters?"

"That was him. If there was a hall of fame for dipshits, he would be first ballot material."

"I couldn't stand that guy," I said, looking at Pam, who had walked back to our end of the bar.

Buzz laughed. "He thought it was funny to make everybody jump off the high dive the first day of freshman swimming. The funny part was including the guys who couldn't swim. I remember you acting real scared climbing up the ladder. Then you went right to the bottom and stayed there. So, McMasters panicked and dove in to save you. When he found out you could swim like a fish, he wanted to kill you. I still laugh when I think of that."

"Maybe him taking off was his way appreciating a good practical joke." I said. I couldn't have been happier when the gym teacher and aging Lothario disappeared. After my stunt in the pool, he did his best to make life difficult for me. I used to dread days with gym class.

"The girl came back in a few days, not much worse for wear. She claimed he never laid a hand on her. On the other hand, he was never seen in these parts again. Statutory sodomy, even if just alleged, will do that to a fellow," Buzz said.

"How old was the professor?" I asked.

"Around fifty, I think," Buzz replied, then drained what remained of his beer.

"There you go. Some just buy a sports car when they feel time slipping away. Other guys get an eighteen-year-old girlfriend."

"No, this one's a little bit older than that. Working and going to school part time, from what I understand. In any case, she's still around, which lets the air out of that theory."

"Maybe she wanted more than an "A" on her history paper, and he panicked and split. Maybe the wife found out about the girlfriend and put anti-freeze in his coffee."

"Our local constabulary checked that out." Buzz replied. "The wife was in Chicago most of the week. Didn't get back until almost two days after Matthews was seen last. The girlfriend doesn't seem to know anything about what happened to him. By the way, that Matthews had a girlfriend isn't common knowledge. At least it hasn't made the papers yet."

"So, what's your interest in this?" I asked. "I'm not surprised you are getting confidential information about an ongoing investigation, seeing as how everybody in this town would fall all over themselves to do you a favor."

"I shouldn't have said that last part. It's not really confidential—they are just trying to spare Jackie a little embarrassment."

"Jackie?"

"Jacqueline Matthews. The wife. I know her through the local bar association. Worked with her on a pro-bono thing a while back. She knows I used to be an assistant DA and asked if I had any advice for getting the heat turned up on finding her husband. Apparently, she didn't feel like she was getting a whole lot from Bill Hanlen." Hanlen was the long-time sheriff of Prairie County, and a close friend of Buzz.

"Well, no offense to Hanlen," I said, "but she may be on to something. I'm not sure locating a missing person would be right up his alley, unless he or she was hiding behind the counter at Vic's Diner."

"No need to be sarcastic. I hate to admit it, but you got a point. Bill's men handle a few homicides a year, if that, and most of the missing person reports they get are kids running away from home. The state guys have more experience, but they're going to steer clear of this until Bill begs them to come in. I don't think he is quite ready to do that. He thinks Matthews just took off and will come back sooner or later with a grin on his face and lipstick on his collar." Buzz paused. "That's why I was thinking about you."

"You better connect the dots for me."

"Maybe you could do some checking around, kind of low-key, see what you can turn up. Heck, you and I both know you're better than anybody Bill has."

"Was, maybe, but exactly how low key do you think I could be in a town this size? Besides, as soon as Hanlen finds out, he's going to blow a gasket. As you alluded to, he doesn't like other people stepping on his turf."

"I'll talk to Bill. I'll tell him you won't be too obtrusive and won't get in the way of anything his crew is doing. Plus, if you find something out, you'll let him know right away."

"I don't know about that. I'm a civilian now. If something hits the fan, he and Shannon are going to have lot of explaining to do." Bob Shannon was the County Prosecutor and my former boss.

"I thought about that too. Your status with the county is a little up in the air. You're on disability, but you can apply for reinstatement with thirty days' notice, at which time a doctor appointed by the county will decide if your fit to go back to work. You still got your badge and gun, don't you?

"Yeah, but ..."

"So, who is to stay you aren't still a special investigator with the County?"

"That's awful thin ice, Buzz."

"I prefer to think of it as muddy water. Asides, what can go wrong? You find the professor, or what happened to him, and you're a hero. You don't find him, who's going to know or care?"

Then Buzz added, "You'll be doing me a big favor. I told the wife I would try and help her. Aside from that, what else you got going on?"

I had misgivings about working a missing person case. They typically didn't have happy endings. I also sensed something peculiar about this one. Whatever may have been going on, and from what I had read, Professor Matthews didn't seem to have a life that he would voluntarily just walk away from. On the other hand, my curiosity was roused, and I always had a tough time saying no to Buzz. I needed a second to think and looked up at John Wayne for guidance.

"How big you figure John Wayne was?" I asked.

Buzz gave me a perplexed look. "No idea. I'd guess six four, six five, two-forty. Although I heard that he wore elevator shoes. I think he played ball at USC, too. Why?"

"You ever notice in a John Wayne movie, when the Duke is in a bar, somebody always walks in and starts a fight with him? I mean, it's a standard part of the plot."

"What's your point?"

"Well, if you walked into a bar looking to fight with somebody, would you seek out the biggest guy in the place to pick a fight with? It's just not believable."

"They're movies. You're supposed to suspend disbelief. Now, what's my answer?

"Let's just say that I take this on. Exactly what do you envision me doing?"

Buzz raised his beer to toast my assent. He seemed pleased.

"I knew I could count on you. The Tracker is on the case."

I cringed when I heard that. Back when I was in uniform, I handled a case where a five-year-old had disappeared. The immediate, disturbing, assumption was that he had been abducted. I located the boy at his grandmother's house. He had gotten mad at his mother and walked the three miles there without bothering to tell anyone. The grandmother was at the next town over, visiting a cousin, so he had let himself in and was watching cartoons and eating graham crackers when I found him. A reporter who knew my Indian heritage wrote a humorous story about the incident in which he nicknamed me the "Tracker", to the never-ending amusement of Buzz.

"Don't call me that, and don't count me in yet either. Answer my question first."

"Heck, you know the drill a lot better than me. Work it like you would any missing person's case. Go talk to the wife. Go out to the college and nose around. Talk to the girlfriend. Get to know Professor Matthews and figure out what made him tick. As you say, this is a small town. If there is something, keep turning rocks over until you find it."

"What if I find a big old nasty spider?" I asked.

"I guess you'll either have to step on it or let it go," he replied.

We left the bar and walked over to his office, which was only a couple of doors down. He pulled a three page form out of a desk and handed it to me. On it there was a lot of fine print. I asked Buzz what it was, and he replied that it meant that I was now a consultant in the employ of his law firm. He said that way attorney client privilege was assured. I signed it. Also, over my mild and not remotely sincere protest, he handed me a check for $2,000 as a retainer. Then he wrote down Jackie Matthew's phone number, and that of Ivan Rich, the Prairie County detective who was handling the case. He asked me when I would get started, and I told him in the morning. He said he would call Jackie Matthews to let her know. It was starting to sleet again as I left. Buzz said he was going to stay and catch up on some paper work.

CHAPTER 2

The sleet stung my face as I walked to where I parked. There were few cars left on the streets and nobody in sight. Most of the shops downtown closed early on weeknights, plus the weather probably discouraged all but the hardiest from venturing out. All the lights in the courthouse were out now and it rose like an intimidating dark citadel above the town square. When they had done an extensive renovation of the building many years ago, an elaborate lighted dome had been installed at its top. Once, on a foggy night, due to the proximity of the courthouse to the county hospital, an airlift helicopter almost landed on the dome. After that, it was only activated on special occasions, with thorough notice given.

Even though I had expressed reluctance to Buzz about trying to find the missing professor, now that I had committed to it, I started to plan in what I needed to do. The first step would be to talk to Ivan Rich. I started to compile a list of questions for him. I also thought about what I wanted to ask the professor's colleagues. Then there was the wife.

I was halfway down the block when I realized I didn't have my car keys. I cursed my carelessness and walked back to the Lincoln, figuring I left them there. I just hoped they hadn't shut down yet.

The place was empty when I went back in. Pam was leaning against the back bar and working a cross word puzzle. She smiled when she saw me, put the puzzle down and reached for something beside her.

"Looking for these?" She held up my keys.

"Thanks. Guess my short-term memory isn't as good as I thought."

"For what it's worth, I lose my keys all the time, and I haven't been run over by a car in years. And I'm glad you came back. I was getting lonely."

"Glad I did, then." I looked at my watch. "Better get going. Thanks for the keys. I hope I didn't keep you."

"Not at all. I have to stay another half hour to get my time in, and then I'm locking up. Like another beer before you leave?"

"Nah. Need to get going before they start rolling the sidewalks up."

"Can I ask you a favor?" She gave me a small smile.

"Sure."

"Would you mind sticking around and walking me to my car? The cook usually stays, but he left early."

"Be glad to, although you don't have much to worry about. There aren't many muggers in Prairie Stop, and I think their union deal keeps them home on nights like this."

"Thanks. Have a beer on the house."

I was going to decline again, but she had already started to pour, so I sat down. When she pushed it over I took a sip. Pam seemed edgy, like she wanted to ask me something but was hesitant to do so. She had turned the TV off and an oldies radio station was playing. I instantly recognized the song that was just starting and pointed at the radio.

"Ten bucks if you can tell me who wrote this song." I said. "Twenty if you tell me what he goes by now." I was feeling heady about money since I had a check for two grand in my pocket.

"I'm not good with trivia, especially music."

"This is the Tremelos doing 'Here Comes My Baby', written by Cat Stevens. He shucked his musical career at the height of his fame, converted to Islam and now calls himself Yusuf Islam. Talk about putting your mullah where your mouth is."

"Anybody ever tell you, you talk funny?"

"I can amuse myself for hours," I replied.

"I bet."

There was an awkward pause as Pam distractedly polished a shot glass.

"If that glass was any cleaner, it would be invisible," I observed, after a minute went by.

She laughed. "Sorry, I have a bit of an obsessive personality." She put the glass down on the bar. "So, you and Buzz have been friends for a long time?"

I gave her a puzzled look.

"That guy in here a while ago? Never laid eyes on him. I think maybe he followed me here from the movie."

"And me, naively hoping for a straight answer."

"Don't tell me you got a crunch on Buzz."

"A crunch?"

"It's like a crush, only worse," I said.

"If I did, I hope it wasn't that obvious."

"It's ok. He's the proverbial man every woman wants, and every man wants to be. He's wrecked more hearts than bad cholesterol."

"He's hard not to like, but it's more concern. He's in here an awful lot. He holds it well, but he drinks too much. My bartender's intuition tells me something is going on with him."

"Your intuition is on the mark. I can tell you he hasn't always been like that. He's going through what you would call some family difficulties."

"He talks about his daughters, but I've never heard him mention a wife."

"They are still married, but Beth, his wife, is currently living with her folks in Florida. So, I guess you could say they are separated. Now you are probably going to ask why."

"You think I'm nosey," Pam said.

"You're curious. It's natural to be curious. By the way, it's none of the usual reasons."

"Usual reasons?"

"For marital discord. You know, the husband's flagrant philandering, inability to hold a job, or, until recently in Buzz's case, undue drunkenness. Those seem to be the ones most marriages succumb to."

"That sounds like male bashing, but then again, my ex could check all three boxes. Plus, he was emotionally distant."

"Another good one, although in my experience, most woman don't go for the guy who shows his feelings. You know, the sensitive, emotional type. They prefer the controlling brute who occasionally might get a little sentimental. Their ideal man is one who will kick the crap out of somebody and sob about it later."

She smiled, and I noticed I was starting to like making her smile. "Really? And what type are you?"

"The guy getting the crap knocked out of him. But, in any case, none of that applies to Buzz and his wife Beth. Their son died."

"Wow," was all she could say.

"Wow is right. You ever hear about someone who seems to be in perfect health who just keels over and dies? When Buzz and I were little, we watched it happen with the kid who used to deliver the evening newspaper. Fell off his bike and died, just like that. We thought he just was kidding around, but he never got up. Some type of rare genetic heart problem that nobody knew he had. A couple years ago, Buzz's son died the same way after junior high football practice. He was a great kid. A real tragedy."

"How awful for them."

"Yeah."

"How did they cope?"

"They didn't. I've read since that a lot of marriages fall apart after the loss of a child. Buzz had clients, partners, and employees, so I guess out of a sense of duty to them he didn't go entirely to pieces. On the other hand, Beth couldn't get over it. Putting it mildly, and without going into detail, she had some serious grief issues. Tried to ease the pain by self-medicating with wine and tranquilizers. Probably like most normal people would have done. Buzz tried to get help for her. She was in a couple of high end treatment places, but eventually they thought it would be better for all concerned if she went to Florida to be with her folks."

"How is she now?"

"Not sure. It was around that time I got hit by an old guy driving a Buick. Oh yeah, did I tell you they were a couple almost from when they were in grade school?"

"I guess I see why he drinks." She paused. "What was she like?"

"Is. She's still around, just in Florida."

"Sorry, you said that."

"Well, she was beautiful, for one. Looked like a young Martha Hyer."

"Who's that?"

"Ever hear of a movie called *Some Came Running*? Frank Sinatra and Dean Martin? Shirley MacLaine in one of her first big roles. Based on a book by the same guy who wrote *From Here to Eternity*. Came out in the late fifties."

"That was a little before my time," Pam said.

"Yeah, mine too. Anyhow, Frank plays a cynical war veteran who returns to his home town after a long absence. Martha Hyer was the actress who played Frank's love interest and got nominated for an academy award."

"I told you I didn't know much about trivia."

"They filmed it in southern Indiana. Apparently, Buzz's dad and a friend drove down to see what all the hoopla was about. Buzz's mom used to kid him about almost leaving her for Martha Hyer."

"She looked this actress. Other than that, what was she like?"

I took a pull on my beer and looked down at the bar.

"It's hard to explain, really, but did you ever know somebody who, when they walked into a room, everybody kind of stopped what they were doing to look at them? Like a light in a dark room. Whatever that is, Beth had it in spades, and it wasn't just on account of her looks. Buzz is the same, as you seem to have noticed. But a lot of it went away for Beth when her son died."

I looked up at Pam and noticed my face was flushed in the mirror behind the bar.

"Look at me, blathering on like a schoolgirl," I said.

"I'm sorry. I didn't mean to bring up an unpleasant memory."

"By the way, I'm just telling you, so you know. It wouldn't be a good idea to bring it up in the presence of Buzz. Nobody who knows him would. And don't feel sorry for him either. He wouldn't like that either."

"Thanks for telling me."

"More than you wanted to hear, I guess." I felt a need to change the subject. "Speaking of Florida, how did you wind up in this rust belt hell hole?"

She laughed. "I've worked in worse places."

"I don't mean the Lincoln. How did you end up in a small town in Indiana?"

"I like it here. It's quaint. I love the big old homes near downtown. Somedays I show up early just, so I can walk around. People are friendly. No traffic, no crime. The weather is ok, except in winter. But to answer your question, my husband left me for a younger woman. He cleaned out our bank accounts and left me with a stack of credit card bills as a goodbye present. My father works for U.S. Steel and has a house over in Porter. I had no money, a lot of bad memories, so here I am. I took this gig to get me out of the house and maybe meet some people. I live a boring life."

"I don't know. Sometimes boring isn't bad," I said.

"Now that I told you my story, and if you don't mind me asking, how about you?"

"I'm an open book. What do you want to know?"

"I know you and Buzz are longtime friends, and you were in a horrible accident, but have you lived here your whole life?"

"Most of it. My dad was an ironworker. He worked for Bethlehem Steel at their Lackawanna Plant in New York, then got a job out here with National Steel when they built their plant up by Lake Michigan. A few years later, Bethlehem Steel began to build their Burns Harbor Works down the road, and he went back to them. I met Buzz when we moved. He lived a couple doors down."

"You've been here ever since?"

"No, but close. I went to Wallace College, in Dyersville, which is only a couple hours away. After graduating, being at loose ends, and not wanting to come back here, I hung around Dyersville for a time. Worked odd jobs, drank too much, that type of thing."

"Bad choice of major?"

"You should have been a detective." I saluted her with my beer glass. "You wouldn't know it to look at me, but I was once on the fast track to be an accountant."

"What happened?"

"Well, there I was in college, racking up the business and accounting credits. I never found any of it to be particularly challenging, and while I didn't really like it, I didn't hate it either. I figured I needed to get a job when

I graduated, and accounting seemed as good as anything. But then one day, in the middle of my junior year, I had what you could only call an epiphany."

"An epiphany? Like a religious thing?"

"For all practical purposes, yes. I had a moment of profound insight," I replied.

"Which was?"

"I was taking an exam one day, with my fellow would-be accountants. I finished early and as I looked around at my classmates and then at the pages full of numbers I just completed, I had terrifying vision of my future, which was the rest of my life surrounded by accounting guys and pages with numbers on them. The very next day I went to see my faculty advisor and changed my major to history. He tried to talk me out of it, of course, and eventually convinced me into a dual major of business and history. I already had most of the business courses done, so there was no point in wasting them. But I wasn't going to be an accountant."

"Well, I admire you for doing that, no matter the consequences."

'Yeah, well, the main consequence was my folks wanted to kill me. So, when I graduated, I didn't go home, or get a serious job for that matter. I found part-time work and hung around Wallace with some like-minded renegades from adult life. Then Buzz called. He was back at Notre Dame, going to law school, after a couple of years on the Chicago Bears taxi squad."

Pam pondered that. "Buzz drove a cab for a football team?"

I laughed. "I like your deductive reasoning, but no. The taxi squad is a somewhat dated term for a team's practice squad. Guys who practice but don't suit up for games. Think it may have originated from a team owner who also owned a cab company and had his non-roster players drive taxis. Anyhow, Buzz suggested I move to South Bend, so we could hang out together. He was married by then, and Beth was pregnant with twins, and I think what he really wanted was a potential baby sitter. My life of dissipation was getting a stale at that point, so I moved to South Bend."

"Then what?"

"Buzz had a connection in the South Bend police department. He has connections everywhere. He put a word in for me, and I got on as a part-time dispatcher. I liked it, so I took a couple courses in criminal justice at the local community college. Then I applied for a job as a police officer, made it through the academy, and began my storied career in law enforcement."

"Storied sounds exciting."

"Not really. But I did make detective rather quickly. Think I may have had an edge on my brother officers because of my accounting background. I was the shining star of the fraud unit."

"I guess with all this activity, there was no time for a girlfriend," Pam said.

"I thought we were just going over my professional resume. I didn't know you wanted the personal stuff."

"You said it was ok to be curious."

"It is. Well, Beth was a nurse, so from time to time she would introduce me to co-workers of hers. One in particular, I hit it off with. We went out for a year or so and figured we might as well get married. Turned out to be not such a good idea."

"Why not?"

"We got a water bed, then we drifted apart."

"Your memory doesn't seem to have failed for remembering corny jokes."

"That's the one inexplicable feature of my condition. Well, she did shift work, and so did I, and we both put in a lot of overtime, so after a while, it was like we were ships passing in the night. But we could have worked through that. The bigger problem was she was obsessed with doctors. Specifically, being married to one. Eventually she found on who would oblige her. That reminds me of another joke. Where did the nurse learn how to swim?"

"I have no idea."

"Under the dock. Anyhow, I came home from work one day and there was a note from my soon to be ex-wife. It said, 'Dr. Steven Hetlage and I are in love and have decided to get married.' I thought it was interesting that in the note she referred to him as 'doctor'. "

"How cruel."

"That's harsh way to put it. I would prefer to think of her as pragmatic. She wanted something I couldn't give her, so she went out and got it." I thought about that for a second. "Maybe that's not pragmatism, maybe that's gusto."

"How long were you married? Do you ever hear from her?"

"Seven years. Not from her, about her. Beth and Noreen used to keep in touch. She lives in Chicago area now, Evanston, I think. In a big house with four kids."

"What did you do?"

"Could think of anything better to do, so I came home. I called Buzz, who by that time was back here, with a thriving law practice. He put in another word for me, and I got on with the County Prosecutor. It was providential timing, I suppose. My dad had just been diagnosed with cancer, so I was able to help my mom through that. That was a few years ago."

I looked at my watch. "And speaking of timing, what do you say we get out of here?"

Pam's car was in the alley behind the Lincoln. When we got there, Pam turned toward me and extended her hand.

"It was nice talking to you, Logan. If you ever want to do it again, and I hope you do, you know where to find me." There was a pause. "Or I can give you my number."

I was a little taken aback but pleased nonetheless.

"Well, if you give me your number, I probably won't call, because I'll chicken out. But I know where the Lincoln is, and I'll be back."

CHAPTER 3

I called Ivan Rich early the next morning. We had worked together many times over the years, and he was a decent cop. My impression was that he was competent, but not particularly adept in deductive thinking. He was a stickler for procedure, and if he could find the guilty by following an easily marked trail, he would certainly do it. If more than that was required, then he might be overmatched. That he made detective at all seemed to be due not to his ability, but that he seemed have friends or relatives everywhere, some in influential places.

Despite that I hadn't talked to him in a while, Ivan didn't seem too surprised to hear from me, and registered even less surprise when I told him what I was working on. I inferred from that that someone had given him a heads up. He told me he hadn't had breakfast yet and said he would meet me at the Town Square Restaurant in an hour.

The other thing I remembered about Ivan Rich was his obsession with food. Not just eating it, but all the details that went along with always having it available. A good part of how he organized his schedule seemed to revolve around making sure that a food service establishment was in close proximity to wherever he was going. I wondered how many criminals in Prairie Stop had escaped justice due to their crimes being committed more than a quarter mile away from the nearest restaurant.

It was about 45 degrees and cloudy when I went outside. There was a cool breeze coming from the north, off Lake Michigan. Looked like maybe we were in store for some more precipitation.

Ivan was standing outside the Town Square when I got there, a little after 9, and made a point of glancing at his watch when he saw me. It appeared that he had put on about thirty pounds since I had seen him last, if indeed that was possible. A short burly man to begin with, his neck now seemed to have disappeared totally, and the cheap tie he had on abruptly vanished into his chins. He was wearing a worn and ill-fitting gray suit, the jacket lapels of which appeared to be in dire need of dry cleaning. He stuck out an arm and gave me a vice like handshake. I felt like dropping to one knee in mock agony but decided against it. One other thing I recalled about Ivan was that he didn't appreciate my sense of humor.

"Ivan … good to see you. Thanks for meeting me."

"Don't mention it, Logan. You're buying."

After that warm greeting, we went into the restaurant. Much like the Lincoln, the Town Square hadn't changed much since the last time I was there, and for that matter, probably not much in the last twenty years. Faded orange vinyl booths, stained Formica tables and a carpet that looked like dirt was the only thing holding it together.

At that time of morning, the people who had to go to work had already eaten breakfast and departed, so most of the customers left were old people. A couple of them looked at us with tired interest as we took a booth in the back. Ivan nodded hello to some of them but didn't stop to talk. He looked like a man on a mission.

Ivan grabbed the menu and eagerly opened it up.

"The blueberry pancakes are good," he said, and then added with a note of caution, "but you got to find out if the blueberries are fresh."

I pointed out the obvious.

"It's November. How fresh you figure the blueberries are going to be?"

He gave me a look as if I told him he had stepped in dogshit on the way in.

"Yeah, well, maybe I'll have the Denver omelet. How about you?"

"I'm not much on breakfast. Maybe I'll just get a cup of coffee." The thought of sitting there watching him shovel food into his face made me lose whatever appetite I might have had.

"Suit yourself. You look like you could use a couple meals. Been on a diet?"

"I'm on a hunger strike. Until there is world peace, or the Cubs win the World Series."

"You're gettin' close. Some better pitching against the Giants in the playoffs, and they would have been in the Series. Course, the Giants lost to the A's in four straight. Doubt the Cubs could have done much better."

"You may have heard I was in the hospital for a stretch. I can recommend it highly for losing weight. You should try it."

"Yeah, I heard. Sorry I didn't send you flowers."

"I did get the chocolates you sent. Funny, someone had picked out most of the ones I like."

"How you been?" There was small note of concern in his voice. I wondered if he was sincere or not. I guessed not, but at least he asked.

"Good days and bad. I wake up most mornings stiff as a board." I waited until Ivan was taking another bite of his omelet, then added, "plus, my legs are tight as hell." He snorted and some of the egg in his mouth went onto the table.

"You're a funny guy, Logan. Do you ever give anyone a straight answer?"

"Once in a while," I said "Ok, it was like I was in a fog for a long time, physically and mentally, then I started to come out of it, out of it, if that makes any sense. Still not one hundred percent, I guess. Discomfort really, not so much pain like before. That's the physical part. Mentally, feel like I'm almost as good as new. Anyhow, the doctors said the effects of severe trauma can last for months if not years."

Ivan nodded. We sat in silence for a minute while the waitress came over and took our order.

"So, you're trying to locate our missing professor," he said, eyeing me and then taking a long deliberate slurp of his coffee, part of which immediately dripped down his chin.

"You don't seem like I caught you off guard."

"Chief told me the other day you might be giving me a call."

I smiled. Buzz knew he had me roped in before he even talked to me.

"What's so funny?" Ivan asked.

"Nothing. What did Hanlen say to you?"

"Just that you were going to be looking into my case, and that I was to give you all the information I had. I wasn't too happy about that, but what the hell. We got a lot of nothing."

"Hanlen said everything?" I asked. That surprised me.

"Sort of. He said not to give you any leads that might jeopardize the investigation." Ivan's brow furrowed. "Which is odd, when you think about it, because like I said, we don't have much."

"I heard he had a girlfriend."

"So, you know something already." He reached into his jacket pocket and pulled out a small bound pad. "Name is Roseanne Parker. Age 25. Divorced with a six-year-old kid. Works part time at the Video Warehouse out on 49, plus tends bar a couple of nights a week. Different places. She takes courses at BHU. Ask me, I don't think she knows anything"

"She met the professor at school?"

Ivan looked up from his notebook. "I would have asked that first, too. No, they met at the video store. The professor liked to watch a lot of movies."

"What kind?"

He laughed. "Now you're two for two. You must have been in the back room before."

Ivan was referring to the large room at the back of the Video Warehouse where the adult videos were kept. A couple of years ago a local church group picketed the store demanding that they cease renting the adult material, but the store politely refused. Then they indicated that they might let slip the names of some of the people who rented the adult fare, and the church group abruptly ceased picketing.

"I've been back there to look, but now I'm too chicken to check them out. It might be my imagination, but the clerk always looks at me with disgust. Or maybe it's disdain. I'm still having a little trouble with words."

"I know what you mean. I let my wife do it. A pillar of the community such as yours truly can't be seen pandering. I always wonder what they think when she's checking out Beauty and the Beast, and Beauty does the Beast. It gets her motor started, I'll say that. The other night we were watching this one where this chick …"

I broke into a contrived coughing fit. In addition to his obsession with food, one of Ivan's other foibles was discussing his sex life, which he did at length and with great candor. A couple years ago, I bumped into Ivan and his wife in a fast food place. From listening to his stories for years, I imagined her to be a voluptuous sex kitten. Instead, she looked and acted like a female Ivan. After that, whenever he started to tell me about his latest sexual encounter, I tried to cut him off as soon as possible.

He looked annoyed. "You gonna live?"

"Yeah, sorry. You were saying about the professor's movie choices?"

"Let's just say the professor's tastes weren't strictly PG."

"Maybe he didn't rewind one of the tapes and disappeared rather than face the shame. How did you find out about her?"

"During our initial interviews. One of Matthew's colleagues, another professor, mentioned that he had seen him with the girl up at restaurant in Lakeside, acting kind of friendly. Thought it was peculiar."

"The professor's name?"

"Morgenfeld. Harold Morgenfeld. Old Jewish guy, kind of fussy. Teaches political science. Probably gay. He seemed reluctant to mention the girl, but I gave him the old 'any small part of the puzzle' bit."

I made a note of the name.

"What did Ms. Parker have to say?" I asked.

"She and the professor were just friends. Doesn't know anything about what happened to him."

"You believe her?"

"Yeah, mainly. I get the picture that they were more than just friends, but I don't think she knows what happened to him."

"The wife?"

"The wife was in Chicago starting Tuesday of the week Matthews disappeared, and didn't come back until Saturday evening. If you figure Matthews vanished either Thursday night or early Friday, then that would seem to put her out of the picture. Unless she got someone to get rid of him for her."

"What's she like?" I asked.

"A looker. A lawyer. A lot younger than the professor. I don't see her involved in offing him, but you never know."

"Any incentive for her to do so?"

"A couple. Matthews had almost a million in life insurance. Plus, he was a trust fund baby. His grandfather made a killing in Chicago real estate."

"That supports a theory of mine. Behind every successful man is a successful grandfather," I said.

"Or a successful father in law."

"Yeah. Speaking of Chicago, it's an hour away. She could have come here, then been back in Chicago before daybreak."

"Thanks for the geography lesson. I called the Chicago PD and asked them to go over to the hotel to make sure she was there. Her car didn't leave the parking garage from the day she got there until Saturday. The maid saw her most mornings, plus they got room service, movie rentals, or phone records that say she was there."

"Most, but not all?" I asked.

"It's a big hotel. Lot of people coming and going all the time."

"Who did you talk to at Chicago PD?"

"Liz Parilli. Used to be work here. Remember her?"

"Not sure."

"Blonde, on the chunky side. She was a uniform in the county for about five years, and then went on to the big time."

"Doesn't ring a bell. Did anybody check the bank accounts?"

"Gee, Colombo, that didn't occur to us. You think we should have?" Ivan said and shook his head.

"To answer your question, yes, I checked the accounts. No large withdrawals. Also, no clothes or suitcases missing. No airline tickets booked. Heck he even had a bunch of videos that needed to go back to the movie store. Wherever Matthews went, it didn't look like he was expecting to go there."

"Any chance he got one of his students pissed off enough to want to get rid of him?"

"Judging from what I found out, he wasn't regarded as a real ball buster. Tough but fair. Aside from that, how many twenty-year-old college kids do you know that have the savvy to make somebody disappear? Heck, my fourteen-year-old couldn't find his dick unless it wasn't always in his hand."

"Any of his fellow professors have it in for him? How about Morgenfeld?"

"An old gay Jew? I don't think so."

"A rat for a co-worker is still a rat, right?"

"Maybe. But teaching isn't like guys slinging sacks of mail around over at the post office. One guy, Davis, though apparently wasn't in the professor's booster club. I talked to him. Black guy with a bad attitude."

I laughed. "A black guy and a Jew. Any cripples involved, Mr. Secretary?"

He gave me a disgusted look and slowly shook his head.

"Oh, I get it, a yokel like me doesn't read the paper and doesn't know who Regan's Secretary of Interior was. Believe it or not, Logan, I got better things to do than sit around and shoot the shit with you." He made like he was going to get up to leave, which I knew wasn't happening because he hadn't finished his breakfast.

"Ivan, now take it easy. I didn't mean any offense. I appreciate your help, really. Did this Davis with the bad attitude seem like he disliked Matthews enough to get rid of him?"

"Nah, unless he could have talked him to death. He seemed to have a high opinion of himself."

I let Ivan finish his breakfast and hoped that he wasn't going to order up any more food. He looked like he was still hungry. When he wiped up the last morsel of egg on his plate with an English muffin, I asked the obvious question.

"What do you think happened to him?"

"A UFO took him." He said that with a straight face.

For Ivan Rich, I thought that was pretty funny.

"There's been a rash of that," I said. "Did you know that Northwest Indiana is a veritable hotbed of UFO activity?"

"Yeah, too bad the UFO theory doesn't rate a lot of credibility with my supervisors. I personally like it. It takes care of all the facts, plus leaves open the possibility that the missing person will return. Unfortunately, nobody likes it but me."

"Ok. What are your other theories?"

"Other than that, I've got a couple of thoughts. Nothing concrete, but since you asked …one, maybe the marriage wasn't that happy. Considering he had a girlfriend and all. Plus, I mentioned that the wife is a lot younger, didn't I?"

"Yes. Matthew's was in his fifties, right?"

"Yeah. Jackie Matthews is mid-thirties. Sometimes that can be a problem. The age difference doesn't seem much at 25 and 40 but looks a little different at 35 and 50. I got the feeling he wasn't in real good health, either."

"How so?"

"She downplayed it, but I got the impression he was having heart issues. She said he was on a couple blood pressure meds."

"Any reason to think she was looking to get out? Like a boyfriend on the side?"

"No, but if you told me there was, I wouldn't be too surprised. When you meet her, you'll see what I mean. It's kind of hard to see her with a bookworm like Matthews. Plus, you got the life insurance. Make a nice going away present, assuming he was going away and not coming back."

"What's your other thought?"

"This one's more of reach. According to the wife, he was acting kind of strange lately."

"In what way?"

"The usual. Not coming home when he was supposed to. Being secretive. Not talking to her. Probably goes along with having a girlfriend. But she also claimed he was having a lot of peculiar dreams."

"Define peculiar," I said.

"Get this. Matthews was a history professor. You know what his specialty was?"

"History? I think that's about stuff that happened in the past."

"Wiseass. You probably also figured out most of your history professors have got a specific period or event that they become experts on. You know, like if they are going to write a book or paper, that's what they write it on."

"And Matthews' specialty was?"

"When you were a kid, did you ever to go Camp Tecumseh?" Ivan asked.

Camp Tecumseh was an outdoor recreational area about thirty miles south of Prairie Stop. Most Boy Scout troops in the area went there at least a couple of times a year. Buzz always went there for a week each summer. I was jealous that he got to go, until one summer when he came back and told me one of the counselors tried, as he put it, to be his "special buddy." After that he didn't go anymore, and I was glad I never joined the Boy Scouts.

"No," I replied. "My dad didn't let me or my brother join the Boy Scouts. Claimed they were communists."

"Communists? The Boy Scouts?"

"Well, when you think about, they all wear the same uniforms and recite the same slogans. And what's that thing about "merit" badges? Sounds like something Stalin invented. But no, in my dad's case, I think he just didn't want to have to take me and my brother to the den meetings. He hated meetings.

He probably would have quit drinking years before he did if he could have handled meetings."

"I just figured out why you turned out like you did, Logan."

"What's that?"

"You didn't get to join the Boy Scouts. So, I'm guessing you know Camp Tecumseh is named for Tecumseh, the Indian. When I went to camp there, we used to say that Tecumseh was Indian talk for, 'something smells bad in the woods'. "

"If I was you, Ivan, I wouldn't kid around about Tecumseh. He may be dead, but he had a powerful spirit. He might be standing over you now with a karmic tomahawk."

"Oh yeah, I forgot, you are part Indian. He was some big chief, right?"

He seemed like he was waiting for me to add more. Like me being part Indian would automatically qualify me as an expert on Native American history. I obliged him.

"Tecumseh was a war chief of the Shawnee tribe. His name means Panther Passing Across. With his brother, known as the Shawnee Prophet, he tried to form an alliance of tribes to oppose the whites taking over Indian lands in present day Ohio and Indiana. That was back in around 1800 or so. The brothers started a settlement of Shawnee and other tribes near Lafayette. It was known as Prophetstown. Territorial Governor William Harrison attacked and destroyed it in 1811. Tippecanoe and Tyler too. One of the events leading up to the War of 1812."

"Yeah," Ivan said, distractedly. I think I must have told him more than he wanted to hear, because now he didn't seem so interested.

"Anyhow," he continued, "turns out Matthews specialty was Tecumseh. Wrote a lot of papers and articles on the chief and is regarded as a leading expert on him. I think he may have even been working on a book about him. Supposedly, Tecumseh spent some time in these parts."

"Like I said, Prophetstown was south of here. Near Lafayette. It was resettled after the battle of Tippecanoe, but then destroyed again when the war started. Some think Tecumseh and the Prophet spent the first winter of the War of 1812 closer to this area, further away from the whites. Nobody is sure exactly where."

"Sounds like you took a couple of the professor's courses," Ivan said.

"What does that have to do with the dreams?"

"His wife seems to think he was having a lot of strange dreams about Tecumseh."

"That doesn't sound odd. Did you ever dream of a case you were working on?"

"Hell, yeah. They were more of nightmares, though."

"How does she know the dreams were about Tecumseh?"

"She claims he was even speaking Shawnee in his sleep."

"Doubt that. I would be real surprised if anyone speaks Shawnee anymore. In fact, I'd be surprised if there are more than five thousand of the tribe left, and probably most of them don't know much Shawnee. How did she know it was Shawnee?"

"Because he told her, that's why. She wrote down what he said and then asked him about it the next day."

"How does this fit into Matthew's disappearance?"

"I didn't say it did, necessarily. But let's say this guy goes a little nuts, mid-life crisis, young demanding wife, whatever. Then he starts imagining he's this Indian chief he done all this research on over the years and goes off looking for the happy hunting ground."

I couldn't help myself. I started laughing and said, "I like the UFO theory better."

"Screw you, Logan. You ask what I think, I tell you, and then you bust a gut laughing at me." He looked like he was going to take a poke at me.

"I wasn't making fun of you. It just sounded funny the way you said it, is all."

Somewhat to my surprise, after a second, Ivan gave me grin.

"Yeah, I guess it did." The grin turned into a pensive look as Ivan finished his coffee.

"Look, you and I both know either somebody, for yet unknown reasons, killed the professor and did a good job of covering it up, or he just got sick of his life and went off to find another one. I work a few of these cases every year or so, and they are usually teen runaways, so I'm no expert. My bet is Professor Matthews isn't coming back anytime soon." He looked at his watch and stood to go.

"Thanks for breakfast. I got to get back to work. Call me if you find out anything worth calling about."

CHAPTER 4

After I left the restaurant, I drove out to BHU. It was just a few minutes northeast of downtown, the campus beginning right next to the Prairie County Hospital. The hospital was a large four story brown brick building that had been built in the late thirties and was showing its age. It routinely operated in the red and they kept losing staff to more prestigious and profitable hospitals in Chicago. There were rumors the county wanted to get out of the healthcare business altogether and sell the property to the university. I could see the economic sense it that, but since it was the only full-service hospital in the county, wondered where people would go for care. In addition to my accident, Buzz and I had been there plenty of times when growing up for various broken bones and assorted other injuries.

BHU was a small school, with student body, graduate and undergraduate, of around 5,000. The university had been founded as Benjamin Harrison Academy in 1898 by a group of local civic and religious leaders. They named it after Indiana's own Benjamin Harrison, the 23rd President, and grandson of William Henry Harrison, Chief Tecumseh's arch foe. The school was dedicated to providing a "higher Christian education for young men of solid moral background." The college had almost folded after World War I, when a flu epidemic caused it to shut down for three years. Gradually it had expanded, being helped immensely by an officer training program run by the Navy on the campus during World War II, and then by the GI Bill after the war. Many buildings were added during this period, and the school started admitting women in 1950. BHU earned a reputation as a high quality regional university, if you didn't mind one with a conservative tone. They had some pretty good basketball teams, too.

As I entered the campus, I remembered my dad taking my brother and me there when we were little to watch football and basketball games. At time I thought how massive the campus was and how enormous the stadium and gym were. My adult perspective was much different than the one I had when I was six years old. I'd be surprised if the football stadium held more than a few thousand people, and the buildings now seemed of normal size and close together.

Students were scurrying between buildings, trying to minimize the effect of the chill of the late fall morning. After I parked, I stopped one of them and asked him to direct me to the history department offices. He jerked a hand up to point a finger at an older three-story building that was near where we were standing. A sign at the front of the building identified it as the Moore Liberal Arts Center. When I stepped inside, the directory showed that the offices of the history and political science departments were on the third floor.

A stern looking middle aged woman sat behind a desk facing the glass door to the stairway, obviously placed there so she could observe all that came and went. She looked familiar, but I couldn't place her. She glanced up from what she was doing as the door shut and eyed me warily.

"Hello," I said, giving her my winning smile.

She skipped the hello back. "May I help you?" The tone of her voice gave me the idea she was hoping she could tell me I was on the wrong floor, which didn't surprise me. I seldom make a good first impression on people.

The nameplate on her desk identified her as Virginia Hanlen. I pointed at it.

"The county sheriff in Prairie County is named Hanlen," I said.

"What a coincidence. I've a husband named Hanlen, who also happens to be the county sheriff."

Now I knew why she looked familiar. I remembered somebody once telling me Hanlen's wife worked at the university. I probably had even met her before, but where and when escaped me.

"My name is Logan Wells, Mrs. Hanlen. I'm investigating the disappearance of Professor Matthews."

She gave me a puzzled look. "I don't recall my husband ever mentioning an Officer Wells."

"Point of fact, I'm not with the county police. I'm an investigator with the County Prosecutor's office, but I'm on an extended leave right now. The Matthews family has retained me." Not exactly true, but close enough.

"Logan Wells? Oh yes. You were the one in that awful accident last year." When I nodded, she added, "Bill said you almost died." Her tone and demeanor visibly softened. "How are you?"

"I'm ok, thanks, getting better every day."

"You know, I think I might have played bridge with your mother, many years ago."

"It would have had to have been many years ago. She moved to Florida some time ago, after my dad died. She hated the winters here. She did love her card games though. Still plays bridge at least a few times a week."

"Have a seat, Officer Wells," she said, gesturing to the chair by the side of desk. "Could I get you a cup of coffee?"

"It's just plain Logan, Mrs. Hanlen. I was a cop once but haven't been for a long time. No, on the coffee, I had my limit today. Thanks anyhow."

"How can I help you, Logan? I'm afraid I already told another detective all I knew about Professor Matthew's whereabouts on the day he … I still feel funny saying it, disappeared. It makes it sound like he is never coming back."

"That would have been Ivan Rich. I met with him this morning. I just wanted to see where the professor worked, talk to some people that knew him, kind of get a feel for what kind of man he was."

She nodded slightly, which I took as encouraging.

"Can you tell me, Mrs. Hanlen, was the professor well-liked by his students?"

"Call me Ginny. The students seemed to like Professor Matthews well enough, although he wasn't one to try and be popular at the expense of being a poor teacher. Some of the younger ones are like that."

"How do you mean?" I asked.

"I shouldn't have said that. It just seems that some of the younger professors act as if they are in a popularity contest. I guess they think they aren't supposed to give anyone below a C, no matter how badly the student does on his tests or papers."

"How many professors of history are there?"

"The History Department is rather small. We have four full-time tenured professors, and another two visiting professors. Plus, two-part time associates and a graduate assistant. Jason was the chairman of the department."

"The professor's area was American History, right?"

"Yes. He taught courses covering all periods of American history, but his specialty was the early nineteenth century. He was considered an expert on the history of this region, including the Native Americans who were here before it was settled by the whites. He was always being asked to speak at meetings of the historical societies in the area. In fact, recently there was an article in the paper about how Jason was spearheading an effort to preserve a couple of artifact sites near here."

"I think I missed that," I said.

"Oh, it was on the front page some weeks back. A developer is talking about building a big shopping mall north of Prairie Stop. Jason identified the area as being possibly the former site of an Indian village and was leading an effort to keep it from being bulldozed under."

"How was that going?"

"It wasn't going well, I'm afraid. It seems all people care about nowadays is making a buck. You would think we had enough Wal-Mart's and fast food places."

"I understand he had a special interest in Tecumseh."

"Oh, yes. He wrote several articles on Tecumseh that were published in national magazines and journals. He was even writing a biography."

"How was the book coming along?"

"I'm not sure, other than that I know he has been working on it for a long time."

"How did Professor Matthews get along with his colleagues?"

Her brow crinkled, and it almost seemed like she squirmed in her chair.

"You don't think one of them had anything to do with this?" she asked, hesitantly.

"Doubtful, but I'm not sure I think anything at this point. Part of any investigation is eliminating all the possibilities, no matter how farfetched they seem."

"That sounds like something my husband might say."

"He could have. I should tell you, I stole that one from Sherlock Holmes."

"Well, Jason was certainly liked and respected by all of his colleagues."

"To paraphrase another famous detective, Abraham Lincoln, nobody is liked by everybody all the time."

"I probably shouldn't be saying something like this …"

"I can assure, you, it will just be between you and me." I was lying, of course.

"I think it was well known that he and Professor Davis didn't get along, so I'm not telling you any secrets."

"Professor Davis?"

"Lavon Davis."

"Why did you think they didn't get along?"

"They had some arguments. Last June, Professor Davis was up for tenure. Jason was on the tenure committee."

"I'm assuming that Lavon Davis didn't get tenure."

"Oh, no," she said. "If he didn't get it, he wouldn't still be here. He was awarded tenure."

"But Professor Matthews wasn't in favor of it."

"Well, the tenure consideration is supposed to be confidential, but I know Jason was against his appointment. At least initially."

"Do you know why?" I asked.

"No, other than perhaps he thought he wouldn't be a good fit with the department."

"Because?"

"I think maybe Jason thought Lavon was a little too popular with the students."

"In what way, exactly?" I asked.

"Kind of what I mentioned earlier. He didn't seem as regimented as the older professors in terms of exams and grades."

"Which is to say, he gave good grades for not so good work?"

"I shouldn't really say anymore."

"Let me ask you something else, Ginny. Assuming Professor Matthews, God forbid, doesn't come back, what happens with his position? You said he was chair of the department."

"His classes are being taught now by one of the part-time professors. I imagine eventually the dean of the liberal arts will appoint a temporary department chair."

"And that would be one of the other senior professors?"

"Not necessarily. They may not be interested in doing it."

"Then conceivably Professor Davis could wind up in the position? That would be something good to have on a resume."

"I wouldn't know about that."

"Is Professor Davis around right now?"

She looked at the clock. "He should be returning from his eleven o'clock any minute now."

"Do you think it would be alright if I hung around? I'd like to talk to him."

Before she could answer, as if on cue, the door opened and a tall black man who appeared to be in his mid-forties walked into the hallway. He had a short precisely trimmed beard and was wearing a gray tweed coat, dark blue button-down shirt, and jeans. Rimless glasses were perched halfway down his nose. Who I took to be Professor Davis gave me an appraising and somewhat peeved look, as if me being there could only mean aggravation for him.

Ginny broke the ice.

"Dr. Davis. This is Logan Wells," she said. "He's here about Jason."

"Don't tell me. They found him working as a female impersonator in Reno."

Ginny's jaw dropped.

Davis gave a wan smile. "I'm sorry, that was terrible wasn't it? It's just that we have all found Jason's disappearance so disturbing. I can't even begin to deal with it, hence the flip remark. Was it Freud who said humor is a defense mechanism?"

"I'm wouldn't know, Professor," I said. "I was a history major. I was wondering if I could have a few minutes of your time."

He glanced at his watch. "I've got a lunch meeting shortly, but we can talk until then. Please hold my calls, Ginny."

"Why don't we step into my office?" he said, pointing down the hall.

His office was at the end at the hallway, and I wondered if the location and size had to do with his status as recently tenured. The room was small and had one tiny window, high on the wall. Books and papers were everywhere, in shelves, in boxes, lying in piles on the floor. To say it seemed cramped would have been an understatement. And since Davis was a large man it made it even more noticeable. He cleared some papers off a chair in front of his desk, so I could sit down.

"I like what you've done with the place," I said. "You've really captured the early U-Boat feel."

He gave a small smile.

"It's like a sports team where the rookies get the smallest lockers," he said. "The newest professor usually has the tiniest office."

"Not sure why, but I had the idea you had been here a while."

"I have been, but most of the same colleagues I had when I got here are still here. Change is a slow process here. I'm not sure I understand. Are you with the police, Mr. Wells?"

"Not exactly. As I told Mrs. Hanlen, I'm an investigator on leave from the County Prosecutor's Office. I've been retained by the Matthews family."

"Because a week or so ago I spoke with a detective. Short stocky fellow who looked hungry. I know, that's an odd way of describing someone, but he looked like he wanted something to eat. Lucky somebody brought in doughnuts that day. He polished off two of them while he was here. Kind of validated a stereotype, in a way."

"That would have been Ivan Rich. He's the Prairie Stop detective assigned to the case."

"I take it you know him?"

"We've worked together before, a number of times."

"No offense, but if he is in charge of finding Jason, I think Jason is going to be missing for a long time."

"Rich is a good cop, but they don't handle many cases like this."

"Which explains why Jackie hired you."

"Actually, a friend of hers thought I might be of some help," I said, not wanting to elaborate.

"I see. And have you?"

"I'm just getting started. That's why I wanted to talk to people who knew the professor. Like you."

"I'm not sure what I can say. I have no idea what happened to Jason. We weren't that close."

"Can you think of anyone who might have wanted to harm him?"

He laughed. "You mean, like me? I suppose Ginny told you all about my obsessive hatred for the great Professor Matthews. She should stick to her administrative work and leave the office politics to others. I can imagine my lame attempt at humor in the hallway has already made it all the way across campus."

"She just said you two didn't get along."

"That's not true at all. We got along fine, considering our cultural differences."

"Cultural differences?"

He smiled. "In case you hadn't noticed, I'm a Jewish kid from North Philly. Jason family is old money from some affluent Chicago suburb. I went to Temple. Jason went to Dartmouth. Jason's specialty is early nineteenth century rural America. Mine is urban history. Jason is something of a legend here. I will be quite frank with you—I don't intend to spend the rest of my career at BHU. I mention this because if you haven't already, you will find out that Jason opposed my tenure, but had I not received it, I would have just gone somewhere else. No big deal. In short, we didn't see eye to eye on a lot of issues, but the idea I had it in for him, or him for me, is ridiculous."

"If someone was reading between the lines, your remarks might be construed to imply that Matthews was a racist."

"I didn't say that, but to coin a phrase, if the construe fits, then wear it. In point of fact, Logan, I think we are all racist. Wouldn't you agree?"

"Perhaps. But that doesn't mean people can't get along."

"If getting along means the oppressor and the oppressed can sit peacefully next to each other in history class, or church, or at the movies, or be on the track team together, I agree with you. But sooner or later the nature of the relationship will be revealed for what it truly is. Tell me, as you made your way here, how many people of color did you see?"

"I didn't notice, to be truthful," I replied.

"Well, I can tell you that less than 2% of the student body at BHU are people of color. Would you find that unusual for a university that is regarded, at least by some, as a top regional institution, and within an hour of a major urban area?"

"I'm not sure. If you put it like that, I guess, yeah, that seems unusual."

"And what or who would you say is responsible for that fact?"

"My standard answer to questions like that is 'the guys in charge.'"

Davis laughed. "In this case, your answer is very prescient. The people in power at this institution have shown at best indifference, and at worst, a reluctance to bring people of diverse backgrounds to this institution. Either as students, faculty or staff."

"I'm guessing that you consider Jason Matthews a person in power," I said.

"Jason is or was on about every committee here you could name, from the campus darts tournament to long range planning."

"And he opposed inclusion of minorities?"

He gave me a scowl. "Don't patronize me. Even a conservative institution like BHU doesn't permit blatant racism. What I'm talking about is much subtler than that. It means setting up standards that make it impossible for a person from a disadvantaged background to succeed."

"You mean like giving a student a failing grade when he deserves one?"

Another scowl.

"You are a bit of cynic. Anybody ever tell you that?"

"Yeah, but I don't have a real high opinion of any of the ones that did."

"Your contention is one I've heard before, usually espoused by so called conservatives with an ax to grind. That to avoid criticizing a person or not to hold him to the same standard as others because of race is in itself an insidious form of racism. That's not what I'm talking about. I am talking about modifying some standards to level the playing field."

"And that was a point of disagreement between you and Professor Matthews."

"I would call it more of an abyss than a point of contention. Jason was one of the individuals who had been given every break but did his best not to cut anyone else one. Especially if they didn't hang around in his social circles. Where I came from, that's called white privilege."

For some reason, part of me wanted to launch a diatribe into how people of my ancestry had been treated, but let it go. It wouldn't have been exactly true in my case, anyhow.

"Speaking of social circles, did you ever hear that Professor Matthews was having an affair with a student?" I asked.

Davis again laughed. Apparently, I was brightening up his morning.

"I've been teaching for over twenty years, at a number of different schools. I don't think I ever worked anywhere where I didn't hear a rumor that a professor was having an affair with a student. It goes with the territory, so to speak. Whether it's true or not in Jason's case, I have no idea. But I can tell you, Jackie was a student of his as well, so it wouldn't be the first time."

"His wife was a student here?"

"As an undergrad," Davis replied.

"Speaking of his wife, was there any problems in the marriage that you were aware of?"

"I could hardly express an opinion on that. It wasn't like they invited me over to brunch every Sunday. I saw them together at faculty meetings and the odd cocktail party. They seemed to get along ok. You would have to wonder about the age difference."

"Were you aware of any personal problems that Matthews might have been having?"

"Like I said, you are asking the wrong man, but to my knowledge, he didn't gamble, drink excessively, or use drugs—the usual stuff problems are made of. He was also apparently independently wealthy, well respected by his colleagues, most of them anyhow, and had a beautiful, vivacious wife. If Jason had problems, I would have liked to have had some of them."

"Can you think of anyone who might have wanted to have harmed him?"

No laugh, but a smile. "Back to me again?" Then the smile was gone. "That, to me, is the most puzzling aspect. Assuming for a second, Jason's disappearance isn't voluntary, I can't think of anyone who had any reason to harm him. I don't know anybody who would even own up to actively disliking the man. That includes me, by the way."

"You said that the Professor didn't have any problems. How would you ..."

Davis interrupted me, raising his right hand in emphasis. "In point of fact, I said I wished I had problems like his. I was also being facetious. I would say Jason had reasons to be depressed."

"Which were?"

"He was a dinosaur among dinosaurs. He had become irrelevant."

"I'm not following you."

"Think about it. He graduates with honors from an Ivy League school. Shows a lot of promise at an early age. What does he end up doing? His whole career is spent teaching at Small-town U. History, no less. Nobody goes to school to major in history anymore. Kids today want to be accountants and engineers and nurses."

"What about you?"

"Like I said, I'm not going to be here forever. I shouldn't tell you this, but I've got a book deal with a major educational publisher in the works. When that goes through, my days here are going to be numbered. Not that I wouldn't like to stay here and change some things, but you have to pick your battles."

"Speaking of books, do you know anything about the biography Matthews was working on Tecumseh?" I asked.

That brought a contemptuous chuckle.

" 'The definitive biography of Tecumseh'? That's another reason I would be depressed if I were Jason. I think he started working on it the year Tecumseh died."

"Writer's block?"

"One wonders. Perhaps it is difficult to get too excited about an obscure Indian chief who failed to achieve anything."

"Funny you say that. We got a street here in town named after him."

"That's says a lot about the town," Davis said, dismissively.

"You mentioned you knew of no one who had a reason to dislike Matthews. How about the developer of mall that Matthews is trying to stop?"

"I doubt it. First, the mall opposition is Jason and three blue haired old ladies who don't have anything better to do. As I just mentioned, perhaps Jason was feeling irrelevant and getting his name in the paper would be a boost to his ego. Point two, there is little evidence that an Indian village existed at the proposed mall site. Jason might have found an arrowhead there once when he was walking his dog. Point three, if someone wants to build a mall it is going to get built, even if they find Tecumseh's and Adolf Hitler's lunch boxes out there. Crass developers and urban sprawl are, unfortunately, inevitable facts of life, even in Prairie Stop. Now, I must be going."

"Just a couple more questions," I said. "When was the last time you saw Matthews?"

"The morning of the day, I believe it was Thursday, he apparently vanished. We passed in the hallway, between classes."

"Did you notice anything unusual about him?"

"No, not really."

"That didn't sound like a firm no."

"Ok. I didn't mention this to the doughnut detective, but Jason looked preoccupied."

"What made you think so?"

"This might not sound like much, but whenever Jason greeted me, when there were students around, he always called me Professor Davis. As in, 'Good morning, Professor Davis,' or 'How are you today, Professor Davis?' He did that with the entire faculty. Very formal. When we were alone, of course, he called me Lavon. That morning, as he passed me, in the hallway with plenty of students around, he didn't seem to see me. I said, 'Hello, Jason.' I'm not sure if I startled him, but he looked at me in an odd way, then gave me a jaunty, 'What's up, Lavon?' Took me aback. It just seemed peculiar." He started to get up. "Now I really must get going. Can't keep the dean waiting."

"One last question. Assuming Matthews disappeared Thursday night, where were you that evening?"

"I was at home, grading papers. If your next question is doing I have any witnesses, the answer is no. Goodbye, Mr. Wells."

After I left Davis' office, I walked down the hall to the Political Science Department to see if I could find Professor Harold Morgenfeld, the one who saw Matthews with the Parker girl. He wasn't in his office, but the department secretary, after an initial impasse of suspicion, said he would be back shortly and I could wait for him.

CHAPTER 5

I was about halfway through a journal of not so good student poetry when a short round man came through the office door. I'm guessing he was around sixty. He had a trimmed grey mustache to go with short cropped grey hair, and owlish black glasses. He was on the heavy side, but he had on a black cashmere double breasted blazer and grey wool pants which fit him well. They looked expensive. The effect was completed by a crisp sky-blue dress shirt with white point collar, and a paisley silk tie. I could also smell his cologne shortly after he walked in. He was obviously a man who just didn't jump out of bed and throw the first thing he could find on. The secretary had a couple hushed words with him, and then pointed at me. I put the poetry journal down. When I did, noticed someone had taped a small card on the table, with "NO GUM" in red ink on it. I got up as Morgenfeld walked over to me. I thought about breaking the ice by asking, "How's the gum problem?" but decided against it.

"I'm Dr. Morgenfeld. Sharon informs me that you wanted to speak with me concerning Jason." His voice had a slight effeminate quality, which along with the stylish clothes was what probably made Ivan figure he was gay.

"That's correct, Doctor. My name is Logan Wells."

"Are you with the police?"

"No, although I was formerly a investigator with the county prosecutor's office. I've been retained by Jason's wife to investigate her husband's disappearance."

"I see. I did talk to a county detective about Jason."

"Yes, I know. That would have been Ivan Rich. He gave me your name."

"I'm not sure what assistance I can be, but if I can be of help, of course I will do anything I can. My office is just down the hall."

Morganfeld's office was substantially bigger than that of Davis. It definitely had a more spacious feel to it, due to there being two large windows as opposed to one small one. It was also impeccably organized. All the books were neatly shelved on two massive cherry bookcases, in front of which was an equally massive cherry desk. There were no books or papers strewn about, like in Davis' office. On the other hand, I'm always a little wary of someone who has a tidy desk. It's tough to make a fire without leaving some ashes.

I sat in one of the two red leather winged chairs facing the desk. On the wall were mainly pictures of a younger and thinner Morgenfeld with various people, some of whom I recognized. In one he was shaking hands with Robert Kennedy. He saw me looking at it.

"I helped manage the RFK primary campaign in Northwest Indiana, he said. "You may recall Indiana was one of the four state democratic primaries he won in 1968." There was a trace of wistfulness in his voice.

"Oddly enough, I do recall that. But he wasn't going up against Humphrey was he?"

"Yes, very good, Mr. Wells. Most people don't recall that Humphrey chose not to run in Indiana. Things got a bit chaotic when Lyndon Johnson suddenly announced he wasn't running again. That was during the height of the Vietnam War. Indiana Governor Brannigan was the dark horse candidate in the state."

"Call me Logan, please. My brother and I wanted to go see RFK when he spoke at the university, but my dad wouldn't take us. He thought all the Kennedys were rich phonies. Claimed that all JFK ever did was get his boat sunk in the war."

"Hah. A Nixon man, then?"

"No, he didn't have much use for Nixon either. Thought he was a weasel."

"I might agree with him on that one. Sounds like your father was an opinionated man. Did he vote for George Wallace in '68?"

"You know, I'm not sure. He could have, I suppose. He was part Native American though, and consequently couldn't stand racists either."

"Really? What tribe?"

"Mohawk. Although he seemed think some of our ancestors migrated to Ohio, where I believe they were known as Mingo. Apparently, that group of Mohawks had converted to Catholicism, and consequently were not too popular with either their fellow tribesmen or English allies."

"Interesting. Strictly speaking, I think Wallace was more a political opportunist than a card-carrying racist. He didn't do too badly in Indiana. But there have always been strong southern sentiments in Indiana politics.

You may know, in the Civil War, the so called "Copperheads", who favored immediate cessation of hostilities with the south, garnered a majority in the Indiana legislature. And members of the Ku Klux Klan had similar control of legislature in the 1920's. Rather hard to believe now, isn't it?"

"I'd be the last person to call myself particularly enlightened, but that the KKK even exists seems hard to believe. You might think people would have better things to do," I said.

He smiled. "Yes. But you didn't come here to discuss Indiana political history or race relations."

"No, not exactly, but it occurs to me you would be the one to discuss them with, if I was. So, were you close with Jason Matthews?"

"We started here at the same time. Lowly non-tenured assistant professors. By coincidence, we each got an apartment in the same building. We used to walk to and from campus together. We had many a lively conversation on those walks. Then, when Jason bought his first house, over off of Lincoln Avenue, I ended up buying the one three doors down. His was much nicer, I admit. Jason had some family money. He could also afford a housekeeper. Betty Clarkson was her name. She made the best apple pie I've ever had in my life. Not sure I've ever had one that good before or since. Needless to say, you could probably tell from looking at me, I was over at Jason's for a lot of dinners. In the fall, after classes started, he would host gatherings for selected faculty on Sunday afternoons. There was a lot going on both in the country and the college at that time. Interesting times as they say. I have very fond memories of those days."

"So, I'm guessing, you were close?"

He laughed. "Yes. I should tell you, like most old college professors, I have a tendency to run on. If need be, please just tell to get to the point."

"How about recently?"

"Well, when Jason got married, our relationship changed of course. Then when they moved, I didn't see as much of him, except on campus. We were still friends, just not as close as before."

"When did they move?"

"Oh, five years or more, I think. They bought a large home north of the city, where a lot of those new exclusive subdivisions have been going in. I said a large home ... it's a mansion really. Then they spent quite a lot fixing it up. I don't think it was Jason's idea. Despite the family money, he's not an ostentatious person and the idea of him living in a mansion is almost laughable."

"It was his wife's idea to move?"

He hesitated before answering.

"Now there, I've gone on again, and perhaps I gave you the wrong idea.

Jason wanted to make his wife happy, and she apparently felt his house on Lincoln wasn't opulent enough. It was a shame, though. Betty had to go too. She lived only a few blocks away and walked to the old place. She seldom drove, so when they moved she had to quit."

"What is Betty up to now?"

"Retirement home, unfortunately. She is in her late seventies. I visit her occasionally, and she appears to be glad to see me, but I'm not sure she recalls who I am. She kept active taking care of Jason and once that went away, she went into a bit of a decline. I see that a lot. The moral to the tale seems to be one way to have a long productive life is to remain active."

"Not sure I'll have to worry about that," I said. "My dad was in his early sixties when he died. His father didn't even make it to sixty."

"My colleagues in the biology department have informed me that, despite common perception, the mother's lifespan is more the determining factor in aging and lifespan than the father's."

"That's good to know. Speaking of their marriage, Detective Rich told me you saw Jason with another woman up in Lakeview sometime back."

"Yes, I was having lunch with a friend on a Saturday afternoon up at Redenbach's, and I saw Jason come in with a young woman. I had seen her talking with Jason previously on campus, so knew she was a student of his. I don't know what to make of that, honestly. Irregular, I suppose, but it probably was something very innocent. Your police colleague got animated and seemed to assume something unseemly was going on."

"Did Jason see you?"

"No. Not sure if you have ever been to Redenbach's on a nice weekend afternoon, but it's usually wall to wall people. Sometimes you can't even find a place to park. They didn't notice us when they came in, and we left shortly after. I have to admit I couldn't help but constantly glance over their way. I should have just gone over and said hello, but for whatever reason, didn't do it."

"So, there was something about seeing them together that made you at least a little uncomfortable?"

"I suppose."

"Did you consider the possibility Jason was having an affair?"

"I would be flabbergasted if he was. But as I alluded to earlier, we aren't as close as we once were."

"How well did you know Jason's wife?" I asked.

"I'm assuming that you know Jackie was an undergraduate here when she met Jason. She was in a couple of classes of mine. And, of course, she married one of my closest friends. But I can't say that I knew her that well."

"What was your opinion of her?"

"She was good for Jason, I suppose. He was a social person, by upbringing, but not by nature, if that makes any sense. Well-mannered and polite, but not outgoing. He had a tendency to obsess over his work. He would have spent all his time doing research if it hadn't been for Betty and me, and later, Jackie. In that sense, she was good for him."

"But in other ways?"

He didn't answer right away and started fiddling with a paperweight on his desk. Then, as if making up his mind, he continued. "As I said, Jackie was in some of my classes as an undergraduate. She was very bright, there is no question about that. In fact, although she majored in political science, I believe she took a number of engineering courses and seriously considered having a double major. As I recall, she was only a course or two from doing so. Mechanical engineering, I think it was."

"That sounds challenging. My sister's a chemical engineer. I looked at one of her textbooks once. It might as well have been written in Chinese."

"Exactly. She was very driven, almost to the point of obsession. Yet, I would not be able to say she stood out, if that makes sense. And I don't mean that necessarily in a negative way. Plenty of students of mine have gone on to be successful, yet I don't recall anything that stands out about them. On the other hand, I I've had a number of students who seemed to do well in my classes who did not achieve much after graduation. But I would have to say, that the ones who impressed me the most eventually became very successful. Not to be a name dropper, but I'm sure you have heard of Micah Smith."

"Sure. Lawyer and civil rights leader. Advisor to host of liberal political heavyweights. Under Secretary of Urban Affairs. He graduated from BHU."

"Yes. Micah was a student of mine, and it was clear early on he was going places."

"So, Jackie was no Micah Smith."

He laughed. "Point made. I believe what I was trying to say was that Jackie was a late bloomer. Certainly, in appearance. Please don't repeat this, but she was somewhat dowdy when she and Jason first became an item. A little pudgy and dressed like a Russian factory worker. Maybe all the engineering courses she took had something to do with it. Later, over the years, she became quite stunning. Lost weight, different hairstyle, makeup, flattering clothes that sort of thing."

He lowered his voice. "And I don't mean to be catty, but she also had cosmetic surgery. A nose job over Christmas break one year. Claims she broke it in a skiing accident and had to have it fixed. Like anyone believed that."

His voice dropped further. "Then one summer, she left a 32A and came back a 34B."

"My kind of girl. Sounds like was trying to project greater self-confidence."

"I suppose so. But, of course, Jason was a big part of it. Not sure she could have spread her wings without him being there for her."

"Sort of an A Star is Born type relationship?"

"The 1937 version or the 1954 version?"

"I was thinking of the Barbara Streisand version."

Morgenfeld smiled.

"I've often thought there was a similarity in manner between Jason and James Mason."

"I'm glad you didn't say Barbara Streisand," I said.

"You have a dry sense of humor. By the way, your first name isn't one you hear too often. Not unusual, but not common. I'm curious … is it a family name?"

"Indirectly, I suppose. As mentioned, my father had some Indian blood and named me after a chief of the Mingo tribe. He seemed to think the Mingo Chief Logan could have been a distant relative of ours."

"Of course. 'Logan's Lament' … 'who is there to mourn for Logan? Not one.' Said, I believe, after some white marauders murdered his family at the start of the Revolutionary War."

"Now you surprise me. Not many people, even college professors, would know that."

"I certainly could not have been close friends of Jason's for all those years without learning a thing or two about his area of interest. In fact, it is quite fascinating. Makes me wonder if I should have been a history major. You know, of course, Jason was an expert on the conflict between the whites and the Indians in the old Northwest."

"And especially Chief Tecumseh, I understand."

"Yes, Tecumseh and his quest to unify the Native Americans against white aggression was his true passion."

"Speaking of which, I understand the professor was working on a book about him."

"Yes. I believe it will be the definitive account of the life of the Shawnee chief."

"I heard he's been working on it for quite a while," I said.

"Yes, that's true. It has been difficult for Jason to complete."

"Would you have any thoughts as to why?"

"Jason is a perfectionist, and much of what we know about Tecumseh has been colored by myth and bias."

"Well, after all, there wasn't TV news back then."

"Thank God. You think TV news is accurate? When I was a youngster, I recall watching a news show that showed cooked spaghetti being harvested from trees. And I believed it."

"I might have fallen for that one myself," I said. "I would expect there are a lot of myths and legends surrounding Tecumseh."

"I should say so. For example, the average, somewhat educated person might say that Tecumseh was the chief of the Shawnee. Further, he was the principal figure in an organized movement of Indian tribes which opposed white settlement of the lands claimed by the tribes. Would you agree with that?"

"I would agree that a somewhat educated individual would say that," I said.

"But you wouldn't?" He asked, raising an eyebrow.

"In general, I suppose. But I would clarify by saying that Tecumseh was a war chief and had no political status, for lack of a better term, among the Shawnee or any other tribe. In fact, the political chiefs resented Tecumseh and his brother, the Prophet, for disputing the treaties they had signed giving away tribal lands. And speaking of the Prophet, most historians now credit him, and not Tecumseh, for starting the Indian unification movement. When it turned more militant, Tecumseh gradually superseded his brother," I paused. "Oh, I should tell you, I was a history major too."

"Law enforcement's gain has been history's loss. But, your response illustrates what I'm talking about. Also, Jason had what can only be described as an obsessive preoccupation with minutiae."

"Such as?"

"For example, the whereabouts of Tecumseh during the first winter of the War of 1812. Some claim he went south to try and gain support among the tribes living in Tennessee, Georgia, and Alabama. Others say he stayed in Michigan, where the British had captured an American army at Detroit and defeated another one further north. Jason was convinced that he spent that winter in this area, recovering from a wound or illness."

"Is that area where they are talking about building a new mall?" I asked.

"Jason seemed to think so. He was rather adamant that an Indian village had been located there and wanted to do some large-scale excavations to prove it. He was convinced that Tecumseh spent the last winter of his life there."

"But he couldn't prove it?"

"No, I'm not sure it was provable, honestly. I was out there on several occasions with him, his dog, and his metal detector, looking for artifacts. He did find a number of arrowheads, pieces of metal utensils, tools, etc. But he was hoping to find something of more significance."

"Something specific, I take it?"

"Yes. I didn't tell your colleague about it for fear of making Jason look delusional."

"Sounds mysterious."

"Perhaps. And please take this with a grain of salt."

"Salt taken."

"You may know that when the War of 1812 began, the British commander in Canada was General Isaac Brock. Unlike some of the other British high-ranking officers in Canada, Brock was a competent leader and brave soldier. He and Tecumseh had an instant rapport when they met. Their esteem for each other was enhanced when the two successfully orchestrated the capture of Detroit at the start of the war. A disaster for the US. There is story, that after the American surrender, Brock honored Tecumseh by giving him his officer's sash. Early accounts even had Brock giving the chief a British general's coat. If he did, he would have had to have given him the one off of his back ... the British were in short supply of everything."

"Matthews was looking for some old rags with a metal detector?"

Morgenfeld chuckled.

"That would perpetrate the myth of the eccentric college professor, wouldn't it?" He said. "No, but in any case, it is believed Tecumseh gave the sash to one of his principal war chiefs, who is known to have been killed at the Battle of the Thames in southwest Ontario, where Tecumseh himself was mortally wounded. General Brock, of course, had been previously killed by American troops at the battle of Niagara, when he returned east after Detroit fell."

"Then it was something else that Matthews hoped to find?"

"There is a story, more of an obscure legend, that before he returned east, General Brock gave Tecumseh his own officer's sword and gorget."

"A gorget?"

"A gorget was originally a functional small plate of armor worn to protect the throat. Later, its use became ceremonial. British officers wore gorgets inscribed with the royal coat of arms. Most were made from silver or brass, although some were more elaborate. Sometime around 1830, officers stopped wearing them. According to the legend, Tecumseh was seen with the sword and gorget after the fall of Detroit. Jason believed Tecumseh spent the winter of 1812 in this area, and hid them, probably buried them somewhere, with the hope he could return. If not, the items would be given to his son, when he got older. Oh, by the way, I understand Tecumseh returned the favor by giving General Brock his tomahawk. I believe it's still a prized possession of the Brock family descendants. Distant ones, I believe. Issac Brock had no children."

"I wonder why a British general would give his sword to an Indian, even if he was a war chief and an ally."

"That one isn't hard to answer. The British were locked in mortal combat with Napoleon in Europe and could not spare any troops to defend Canada. The French Canadians were dubious allies. The only strong support they had was from the Native Americans, who were brilliant irregular fighters, but not given much to traditional European military tactics or discipline."

"Hence the phrase 'Indian fighting.' " I said.

"Exactly, although I understand that phrase is a probably one of the most widely used misnomers in American history. In any case, the Indians were also a people with strong mystical beliefs. The British had betrayed the Indians after the Battle of Fallen Timbers a decade earlier, and the natives had long memories. For those reasons, Brock giving his sword to Tecumseh would have been a gesture of enormous significance to the tribes."

"Why would he have hidden them?" I asked.

"Tecumseh undoubtedly realized there was a chance he would be killed in battle, in which case the sword, with all its symbolic importance, would wind up in the hands of his enemies."

"He buries it, thinking he will come back and get it later? If things go his way, that is?"

"Yes. From Jason, I understood it was common for Native Americans to conceal their valuables by burying them. They also used caves or dry wells. It was not as if they had access to safe deposit boxes, and the tribal villages were constantly being raided by whites. In fact, there is a story that the Shawnees hid a fortune in silver somewhere in southwestern Ohio, when part of the tribe relocated to Missouri."

"Interesting," I said. "Supposing somebody found the sword and the gorget. Would they be worth a lot of money?"

"Perhaps, to someone who collects those types of things. If its authenticity was confirmed, that is. Brock and Tecumseh are national heroes in Canada. I imagine one of the larger museums in that country would love to display them. The likely scenario would be collector would pay a small fortune to the finder for them, and then donate the items to a museum in exchange for a large tax deduction and naming rights for the display housing them. But that's not why Jason was trying to find it. If he found the sword, another piece of the Tecumseh puzzle would be solved."

"Do you think, if he found it, that someone might have wanted it bad enough to do him harm to get it?"

He thought about that. "You would have to make an assumption that, one, there was such a sword hidden or buried somewhere out there, and two, Jason located the sword shortly before he disappeared. And three, that someone knew he found it, realized its significance and wanted it badly enough to harm Jason."

"Speaking of harming Jason, is there any possibility one of his students, past or present, may have nursed a grudge against him? Bad grade on a paper, made them sit in the corner for talking in class, that sort of thing?"

Morgenfeld didn't answer right away and leaned back in his chair, as if he needed a moment to compose an answer.

"Unlikely. We are a small, high quality institution of higher education. I will add conservative, since that's frequently used to describe the university, perhaps unfairly. We don't get the best and brightest, but most of the young people who come here are reasonably bright and hard working. They are looking to get a decent job when they graduate, not necessarily go on to an Ivy League law or medical school. If they are having a problem or issue in a class, they can speak directly with the professor, not some graduate assistant, and get the issue resolved. You will find that most of the professors here, Jason included, will go out of their way to help a student." He paused. "Now, if this was a very competitive institution, where one's future could be jeopardized by a 'D' on an exam, there might be some hard feelings. I should think that doesn't go on here."

He paused in reflection. "Although I was just remembering something." At that, he pushed his chair back and went over to one of the file cabinets. He came back to the desk with a manila folder.

"I gathered from a remark you made earlier that you've lived in Prairie Stop for a while?" he asked.

"Moved here when I was eight. Went to small college downstate and worked as a police officer in South Bend for about fifteen years yes, so never too far away."

"What college, if I may ask?"

"Wallace."

"An excellent school. One of the last bastion of all male colleges. Why did you pick there?"

"It was either Wallace or go work in the steel mill. Nothing more than that. I think the fact that they didn't go co-ed really hurt them when the sexual revolution came along. Made their brochure rather staid by comparison. No cute coeds sunbathing or playing volleyball in the quad. What's in the file?"

"Yes, sorry. I'm deducing you would not have been in college when Kent State happened?"

"I was a senior in high school."

"Well, although BHU is a small conservative institution in the midwest, we are not immune from events happening on the national stage. When the Kent State shootings happened, a large number of our students were justifiably upset. They, like students on other campuses, didn't know how to express what they were feeling. A few decided passively protesting wasn't enough."

When he mentioned Kent State, it occurred to me what he was talking about.

"I remember," I said. "The BHU Three."

"Very good. The BHU Three. A week after Kent State, three students decided to break into the administration building late at night and ignite smoke bombs. The message being that the college was somehow ignoring what happened. That is, putting up a smoke screen, if you will. A relatively harmless statement, if you think about. It wasn't as if they tried to burn the building down or hurt anyone. I understand that they even planned to open some windows to minimize any damage. And it was after hours when no one was in the building."

"But somebody did get hurt."

"Yes. I understand our security people are now, for all intents and purposes, police officers, and meet whatever physical standards that would apply to same. It wasn't so back then. Our security force was mainly retired men. Night watchmen. Most were sixty or older, and not in particularly good shape. A security guard by the name of Luke Smith had a heart attack while he was running up the stairs in the administration building. He went into a coma and died three days later."

"I remember the man died," I said, "mainly because he lived a couple blocks away from us. My dad knew him. He really raged about 'those damn spoiled kids' when he read the story in the paper. I'm not sure I remember what happened after that."

"The authorities wanted to charge one of the students with manslaughter. Only one of the students actually went into the building with the smoke bombs. The other two stayed outside as lookouts. Luke apparently saw the two outside, wasn't satisfied with their explanation as to why they were there and decided to go into the building to investigate. That's when he had the heart attack. Of course, since he died, he couldn't identify the students involved. But Jason happened to be working late that night, walking by the building, and saw some of what happened. He knew the two students serving as lookouts. When sufficiently intimidated by the authorities, they gave up the name of their comrade."

Morgenfeld paused, drank a sip of water, then continued.

"The top administration at the time were all conservative hardliners, unfortunately, and wanted to send a strong message. The two lookouts were suspended and charged with trespassing. The young man inside the building, whose name was Ted Franz, was charged with trespassing, vandalism and, because of Luke's death, involuntary manslaughter. Technically, I believe the specific legal term is unlawful act manslaughter. That is, Ted was engaged in an unlawful act and a person died as a result. I would have to say the campus was torn by dissent over that, with most being on Ted's side. Some of the more liberal members of the university community even posted his bail."

"Not sure even my own family would post my bail."

"I suppose we were more idealistic back then. Unfortunately, Ted disappeared rather than face trial, which meant we forfeited the bail. I personally lost $500, which was quite a bit of money for me back then."

"But he got caught, right?" I asked.

"Over five years or so later. Not sure I recall the exact timing. There was a flood out west somewhere and Ted happened to rescue two children from the roof of a house. Very heroic. By coincidence, there were news cameras there, and it turns out the footage made the national news. Ted was recognized and within a week he was back in the Prairie County jail. Of course, in addition to the original charges, he was charged with flight to avoid prosecution."

Just then, a small bird flew directly into one of the large windows. Since I was facing the window, I saw it coming a split second before impact, but the loud bang startled us both, Morgenfeld more than me. He regained his composure quickly.

"That usually happens in the spring, during mating season," he said.

"I think he's ok ... I saw it fly off."

"Good for it. Where was I?"

"Ted Franz in custody."

"Yes, well, things had changed since he disappeared. The Vietnam War was over, there was the Watergate scandal, Nixon resigning, etc. People were tired of it all and wanted to move on. The administration of the university now had no interest in punishing Ted. Jason was reluctant to testify against the students to begin with, so he was hoping there would be no trial. The Federal authorities were willing to drop the interstate flight charge. Unfortunately, the county prosecutor at the time had a different idea. Flamboyant man, bit of a boor, as I recall. He made it out like he was only enforcing the law, yet most thought he was mainly beginning his next election campaign. Although, now that I think about it, I believe his assistant actually brought the case to trial. You mentioned you formerly were with the prosecutor's office?"

"That was before my time, but you are referring to Vince Tomasini. He was the county prosecutor. I never worked for him. He died about six months ago, by the way. Car accident."

"I recall reading that in the paper. There was speculation there was a mechanical problem with the car."

"Someone in the sheriff's office may have been trying to go easy for the family's sake. I heard he liked to drive fast. Collected speeding tickets like they were candy. I also understand he was fond of John Barleycorn. Usually the combination will catch up to you, sooner or later. I do know the assistant. He's not with the office anymore. Name is James Wildrick."

"Yes, the very well know Mr. Wildrick. They seem very determined to send Ted to jail. Jason was compelled to testify. People didn't understand that. What was he supposed to do, go to jail for contempt? Jason was denigrated in the student paper and even received some threatening notes. Anonymous, of course."

"That was, what, almost fifteen years ago? You think anyone would hold a grudge for that long?"

"Probably not, if Ted had gotten off with a slap on the wrist, as most people thought he would. But the judge, Garrison was his name, surprised everybody and gave Ted a very harsh sentence. Ten years. Apparently, he was known as a prosecutor's judge. But Ted Franz decided he wasn't going to prison. He hung himself in his jail cell the night of the verdict."

We didn't talk for a few moments. Something clicked when he mentioned Judge Garrison's name, but I couldn't put my finger on what it was.

"Did Jason blame himself for what happened?" I asked.

"He told me once that if he had to do it over again, he would have refused to testify, or even lied on the witness stand, rather than have that boy die."

"Did Ted have a family? Siblings, parents, girlfriend?"

"That I don't recall."

He looked down at the file. "I've have some news clippings related to the incident. I'll have Marie make you a copy, if you like. Thought perhaps I would write a book or article about it someday, but never got around to it. Probably just as well. I'm a lapsed follower of Judaism, myself, but I believe it was Jesus Christ who said, 'let the dead bury the dead' ."

CHAPTER 6

When I got home, there was a message on my answering machine from Buzz, asking me to give him a call as soon as possible. I called and got his secretary. I identified myself and was put through to him.

"I'm with some people," he said. "Can you meet me at the bar at Shaker's at about 7?" Shaker's was a popular restaurant on the northeast side of town. I told Buzz I would be there.

Almost as soon as I put the phone down, it rang.

"Mr. Wells?" A woman's voice.

"This is Logan Wells. If you are looking for my dad, you're out of luck. He died a number of years ago."

"This is Jackie Matthews, Mr. Wells."

"I'm sorry, Mrs. Matthews," I replied. "I meant to call you first thing this morning."

"I believe we should talk as soon as possible. Would you be able to come over to the house this afternoon?"

"Sure. Where do you live?"

"You're acquainted with Shawnee Road, I assume," she said.

Shawnee Road ran northwest out of Prairie Stop, roughly parallel to State Highway 35, which was the busy main thoroughfare between Prairie Stop and the interstates heading west to Chicago, and east to South Bend and Detroit. Most long-time county residents referred to 35 as the Bypass, since it had been built in the early eighties to replace the original two-lane Highway 35. The Bypass was on the east edge of town, while Shawnee Road was on the west. Since Shawnee Road wasn't as busy as the highway, yet still was close the interstates and the South Shore Commuter Rail Line, it was considered a desirable area to live for Chicago commuters. In recent years, a number of pricey new subdivisions had been built off of it.

"Sure. I've got a sister who lives off of Shawnee Road. Right after you get to Route 6," I replied.

"Then you know where we are. Our house is on a private road about a mile off of Shawnee. It's the second road on your right after Route 6. The road is called Hawk Point, but I should tell you, you can't see the sign clearly from Shawnee. Our house is at the far end of the street. There aren't any others around it, so you shouldn't have any trouble finding it. Just keep going to the end of the road."

I told her I would see her in twenty-five minutes and hung up.

When we moved to Prairie Stop, I don't remember a substantial difference between the existing homes and the new ones being built. And there were a lot being built. There were some older, larger, Victorian style homes near the center of town, where the old money of Prairie Stop lived. Maybe a handful you could call mansions. And some shacks on literally the other side of the railroad tracks. But most people lived in modern, but modest, three and four-bedroom ranch or two-story homes. I was thinking about that as I drove out of Prairie Stop. Soon after leaving the city limits, I went by subdivisions where luxury homes, some topping out at half a million dollars, were being built. I assumed they were being built by people who worked in Chicago, because I'm not sure how many folks who worked in or near Prairie Stop could afford homes that expensive. I'm no student of sociology or economics, but it sure seemed that there were more rich people around than I remember when I was growing up. Plus, a lot more poor people, and the divide between the haves and the have-nots seemed to have become a vast chasm.

I drove by where my sister lived, although you couldn't see her house from the road. In fact, since she lived in a gated community, you couldn't even get to it unless somebody knew you were coming. My sister made straight A's all though high school, and received a scholarship to Northwestern, where she majored in chemical engineering. She got her masters there, then married another engineer after she graduated. They got good jobs right away, worked hard, and received raises and promotions. Then my sister invented an improvement to an esoteric process used to manufacture one of her company's products. As a reward, she was offered either a cash bonus or stock options. She took the stock, and when her company was acquired a short time later, she made a ton of money. I saw her and my brother in law usually just a couple of times a year, and then for not very long. They traveled a lot, and when they weren't, they were frequently entertaining for work. Plus, although there was nothing said, I think my comparative lack of material success made them uncomfortable, as if I had a disease they didn't want to catch.

As Jackie Matthews warned me, I almost went by Hawk Point Road. John Mellencamp's "Small Town" had just come on the radio, and I was distracted, turning the volume up, plus, as she said, the street sign wasn't easy to see. I had to hit the brakes hard on the Mazda to make the turn, drawing an angry horn blast from the woman in the candy red Volvo station wagon who had been tailgating me. I glanced over as I made the turn and she flipped me off. I noticed her back bumper had a sticker on it from the local Christian music station.

As I headed onto Hawk Point Road, I read a large sign announcing that the subdivision was private, and trespassers were subject to prosecution. On either side of the road was dense woods, so that the only way to know where there were houses were where driveways cut into the roadway. And there weren't too many of them. I guessed that each home sat on three or acres at least. At the entrance to most of the driveways were notices, repeating in one form or another, the no trespassing warning at the street's entrance. Several also had warnings about the premises being guarded by security services.

The Matthews' home was, as described, at the end of the street, barely visible through a stand of pine trees. A brick driveway passed from the street through the trees, then curved gradually another fifty yards or so up to the large two-story house. I'm not sure I would have called it a mansion, but it was big, and made of brick, the color of which matched exactly the color of the brick driveway. Ivy covered walls and a slate roof gave the home an English estate look, or at least what I imagined an English estate would look like. There were two cars in the driveway; a late model Audi sedan, and what I recognized as a late sixties Pontiac GTO convertible, which looked to be in mint condition. I parked the Mazda next to the Audi, and headed toward the front door. Before I got there, I heard something behind me. I thought maybe I had startled a squirrel, but when I turned, there was a young woman, in a dark blue warm-up suit, running towards me. She stopped when she was about ten feet away from me.

"Mr. Wells?"

"Mrs. Matthews?"

"Jackie. Thanks for coming out on such short notice. I hope I didn't startle you. I decided to go for a run while I waited for you. It seems the only way I can deal with stress right now."

"That's ok. I don't startle easy. Had my startle response removed a few months back."

She laughed. "And how do they do that?"

"Get hit by a Buick."

"I see. Was it worth it?"

"Most definitely. I can't recommend the method, though. Where do you go running?"

"We built a trail through the woods behind the house. There's a small pond back there. The trail loops around the pond."

The first thought that went through my mind was what Ivan Rich had told me; Jackie Matthews was a looker. The second thought was the resemblance she bore to Buzz's wife, Beth. Not enough to cause me to gape in astonishment, but it was there. She was tall, as was Beth, and had the same general build, perhaps not quite as thin as Beth had been. She had the same long black hair and high cheekbones as Beth. But when she got closer, I noticed the difference in their eyes. Beth's were bright blue and her dominant feature, Jackie Matthew's were dark and deep set.

She extended her hand, and I shook it.

"Have we met? You're looking at me like you've seen me before," she said.

"Sorry to stare," I replied. "I was a little taken aback. You look like someone I know. The wife of a friend."

"I hope it is someone you have a good opinion of. Why don't we go inside?"

The entrance foyer was as big as my family room, and I wouldn't have been surprised if the ceramic floor and thick Oriental rug on it cost more than my car did, new. A long mahogany table was against the right wall of the entranceway, above which was a huge brass framed mirror. To the left, under an archway, and down a couple of steps, was what I assumed was the living room. It looked to be about the size of half of a tennis court.

"Let's go to the kitchen. I need to get something to drink."

The kitchen was also spacious and well appointed. Everything looked expensive and new. The appliances appeared to be of commercial grade and had German names on them, some I hadn't heard of. My dad was fond of saying that if the Germans and Japanese hadn't conquered the world with tanks and ships, they would certainly do it with appliances and cars.

"Too bad you couldn't afford to keep the place up," I observed.

She turned and gave me a smile.

"Jason describes it, tongue in cheek, as tastefully ostentatious. We bought the house six or so years ago. We got a great price on it, but the man who sold it to us had been through a difficult divorce and didn't maintain it properly. We decided to do a complete remodel. I think it was worth it, but it was almost a year before we could move in." She walked over to the refrigerator.

"I don't want to give you the wrong idea," she said, "I'm not much of a drinker, and it's early yet, but I like a beer after I run. Can I offer you one?"

I looked at my watch. "Well, it is almost three, and I don't like to see someone drink alone."

She grabbed two cans of Heineken and gestured toward the bar chairs by the kitchen island.

"Have a seat. I'm just going to get a dry shirt."

I pulled up a stool and took the beer. I was taking my first swallow when I heard something clicking rapidly and loudly on the tile floor. I looked around and, before I even had a chance to put the beer down, a large ball of red fur came streaking across the room and leapt up onto me, forepaws landing mid stomach and almost knocking me off the stool. Half my beer went all over the floor.

"Damn it, Beau, get down! Come here!" Jackie Matthews came hurriedly back into the kitchen while pulling a grey v-neck BHU T-shirt down over her torso. I caught got a quick view of her breasts. From the brief look, I concurred with Professor Morgenfeld that they had been surgically enhanced. She had also changed out of her warmup pants and was wearing loose grey sweatpants that she had cut off just below the knee. Her feet were bare and her toenails painted a bright pink.

The dog, a large Irish setter, instantly got off me, and went to its owner, his tail wagging a mile a minute.

"I'm so sorry. I thought he was asleep in the den but he must have heard me when I was going to change. Don't worry ... he doesn't bite." She grabbed the dog by the collar.

"Lie down." She said it several times, and the animal ultimately complied, although without first trying to lick her face.

"Not sure I've ever seen an Irish setter that obedient."

"Contrary to popular notion, they are very intelligent and trainable dogs. You just have to be patient with them. I'm going to let him outside ... be right back."

While she was gone, I grabbed some paper towels from the counter and wiped up the spilled beer.

"Buzz spoke very highly of you," Jackie said as she walked back into the room. "He told me before your accident you were the best detective the county had. Sorry to hear what happened by the way. It sounds like you are lucky to be alive. Are you feeling back to normal?"

"Yes, unfortunately," I said, then added, "I hope Buzz didn't oversell me. We go back a long way."

"He told me. Well, I'm more hopeful already. The county police seem to be doing nothing. My husband has been gone for almost two weeks, and it's like they have already given up."

"I understand how you feel, but don't be too hard on them. I talked with the officer on the case this morning. It sounds like they are doing everything they can."

"I wish I could believe that." She took a long pull on the beer then set it down and leaned forward over the table. I was getting a good shot of her cleavage. Could have been accidental. On the other hand, I've found that the very few women I knew who had boob jobs liked to show them off as much as possible. I tried to keep my eyes level with hers.

"What do you think happened to Jason, Mr. Wells? I know you just started on this, but based on your experience and what you know so far, do you think that he is still alive? Please be candid."

"Call me Logan. I would give you a candid opinion if I had one, but I don't. I can tell you the fact that he hasn't been found may be in our favor." Actually, I believed the exact opposite, but wanted to sound optimistic.

"You mean because he hasn't been found dead, he might still be alive?"

"I realize that isn't of much solace."

"Where do we go from here?"

"Well, I need to get to know your husband, especially his mind set in the time before he vanished," I replied.

She nodded but didn't say anything.

"I was out at the university this morning talking to some of your husband's colleagues," I said. "I'll need to ask you some questions, of course. Probably some of them the police have already asked. I apologize for the repetition. You also might find some of the questions intrusive."

"I'll answer any question you have, as honestly and concisely as I can," she said. Then a quick smile, gone almost before it registered. "I know, that may sound like a lot coming from an attorney."

I smiled at her last comment. "These may not come in any discernible order or pattern, by the way. I've always tended to ask questions as they pop into my head. My recent accident seems to have made this tendency more pronounced, at times possibly even irritating."

"I understand. But please don't hesitate to ask me anything."

"To start, how did you meet your husband?"

"I was a senior at BHU, majoring in political science, pre-law, and signed up for a seminar in early 19th century American History. Jason was the professor. I had heard about him, of course. It would be hard not to at a school the size of BHU. The students always talk about the professors, and the common wisdom said stay away from him. It wasn't that he wasn't unfair or a tyrant, just that he demanded a lot. His courses weren't cake courses that the pre-laws could skate through and get an 'A.' I was toying with the idea of double majoring in mechanical engineering, so didn't need any more tough courses."

"Engineering. Wow."

"That seems to be the usual reaction when a woman says she wants to be an engineer."

"I would have said that even if your name was Ernie. I'm a mechanical ignoramus."

"I've always had a fascination with all things mechanical, especially cars. I did most of the restoration on the GTO you saw outside. At least the mechanical work."

"Another wow. Does that have the high output engine in it?" I asked.

"Yes. I thought you just said you were a mechanical ignoramus."

"I grew up in the sixties, the banner years of the domestic auto industry, before everything went to hell in the late seventies. Every red blooded American male knew something about cars. Why did you decide to take your future husband's class?"

"I attended a lecture he did on Native American history in this region. I found it very interesting, and Jason was so knowledgeable, that I decided before I graduated, I would take a course with him."

"At some point after that, then, the student-professor relationship changed?" I asked.

There was a pause, as she chose her words.

"Here's where the honesty part comes in. We had an affair. I was very attracted to him. He was intelligent, well mannered, kind, and considerate. I didn't know many people like that growing up. My father was a salesman who drank too much and was frequently out of a job. My mother divorced him when I was four. She worked two jobs to support us, but we still never had any money. We lived in a small apartment in a not so nice neighborhood in Chicago. My mother ended up an unhappy and lonely woman and relied on Valium and chablis to get through life." She paused, gave a half smile, and added, "that was probably more than you wanted to hear."

"Not at all. I appreciate your candor. By the way, is your mother still alive?"

"She died a number of years ago."

"Your father?"

"I wouldn't know. I haven't seen or talked to him since I was ten."

"Any siblings?"

An uneasy look came over her face, but it was gone so quickly that I wasn't sure I saw it. She took a quick swig of her beer.

"I have a brother. We were close when I was young, but lost touch as we got older. I haven't been in contact with him for quite a while."

I was curious about that but couldn't see any relevance to Matthews' disappearance.

"Alright, back to Jason. Obviously, he saw something in you."

"I was determined back then not to live the life my mother had. I got good grades in high school and came to BHU on a scholarship. I did well in Jason's class, even though it wasn't in my major, and he took an interest in me."

"And then it became more of student-teacher relationship," I said.

"Not while I was in his class, if you were thinking that, a lot of people did, but afterwards, in my last semester."

"After you graduated, you went to law school. Where?"

"University of Michigan."

"I understand that's a top law school."

"Next to the Ivies, most people would consider it one of the best in the country."

"About four hours away, right?"

"It's a three and a half hours, but I got it down to under three. I knew by heart every pothole, rest stop, and speed trap on I-94 from here to Ann Arbor."

"When did you get married?" I asked.

"After I got my law degree, I did some graduate study in England. When I came back, we got married."

"Must have been tough sustaining a cross continent relationship."

"It was at times. But I can attest to the truism that absence does indeed make the heart grow fonder. Even when I was in London, probably one of the most exciting cities in the world, I couldn't wait to get back to Prairie Stop and Jason. Besides, I was busy, Jason was busy. We talked by phone frequently and I might add, expensively. There wasn't a whole lot of time to be lonely. It worked out."

I was a curious what exactly the "at times" met. My first quick impression was that Jackie Matthews wouldn't be the type to pine away.

"How long have you been teaching?"

"Right after we got married, I worked for a law firm in Chicago. Then a visiting professor position opened up at the law school. It was kind of a dream come true to be back here, with Jason."

"This may be a difficult one, and don't take it the wrong way, but how were you and your husband getting along?"

She hesitated, then asked, "Are you married, Logan?"

"Was. Not now."

"Serious girlfriend?"

"I was going out with somebody before the accident. I thought we were serious, but our relationship apparently didn't include extended hospital stays. She moved on, literally and figuratively. She's got a job down in Indy now, I understand."

"I'm sorry. That sounds rather callous of her."

"Oh, I don't think so. I believe in emotional capitalism. If everybody does what's in their own best interest, the market will function most efficiently."

She laughed. "Doesn't that contradict the very nature of love?"

"What's the saying? You can't love anybody else unless you love yourself first."

"I thought love, in a general and specific sense, was putting someone else's well-being above your own."

"I think that's called sacrifice, and sacrifice without result or even appreciation is pointless. It took me getting hit by a car to figure that one out. But I've gotten off the path. We were talking about your marriage."

"Sounds like you know, maybe too well, that no relationship is perfect, but our marriage is a good one. We share many interests and enjoy each other's company. Our lives couldn't be any better. We love our jobs, we had just finished the house, and we were planning on starting a family."

"Did your husband ever give you any reason to think he wasn't as happy as you?"

There was a silence.

"I assume you are referring to the Parker girl," she said, coldly.

"I was told that your husband was having a relationship with her."

"I'm glad you said relationship, instead of affair. Jason would never cheat on me. He tried to help that girl get her life straightened out and she took advantage of him. That he would have an affair with her is preposterous."

"Why did she need to get her life straightened out?" I asked.

"It isn't hard to figure out. Pregnant, married and divorced before she was twenty. Working in a video store and tending bar at night. Leaving her child in God knows whose hands."

I thought of the comments she had just made about her own mother.

"People do what they have to do," I said.

"You don't think that the choices one makes determines what they have to do?" There was sharp tone to her question.

"Everybody makes mistakes. Some people never get that chance to make the right choice."

"You surprise me. You were spouting cynicism a minute ago and now you're cutting everyone a break. You were a policeman, right? I thought they all had a disparaging outlook on human nature."

"I would agree with that. Maybe I'm just getting soft in my old age. How did you learn about your husband and Ms. Parker?"

"We would talk about out our classes and students. He told me there was a woman in one of his classes who he thought had potential."

"Potential? As in terms of being an exceptional student?"

I recalled her previous comments about herself as a student.

"More than that. He was acquainted with her and her situation and thought she could be doing a lot more with her life. That's why I said he wanted to help her."

"How was he doing that?" I asked.

"Oh, encouraging her to go back to school, attempting to mentor her, I suppose."

"Is that all?"

"This is the embarrassing part: Jason actually gave her money. One day she didn't make it to class. She called him later to apologize and told him that her car had broken down and she didn't have enough money get it fixed. He lent the money to her to get the car repaired. And for other things. When I found out, I was furious. Imagine how it would look for a male professor to be giving money to a female student? No matter what his standing at the university, his reputation and even his position were jeopardized by what he did."

I got the idea Jackie Matthews was more concerned about her husband's reputation than his position. It certainly didn't seem like he needed money.

"I see what you mean," I said. "What did Jason say when you found out?"

"He gave me his bewildered, innocent look, as if he couldn't understand what he did wrong. He told me she was going to pay him back, with interest. I told him not to see her anywhere except class."

"He agreed?"

"Yes, once he realized the impropriety of what he had done."

"How long was this before he went missing?"

"A month, perhaps."

I didn't think I was getting the full story on Roseanne Parker, even from the angry wife's perspective, but I planned on talking with her myself, so I decided not to pursue it.

"Did your husband have any health problems?"

She paused before answering.

"This isn't widely known, but Jason had some episodes last year that indicated he was at a serious risk of a stroke. He had a number of what are called TIAs, or small strokes. They foreshadow a major stroke. He missed a week's worth of classes while we into Chicago had some tests done. His doctor discovered Jason has atherosclerosis, but it can be treated with medication. We told the university he had the flu."

"Why the secrecy?" I asked.

"My husband is a private man. He also likes to deal with people on equal terms, and he didn't want anyone feeling sorry for him. His doctor is in Chicago, so no one here knew what happened."

"Is he on some medication?"

"Yes, a couple different blood pressure medications. He had to radically alter his diet and curtail some activities. I suppose I should also tell you that he suffered from depression after the episodes—it's very common—and he was prescribed something for that."

"If I wanted to talk to his doctor, would you be ok with that?" I asked.

"Of course. I'll contact him and ask him to call you. Richard Cook is his name."

"Other than his health, were there other things worrying him?"

"He had things going on that were causing him anxiety."

"For instance?"

"I think the main thing was the book. You are aware that Jason was working on a book?"

"On Tecumseh?"

"Yes. It's no secret that he was having trouble finishing it. I believe it may have even been a bit of a joke for some people. When he had the strokes, he worried that he might never complete it. It was a vicious circle. He obsessed about the book and that made his health suffer, which made it harder to work on the book."

"What do you think was the problem with completing it?"

"Jason is a perfectionist and the book was his life's work. He didn't want a single word to be not the right one. I told him he should forget about it for a while and come back to it when he was ready. But he didn't do that. He was even having nightmares about it. I think I even heard him speaking Shawnee in his sleep."

"I'm not sure I would recognize Shawnee."

"Neither would I, except I wrote down what he said. And when I asked him about, he told me the phrases were Shawnee."

"Did he say what they meant?"

"I'm not really sure he knew. Except one. Matchee ne that ha."

"And that means?"

"This sounds very strange, but he said it meant 'you are my enemy'."

"That is strange. Did he say who he thought the 'you' was?"

"No, I think I embarrassed him when I asked. He didn't want to talk about it after that."

"Speaking of the Shawnee," I said, "I understand your husband was leading an effort to keep some local Indian artifact sites from being turned into a shopping mall."

"Jason was convinced that Tecumseh and his brother, the Prophet, spent the winter of 1812-13 just north of here. He hoped to find evidence to that effect. That's the area that a developer is looking to build a new mall."

"I heard about that. Also, that your husband hoped to find a sword that a British general gave Tecumseh."

She smiled. "You've been talking with Hal Morgenfeld. He's one of the few my husband shared that particular obsession with. It's true. Jason had reason to believe the sword existed and might possibly be where the Indian village was located. But please don't think he was a lunatic obsessed with finding the Holy Grail."

"Your husband wanted to halt the development?"

"Jason wasn't trying to halt anything. He just wanted to the opportunity to do some excavations before they threw down tons of concrete."

"Who are they?"

"A lot of silent partners, apparently. Jason had trouble finding out who was even involved in the project. The name I hear mentioned most is Steve Coban. He's a developer in Chicago. Plus, there were local interests. The area construction firms and trade unions were probably salivating over a job like that."

I made a note to ask Buzz about the local interests. If anyone had more details, he would.

"What kind of response did your husband get?" I asked.

"I would say tepid, but that would be an exaggeration. The County Commission is in favor of the development. With the steel business declining, anything with jobs attached is viewed as a gold mine. The commissioners thought if they just ignored Jason he would go away. He did have some success with one of the commissioners: Ray Menlo. Menlo promised Jason that he wouldn't vote for any development plan until any possible artifact sites were investigated."

"Ray Menlo of Menlo's Men's Wear?" I asked. Menlo's was an upscale men's clothier in downtown Prairie Stop.

"Yes."

I knew that Menlo was a big booster of downtown and opposed, as a matter of course. any development that threatened its vibrancy, which automatically excluded anything built out of town.

"Did anyone in the pro development group ever make any remarks about or to Jason that might be construed as a threat?" I asked.

"No, not really."

"But?"

"Our mailbox got knocked off the post a few times. I thought it was kids, but then I wasn't so sure. We had a brick one built and that ended that. There were some late-night phone calls with nobody on the other end. I know some people weren't too happy about what Jason was doing."

"Can you think of anyone who might have wanted to harm your husband?"

"I've thought about that endlessly over the last two weeks. I'm sure there were people that might not have cared for Jason, but certainly not enough to have wanted to harm him."

"The day he disappeared … I understand you were in Chicago?"

"Yes. Every fall some of the law schools in Chicago sponsor a mock court competition. We usually enter a couple of teams, and most of the third-year students go into the city to watch. It's a lot of fun for everyone. The competition starts Wednesday morning and goes through Friday afternoon. I went up Tuesday afternoon after class and stayed around Saturday morning because I wanted to do some shopping."

"When you got back home, did you notice anything unusual, of course other than that your husband was gone?"

"No. I talked to Jason Tuesday evening just to let him know what room I was in at the hotel. I tried to call him Thursday and Friday evenings, but didn't get an answer."

"You weren't concerned when you couldn't reach him?"

"No. I figured he decided to meet some friends for dinner. He had talked about doing that before I left."

"Anyone in particular?"

"I'm sure he told me, but I can't remember."

"When you got back and saw he wasn't there, what did you do?"

"I'm embarrassed to admit that I didn't do anything right away. I figured he was out running errands. Eventually I got worried and started calling anyone who might have seen him. Finally, I called the police."

"Did you noticed any of your husband's things missing? Clothes, razor, that sort of thing?" I asked.

"No, not that I could tell."

I paused. I didn't have any more questions for her but did want to take a look around.

"I think I've asked everything I need to right now. I appreciate your candor. One more thing … would you mind if I took a quick look around? I wouldn't be snooping, just for me to get more of an idea what your husband was like."

Like my question about her siblings, that seemed to generate a reaction. I thought for a second she was going to say no, but then,

"Of course not. Snoop away. I'll go see what Beau is up to. I should tell you, the place is a mess since this happened."

"I won't take long, I promise."

"Take your time. You get to the stairway by making at left at the end of this hallway," she said, pointing. "Did you want to go to the basement as well?"

"No, I don't think so," I said. I didn't think I was going to find Professor Matthews buried in the crawl space. "Like I said, I won't be long."

The stairway was built of a dark wood, walnut I guessed. The banister was of the same material, but the rails had been painted an off white, which matched the light textured carpet running down the middle of the steps. A landing on the second floor overlooked the living room. In the opposite direction of the landing were the bedrooms. I poked my head in the first two, which appeared to be guest quarters, since, despite Jackie's admonition, they were in immaculate condition. All the furnishings and appointments were luxurious. Each room had its own full-size bathroom.

There was study opposite the guest rooms, with a desk, a couple of chairs and four large bookshelves. The desk was the only piece of furniture I had seen so far in that didn't look like it belonged. It was an old-fashioned barristers desk, made of light oak and contrasted with the rich mahogany bookcases and brown leather chairs. The finish on the desk was scratched and marked in a number of places, contrasting with the brand-new appearance of everything else in the house. I guessed maybe it had some sentimental value for Professor Matthews. On the desk was an Apple computer, which appeared to be new.

I ruffled through the very few papers on the desk, not really sure what I was looking for. Something told me I wasn't going to find a note from Jason Matthews saying, "Gone to Tuscon for the winter, back in a few months." In fact, there wasn't anything more personal on the desk than an invitation to the BHU faculty holiday party the first week of December. I didn't see anything that looked like a manuscript either, but I figured that was on the Apple.

The master bedroom was enormous. It appeared to me as if they had knocked down the wall of another bedroom to make the room more spacious. Unlike the guest rooms, this bedroom looked like someone actually lived in it. The massive four poster canopy bed was un-made and a variety of women's clothing items were lying about on the bed and floor. There were large matching wood nightstands on each side of the bed. I pulled open the top drawer of the one on the right. It contained typical nightstand stuff: several pairs of eyeglasses, a couple combs, shoelaces, other personal items. In the bottom drawer were two paperback biographies of Tecumseh and some blank writing pads and pens. My detective savvy told me that was Jason's side of the bed.

I opened the top drawer of the other nightstand and it was full of a variety of lotions, creams, and moisturizers. When I opened the second drawer, I was somewhat taken aback to see there were three vibrators, of varying lengths and circumference, on top of a few Playgirl magazines. There were some paperbacks as well, which from looking at the titles, I supposed would be referred to as erotic fiction.

There were two bathrooms, in opposite corners of the room. I went into the bigger one, thinking it was the master bath. There were a lot of pill bottles in the medicine cabinet with Jason Matthews' name on them. I jotted down the names on the bottles: Atenolol, Chlorthalidone, and Trimipramine. There was also a bottle of Anafranil that had Jackie Matthew's name on it.

I looked in the vanity bottom. The shelves were full of more cosmetic and beauty products. There was something in a drug store bag on the very back of the lower shelf that caught my attention. When I opened it, it took me a second to realize it was an early pregnancy test. A package of three, one missing. The receipt in the bag said it had been purchased about a month ago. I put it back the vanity and went back into the bedroom to double check that I had closed all the nightstand drawers.

I had been gone more than a few minutes and hustled back downstairs. Jackie wasn't in the house. I went outside and saw she was tossing the ball to the dog. As soon as he saw me, he came bolting over and jumped up, his front paws hitting me in the chest with enough force to knock me a step back. While he was leaning up on me and trying to lick my face, I reached over and scratched behind his ears.

"Get down, Beau!"

"It's ok. Our dogs used to like jump on people too."

The dog got down and somewhat surprisingly bolted back around the house. He must have seen a squirrel.

"Find anything interesting?" she asked, giving me a small, what I thought, knowing smile.

"I'd like to meet your decorator. This place is a regular Taj Mahal."

"I did it myself for the most part. Another one of my obsessions."

"When I hit the lottery, I'm going to ask you to redo my shack for me. By the way, how long have you and Buzz known each other?"

She gave me a quizzical look. "I'm not sure I remember. I've known him for a while. I think I might have met him at a Democratic fundraiser a few years back. Why?"

"Just curious."

"It was such a shame about his son, and his wife. I know it's been very difficult for him. That's why I'm so grateful he is trying to help me."

I started to walk to my car.

"How do you like your rotary engine?" she asked.

I turned back to her. "I don't know that much about it, to tell the truth. Other than that Mazda is the only one that has it, and it supposed to be somewhat innovative."

"It's used more in aviation applications," she said. She smiled. "I'm a tech nerd."

I had my hand on the door handle and paused.

"What about the dog?" I asked.

"Oh, he's probably chasing a rabbit or squirrel out back. Maybe even a deer."

"No, I mean, your husband apparently went missing Thursday, and you didn't get home until Saturday," I said.

"Not sure I'm with you."

"Our dog would go nuts if we left her alone for more than six hours or so. My dad was a big animal lover. Didn't like humans so much but loved animals. Anyhow, he would make sure that someone took care of her."

She gave me an odd look.

"We leave water and food out for him. He had a few accidents in the house but other than that, he was fine."

I nodded to her and got into my car.

CHAPTER 7

As I drove back into Prairie Stop, I thought about my conversation with Jackie Matthews. She seemed less distraught than I would have expected, although people deal with stress in different ways. Some do it by not giving up the semblance of control; maybe Jackie Matthews' was that type. More puzzling to me was the lack of communication with her husband from the time she went to Chicago. I would have thought her not being able to reach her husband for a few days should have caused her more concern than it did.

The clouds were lifting as I got back into Prairie Stop, and stars were appearing in the sky when I pulled into the parking lot at Shaker's. Shaker's was one the best-known eating establishments in the region. Family owned, it had originally started out as a roadhouse, fried chicken type place, but over the years it had been steadily expanded and become more formal. We used to go the restaurant on special occasions when I was younger, my father never failing to complain about how the prices had risen from our previous visit. They would make non-alcoholic cocktails for the kids, with little plastic swords with fruit speared on them, with which my brother and I would engage in fencing contests with on the drive home.

When we took our family trips to Shaker's many years ago, the male patrons wore suits and the women wore nice dresses. Even my father, who only wore a suit for weddings and funerals, would grudgingly put his on before we went out to eat. When I walked in this afternoon, there wasn't suit in sight. There was a woman in a black dress standing behind a podium by the entrance to the dining room, but I figured she was the hostess. Most of the patrons in the main dining area were elderly couples and wearing the various types of casual clothes old people favor; polyester pants and knit shirts in peculiar colors.

The hostess was on the phone and put her hand over the mouthpiece as she glanced at me, but before she could say anything, I cut her off by pointing to the bar.

The bar, too, had changed. It had been dark, with a lot of wood paneling and flickering candles in red glass holders on the tables. On occasion, they would have someone playing soft pop tunes on the piano. Now, the place seemed positively bright and boisterous. It was well lit, there were some large mirrors on the walls, and plants hanging from the ceiling. Country music coming from speakers on the wall, and the piano had been replaced with a karaoke machine. Somewhat to my surprise, Buzz was already there, sitting by himself at the end of the bar. He was wearing a dark suit, white shirt and black tie, which I thought was slightly out of character for him. He normally wore suits, of course, but his taste in clothes tended to the more colorful and less conservative. I sat on the stool next to him.

"You in court today?" I asked, glancing down at his attire.

"No. Funeral."

"Anybody I know?"

"Old Judge Garrison. Remember him?"

"The hanging judge," I said, recalling how the county lawyers used to refer to him.

"Let's not speak harshly of the dearly departed."

"I think he referred to himself that way."

"I said funeral, actually he's been dead almost a couple months. We had a reception, memorial, whatever you want to call it, in the office. Took us a while to get it on everyone's schedule. Got a good turnout, though. Course we had an open bar. That would bring a crowd out for Attila the Hun's funeral."

"Anybody he put away show up?" I asked.

"They're still all in jail. He believed if you went to jail you should stay there."

"What happened to him?"

"Fishing accident up at Lake Wingo."

"How do you accidently die fishing in Indiana? The great white perch ram the boat?"

"I didn't say a fish killed him. He had an accident while he was fishing. If you are interested, the judge was retired and used to go fishing a few times a week up at Lake Wingo. By himself mainly, which, since he was 85, was probably not a real good idea. They think maybe he got dizzy or something and fell out of the boat. I know he had heart trouble for a long time."

"That's the second time today I've heard his name." I briefly told him about my meeting with Morgenfeld and our reminiscing about the BHU Three. A scowl slowly started to appear on his face as I went on.

I concluded with, "That was your case, wasn't it?"

Buzz shook his head slowly and then, in disgusted frustration, put his head in his hands.

"For Pete's sake, you're supposed to be finding Matthews, not telling me what he did twenty years ago. And it was Tomasini's case. I was his assistant. What was I supposed to do? Tell him to cut the kid a break and we should all go out for a picnic? What about the old guy who died? We were just supposed to forget about that?"

"Take it easy. It's a bit of a coincidence, is all. Within the last six months, something has happened to the judge, the prosecuting attorney and the lead witness."

"Yeah, and maybe if you really let your imagination run wild, you can tie in the Kennedy assassination."

"Which one?"

"Cut the crap. Tomasini drove like a maniac. After my first time in the car with him, I never drove with him again. He was past due for a crackup. And what the hell does any of this have to do with the professor?"

He was getting annoyed, so I changed the subject. I looked around the room.

"What did they do to this place?" I asked.

"I take it you haven't been in here in a while."

"Not since I moved back from South Bend."

"That sounds about right. A few years ago, they had a small fire, started back in the kitchen. Didn't burn much, but there was a lot of smoke damage. Old man Shaker's daughter, that might have been her when you came in, decided it was time to brighten the place up. What you see here is apparently the trendiest in bar décor."

"Bar? This looks more like the lobby of one of those no-frills chain hotels."

"Funny you should say that. You may have noticed that the place right next door is a no-frills chain hotels. Old man Shaker would be turning in his grave. He hated chain anything. Thought Wal-Mart and McDonalds were responsible for destroying small town life. Speaking of which, I saw some self-proclaimed economic expert on TV last week, talking about how many new jobs have been created since the Republicans took over. I'm guessing about ninety percent of them are for shelf stockers or food service workers."

"What about those people living off of Shawnee Road? I doubt if they're flipping burgers for a living."

"No, you're right. Those are the ones who own everything. I know for a fact Shaker had plenty of offers to turn this place into a Red Lobster or Ponderosa. Would you rather eat at a cardboard cutout chain restaurant or a fine dining establishment like this?"

"I dunno. I don't eat out a lot, but this place looks like it's gone downhill. Why didn't the daughter sell after he died? Judging from the dining room, most of her clientele is going to be dead within five years."

"They're here for the early bird specials. I think its pot roast tonight, in case you were interested. Because Shaker put in his will that if she ever sold the place, the trust fund he left for her would be given immediately and in full to Prairie County Hospital. I ought to know, I did the will for him. Course the will didn't say she couldn't tear out the wood bar and replace it with this Formica and particle board crap." He tapped his glass on the bar. "What else you find out? I heard you've been busy today."

"New travels fast," I said.

"It still is basically a small town. Not for much longer though, I fear. The Prairie Stop of our youth will soon be gone forever."

"Especially if somebody puts a big shiny new mall out by the interstate."

He looked up from his drink.

"I didn't know you were interested in commercial real estate."

"I'm always looking for a chance to get in on the ground floor. You ever hear of a guy named Steve Coban?"

"Sure. First and foremost, he's a Fighting Irish alumnus. Second, he's a real estate developer in Chicago. We've done some work for him."

"What kind of work? I understand he's the man behind the mall."

"Nothing too exotic, researching some county ordinances, building and zoning codes, land titles, stuff like that."

"That's interesting," I said. "Jackie Matthews said there were local people behind Coban. Would that include you? I'd guess if he built a new mall there would be pile of legal fees to go along with it."

"What if there was? You apparently don't care about money, but do you have a problem with other people making some?"

"Not at all, especially if it's you. No, it's just that I've had a couple of people tell me the Professor was trying to toss a wrench into the works, mall-wise. That might not have made him too popular," I said.

"If you're referring to that stuff about Indian relics at the site, who cares? From what I understand, this area was like a truck stop for Indians. You can't dig in my garden without finding a couple of arrowheads."

"It's history. It's the heritage of a people who originally lived here."

"So what and who cares? That has as much chance of stopping the mall as Miami does of stopping the Irish this Saturday. If your theory is that Steve Coban made the Professor disappear because of a stern letter to the editor, you may want to come up with another one."

"I also heard Matthews found a sympathetic ear on the county commission."

"Who?" Buzz asked.

"Ray Menlo."

Buzz snorted.

"Consider the source," he said. "Ray's a good man, but he's opposed to any development that isn't located fifty feet away from his place downtown. He could have invented the term conflict of interest. In any case, one commissioner can't do squat by himself except make noise. Menlo is a lonely voice wailing in the wilderness. The other commissioners are for progress, not a return to the good old days. Which, incidentally, maybe weren't so good."

"I assume you are attuned to the inner workings of the county commission. Probably all golfing buddies of yours."

"It's not a crime to have friends, especially ones in high places. If you are working up to another conspiracy theory, at least make it believable."

The bartender came over. I ordered a club soda, and Buzz ordered another beer, and then asked for a shot of Bushmills to go with it.

"How long did you say you knew the wife?" I asked.

He gave me a frown.

"I don't think I did. I might have mentioned that I met her at a bar association function a couple of years ago."

"She said it was a Democratic fundraiser, a few years ago."

"Whatever. We've worked on a couple of pro-bono cases together."

"She's attractive, wouldn't you agree?" I asked.

"No argument there. Reminds me a little of Beth."

The Bushmills disappeared.

"Why are you asking about the wife? Think she got rid of her husband?"

"No, but something about her just didn't seem kosher."

"In what way?"

"A little too cool."

"She didn't seem aggrieved enough for you?"

"I guess you could put it like that."

"What's the motive?"

"Matthews had money, didn't he? And a lot of life insurance."

"You saw their house, right? Did it look like he was depriving her of anything?"

"You've been in their house?" I asked.

"I told you. We did some work together. I dropped some papers off at the house a couple times."

"I saw an end table there that probably cost more than my car," I said.

"Ed Fletcher, of Fletcher's Furniture, wasn't too happy about that. He told me she bought all that stuff in Chicago. Didn't even throw a table or lamp his way."

"Maybe he did away with Matthews to get even."

Buzz looked at his watch. "I got somewhere to be. Next round is on me." He tossed a twenty on the bar. "Far be it from me to give you guidance, except that technically you are working for me, but it seems to me you've spent most of the day spinning your wheels. There is no conspiracy, and the wife didn't do it. I'd scratch those two off the list and start to figure out what really happened to Matthews."

Chapter 8

I was a little peeved after my conversation with Buzz, and as soon as he was gone decided to have another beer to soothe my bruised feelings. Not a good idea, but I did it anyhow. I paid for it with his twenty and gave the rest to the bartender. It occurred to me that I had more to drink the last two days than in the previous several months. I thought briefly about eating at Shakers but the idea of eating alone surrounded by old people too daunting. I decided I'd stop at Foodchopper on the way home.

When we were kids, we were fond of Lujacks, the predecessor to Foodchopper, mainly because of the variety of candy and small toys they stocked. Although, as I recall, the store was dark and dingy, with the shelves seldom being fully stocked. I also remembered the butcher, a large, unpleasant man, who, in hindsight, had a heavy drinking problem. He had the drunk's florid face, with broken blood vessels lining his bulbous nose, and red watery eyes. He liked to make ribald remarks and double entendres to the female customers. It was curious to me that there were at least few who apparently enjoyed making crude banter with him. I heard he was a first cousin of the owner of the place, which was probably the only reason he was able to keep the job. My mother, I remember, took his risqué comments in stride and even gave it back to him, which, as I got older, found confusing. I asked her one time, "Why do you let Mr. Lujack talk to you like that?" She replied, "I know to handle myself. I can take care of an old lecher like him. Did you ever notice he tips the scale in my favor?"

Foodchoppers was a regional chain, and accordingly seemed to have some minimum standards for store appearance. Every time I was in there the store was clean, brightly lit and the shelves were always full. Plus, although they may not have had the most gracious clerks, they generally didn't make crude remarks to the patrons either.

I was standing at a bin back in the meat section that had items "marked down for quick sale." I was trying to decide which package of ground beef had the least amount of gray tinge to it, when I heard a voice behind me.

"Looks tainted, if you ask me."

The voice was immediately familiar, yet I couldn't quite place it. When I turned around, my girlfriend from 20 years ago, Kathy Plemons, was standing there.

I felt my face flush. She gave me bemused look.

"Hello, Logan. Long time no see."

"Hello, Kathy."

I extended my hand. She took it and held it for a few seconds as she stared at me.

"It's incredible, but you've aged hardly at all."

"It's clean living. You look good too."

"If only it were true. I look like a close to age forty-year-old woman should, I suppose. But you, I can't get over it! Is there a fountain of youth somewhere around here?"

Her self-assessment was honest. She was thin and had a good figure when we were younger, but now was heavier, not overly so, but rounder. Her hair, which I remembered as dark brown, long and flowing, was now cut short, permed, and much lighter, maybe to hide some grey. Her cheeks and jaw line reflected the extra weight, yet her green eyes were as bright and curious as I remembered them. She certainly was not hideous, just older, but even so, not having seen her for years, the changes were startling.

As if reading my mind, she said, "You're thinking I got old and fat, aren't you?"

"Of course not."

"I don't blame you if you are, because I did." She laughed. "I should have known you would look the same. The Dorian Gray of Prairie Stop."

"I was in hospital a while back. That's a good place to lose weight."

"I heard that. I bumped into Buzz somewhere and he told me what happened. It's amazing you're still alive, let alone looking like you're twenty-five."

"Now you're overdoing it," I said.

"I was hoping I would run into you somewhere. How are you?"

"Please don't say run into near me. And getting better every day and every way."

"I see," Kathy said.

"Enough about me. I heard you came back to town a couple months ago to look after your dad. How is he?" I asked.

"Not good, I'm afraid," she replied, shaking her head. "He's got lung cancer. Two packs of Winston's a day for 50 years will do that to you. I should talk. Smoking is the one bad habit he had that I picked up. He's already lasted six months more than they thought he would. I think he's hanging around to prove the doctors wrong. He liked you, by the way. Just wondered why you never talked to him."

"He scared me. He always looked at me like he knew exactly what I was thinking, which in my case must have been deeply disturbing. His being sick must be rough for you. I remember when my dad died. It wasn't a good time."

She sighed. "Let's not talk about dying. It's too depressing."

There was a pause as we each tried to collect out thoughts. At least I was. They had country station on in the store and Kathy noticed the song they were playing. It was Willie Nelson singing "Crazy."

"God, I love this song," Kathy said. "For years I always thought Patsy Cline wrote it. Imagine my surprise when I find out Willie Nelson did. I used to cry every time I heard Patsy Cline sing."

"Used to?"

"I guess in addition to getting old, I got jaded. Probably comes from two failed marriages. Now I only cry when the alimony check is late. Which recently has been on a pretty regular basis."

"You don't seem like you lost your sense of humor."

"One thing I have learned is that there isn't much point to going around with a shitty attitude." She moved closer to me and put her right hand lightly on my chest.

"Speaking of which, I've always wondered why you did me like you did. You know, pretending I had died or something. I know it was a long time ago and all, and we were both kids, but still, that was pretty shabby. You broke my impressionable school girl heart." She took her hand away and stepped back. "Now I feel better."

"Wait a second. You went off to an Ivy League school in the city that never sleeps. I went off to a small, all-male college, two hours from here. I could say it was in the middle of nowhere, but that would be doing the term 'middle of nowhere' a disservice. I wrote you two letters a week for three months, but never heard word one from you. Then, at Christmas, I found out you were going out with a Jewish dental student."

"How did you know he was Jewish?"

"You sent me a combination Christmas card, dear John note. There was a naked picture of him in it."

"Now that I really don't remember. I should have married him, though. I understand he has one of the largest periodontal practices in northern New Jersey. And me, needing major gum work now too. So, would you be interested in hearing the real story of my life since I saw you last or not?"

"Here and now?" I asked.

"Well, I suppose we could move over to the canned goods. I thought maybe we could go to Shaker's or someplace."

"Just came from there. How about we go back to my place?"

Kathy hesitated but then said, "Alright."

As we walked to the parking lot, I asked her if she wanted to ride with me or follow.

"I'll follow. That will give your neighbors something to talk about."

"I'm still living on Norwich Drive," I said.

"You got to be kidding me."

"No, it's true. Not long after my dad died, my mom decided she wanted to live in Florida. After thirty years of snow and cold, she decided she had enough of the winters here. She was set with my dad's insurance and asked if I wanted to stay in the house. I had been living there while my dad was sick, so took her up on it."

"You know, Logan, despite what you apparently think, change isn't always a bad thing,'" Kathy said. "I won't need to follow you, by the way. I could probably find it blindfolded."

THE SKY HAD CLEARED, AND the stars were now bright in the sky, much more visible than they had been over at the well-lit commercial area by Shakers. As usually happens, when the clouds lifted, the temperature seemed to have dropped about 10 degrees. The smell of wood smoke hung in the air. I heard a mournful train whistle in the distance. Although there was no more passenger rail service to Prairie Stop, freight trains rumbled through seemingly every hour of the day and night.

Kathy got there before me and was parked in front of my house, her car engine running. When I pulled into the driveway she shut the car off and hurried over to me.

"I almost forget how cold it gets here," she said, shivering.

"It's not even below forty yet."

"It was seventy degrees in LA today, according to the paper."

"I guess you don't want to sit outside then?"

"Now you're kidding me."

"I thought we could sit out back. I've got a heater on the deck, and it turned out to be a nice night."

"Let's go in the house first, and then we'll talk about the deck."

I opened the door and got a few lights on. Kathy walked in and looked around, appraising.

"Now I see why you wanted to sit outside. I like what you've done, or not, as the case may be. Kind of an early American nihilist."

I didn't have a whole lot of furniture. When my mother moved, she took the few pieces she liked and sold or gave away most of the rest of it. She said she thought I shouldn't hang on to the past and told me to buy some new stuff. I hadn't bought much since then except the basics; a leather recliner and love seat, a couple of small tables. All purchased from a secondhand shop. I didn't even have a dining room table. The house wasn't that big but the lack of furniture made it look like a vestibule at funeral parlor. Kathy and I sat on the love seat.

"Sorry, I've never been hung up on acquiring things. In fact, the less stuff I got the better. Call it a tribal mentality," I said.

"Tribal mentality?"

"In most Indian tribes, property was communal. What one had was to be shared with all. Wealth was meaningless unless it benefited the tribe as a whole. That's a different idea, don't you think?"

"You wouldn't last long in California. But I admire a man who doesn't clutter up his house or his life with possessions. Your mother just gave you the place?"

"My dad didn't believe in investing in the conventional style. He distrusted banks and thought putting money in the stock market was the same as gambling. He said the only sure thing he knew was he that was going to die someday. So, he bought life insurance. Lots of whole life policies. They were for small amounts, but in total they added up to a tidy sum."

"And your mother became a wealthy widow?"

"No, not exactly. But enough to buy a beachfront condo in Florida. She still owns this place outright, and I send her a few hundred a month in rent. When I can, that is, which isn't often. She doesn't seem to mind. I think she has given up on me ever making a lot of money. She has my brother and sister for that."

"Sounds like a good deal. Your sister and brother didn't feel cheated out of their inheritance? My one sister has already claimed the dining room set, and my brother showed up a few weeks ago to take my dad's autographed baseballs and signed Ernie Banks cap."

"My brother lives in Washington DC. Does something for the government which he can't talk about. Hence, I never hear from him and he comes to town once in a blue moon. He plays golf though, and uses that as an excuse to visit our mother in the winter so he can get a few rounds in."

"Your sister?"

"My sister lives in a mansion off on Shawnee Road, the garage of which would easily hold this place two or three times over. I see her about as much as my brother. As far as she's concerned, we could tear the old homestead down and salt the ground it stood on."

"Lot of fond memories for her, huh?"

"I think she would just as soon she forget she grew up a steelworker's daughter. In fact, I think she now tells people my dad was an executive in the steel business. The closest he got to an executive was working as a foreman for a couple of years. He couldn't stand it and went back to the union."

"That's funny, that's what I liked about growing up here," Kathy said. "Nobody ever seemed like they put on airs. The doctor and the garbage man went to the same church, shopped in the same stores, and their kids went to the same schools. Maybe they even lived a few blocks away from each other. Where I used to live near LA, who you are is defined by what your zip code is, what kind of car you drive, and the restaurants you eat at."

"Yeah, well times have changed here too. The doctor now lives in a gated subdivision and sends his kids to private school. The garbage man lives in a trailer park off Route 6 and drinks too much. His kids just dropped out of high school and smoke weed. And nobody goes to church anymore. Or if they do, once they are out the door they are running people over in the parking lot so they can get back to coveting what their neighbors got."

I went to the kitchen to open a bottle of wine and get some glasses.

"I understand they have a twelve-step program for cynicism now," Kathy said.

"Yeah, but I need to tell you something, serious," I said, continuing the conversation even though I was in the other room.

"You want to marry me?"

"Not tonight, anyhow. It's about what you said back there at Lujacks, er Foodchopper. When I was in the hospital, and right after, I had a lot of time to think. Plus, I had to quit drinking, so maybe I went through an involuntary twelve step program. Anyhow, I put together a list of all the rotten things I've done in my life, and how I ended it with you was high up there. No matter whose fault it was, I should have kept in touch. We were close. I'd like to say I'm sorry." It was easier for me to say that when she wasn't looking right at me. I took the wine and walked back into the living room.

"OK, you definitely sound like you are in a twelve-step program. Thanks, I accept your apology, but let me tell you a few things. Yes, I was in love with you. As a matter of fact, you were the first man I was in love with. I hope that doesn't embarrass you. But I doubt very much if we had continued we would have wound up happily ever after in Prairie Stop. It's nice to think about, especially having kids, but life isn't that simple. I've had an interesting life up until this point, and I'm not sure I would trade it for anything. I say all this not to minimize your apology or say it doesn't mean anything, but to let you know the past is past."

To my surprise she moved close and kissed me.

"I wanted to do that when I first saw you tonight. Sorry about the cigarette breath."

I hugged her, kind of quickly and awkwardly, almost spilling her glass of wine. She pressed her finger to my lips and stepped away so she could put the glass down. Then she took mine from me and put it on the table next to hers. She turned back to me and we embraced again, this time longer. After another longer kiss, she stepped back.

"You were going to show me your deck, right?" she said, the mischievous eyes flashing.

"Right this way."

CHAPTER 9

We stepped outside into the starlit fall night and I flicked the outside lights on. Once her eyes adjusted, Kathy looked around the deck and whistled.

"Wow. This is incredible. Tell me you didn't do this all yourself."

"Sort of. I needed to do something when I got out of the hospital, so I decided to build a deck. It was therapy, I guess. Unfortunately, I'm not what you call handy. For every board you see, there were probably five that I ruined. So, after a while the guys from the lumber store were coming over after they got off work. I guess they wanted to see the reason for their Christmas bonus. They ended up doing a lot of the stuff. Cost me about fifty cases of beer. Even so, it took most of the summer. Most of the work I did, they had to rip up."

I walked over to a rubber cabinet in which I had installed a stereo. Dylan's Highway 61 Revisited was in the CD player. I turned it on, advanced it to the last song and pushed the volume way up.

"I did do the sound system myself."

The distinctive chords of "Desolation Row", followed by Dylan's dirge-like singing interrupted the still night.

"Logan, turn that off!"

I clicked the stereo off and there was again silence.

"Turn it off? That's like throwing a blanket over the Mona Lisa," I said.

"Don't tell me you sit out here and listen to that all-day long."

"No, sometimes I listen to 'Like a Rolling Stone.'"

"Not only are you a cynic but sounds like you got some major depressive stuff going on. Your deck is darn cool, Logan, but we better get back inside before I turn into a popsicle."

We went back into the living room. Kathy sat down on the love seat again while I poured wine into our glasses. I put on Springsteen's the "Wild", the "Innocent" and the "E-Street Shuffle".

"That's better. Early Springsteen. His sound is so different now, don't you think?

"A few different musicians, including a different drummer. Vini Lopez and Max Weinberg became the Pete Best and Ringo Starr of the seventies."

"When I was in college, we drove over to Asbury Park a few times to see him at the Stone Pony. That was something else. You ever hear of Southside Johnny and the Asbury Jukes?"

"Of course."

"One time, we were there to see Southside Johnny, and Bruce and Ronnie Spector showed up."

"New Jersey music heaven," I said. "You said you were going to tell me your life story."

"That's right, I did say that. I'll give you the Reader's Digest version."

Some of the early part I already knew. Kathy majored in marketing at Columbia University. After she graduated, she got a job in New York City with an advertising firm. She told me within a few years she had worked her way up to vice president and an ulcer. Tired of sixty-hour workweeks and New York, she phoned in her resignation, and, without giving it much thought, decided to become an airline hostess. She got on with Trans World Airlines, eventually being based out of Los Angeles. She started dating a pilot on one of her regular flights, and they ended up getting married. The marriage lasted until a flight she was scheduled on was canceled, and she came home to find him in bed with another stewardess. Shortly afterward, she got both a divorce and a job with another airline. On a trip to Chicago she met her second husband. He was almost ten years older than Kathy, was very charming, and apparently had his own successful business. After they were married, she was rudely surprised to discover, that while her new husband was a hugely entertaining person to be around, he also was a compulsive liar. Or, as he once told her, "I'm a big picture guy, and I don't sweat the details." Details like instead of being married once before, as he told her, he had previously been married three times. And instead of adoring kids and wanting to have more, he was estranged from his only son and already had a vasectomy. He hadn't exaggerated totally about his wealth, although there was some question about where it came from, his businesses or his ex-wives. When they finally did divorce, Kathy walked away with considerably less than she anticipated, but enough where she didn't have to seek full time work for a while.

"So here I am where I started, back in Prairie Stop," Kathy said. "With my old boyfriend, who still lives in his childhood home and still hangs out with the buddies he hung out with twenty years ago. That's strange karma, wouldn't you say?"

"Strange would be an understatement. In my case, it might be better described as sad. Oh, the only person from the old days that I hang out with is Buzz. And strictly speaking, right now I'm working for him, so I'm not sure you could say we are just hanging-out buddies."

"What are you doing for Buzz?" Kathy asked.

I started to explain about Buzz hiring me to check into Professor Matthews disappearance. She was interested, so I gave her most of the details of my activities that day, including meeting Matthew's wife. I tried not to leave anything out. Recapping the day's events for her in detail helped me organize my own thoughts.

"You're trying to find the professor that's missing? I've been following that in the paper. Isn't the FBI supposed to be involved in something like that?"

"Very few rate the FBI trying to find them. Maybe if Professor Matthews possessed some government secrets, the FBI would be swarming all over Prairie Stop. And I'm sure his picture and a description of his car is entered in a law enforcement database with a 'keep an eye out for' tag on it. But it's tough to order a full-blown manhunt for an adult in his right mind who might have just decided to blow town."

"Isn't it peculiar that somebody that prominent can disappear and you are the only one looking for him?"

"I think I've just been insulted," I said, in mock indignation.

"You know what I mean."

"Prairie Stop's finest are on the case. But without evidence of foul play and otherwise nothing to go on, there isn't a lot they can do. It's a helluva mystery though."

"Again, don't take this the wrong way, but what makes you think you will be able to find him when nobody else can?"

"Cause I can cut it, lady."

Kathy broke out laughing. "I remember that line. You used to say that all the time."

"Usually right before I committed a massive screw-up."

"If memory serves, it's from a movie."

"You got a good memory. It's from Hombre, with Paul Newman. I think I've only seen it about 500 times. He played a white man who had been brought up by the Apaches. He got killed at the end trying to save a bunch of white people. This after they wouldn't let him ride in the stagecoach with them."

"I would have let Paul Newman do anything he wanted," Kathy said, and sighed. "I'm a sucker for blue eyes."

"Now you tell me. It was Frederic March's idea to not let him ride in the coach. That was one of his last movies. Richard Boone was the villain. That was after he was Paladin in Have Gun Will Travel. Now that was a show way ahead of its time. You know what a paladin is?"

"I went to an Ivy League school … what do you think? You see yourself as a knight-errant?"

"If Richard Boone could be one, why not me?"

"Tell me some more about the professor. You said the wife has got something going on with Buzz?"

"Point of fact, I didn't say that. He told me he's just trying to help her."

"I suppose helping somebody is a lot easier when that somebody is attractive and has a lot of money. Oh, coincidentally, she happens to bear a resemblance to the love of your life."

"Not sure I'm following you," I said.

"He knew her before her husband disappeared. How long before?"

"Matter of fact, there was a little discrepancy there. Buzz said a couple of years. She thought it was longer than that."

"And what do you make of that?"

"Forgetfulness. It happens when you get old. Why do you think it's unusual that he knew her before? It's a small town. And though there are probably ten times as many lawyers here as twenty years ago, the herd is still manageable. Buzz knows just about everybody in town anyhow. I would find it peculiar if he didn't know her."

"And what about that business with the mall? You don't find it coincidental that Buzz stood to benefit from something the professor was trying to stop?"

"That's a reach," I answered. "Whatever Matthews was doing to stop the mall, apparently nobody took him seriously. Certainly not enough to make him disappear."

"Maybe some people took him more seriously than others. Money does that to people."

We sat in silence for a few minutes.

"Can I ask you another personal question, Logan? It may cause you to eject me bodily from your house, but I feel compelled to ask anyhow."

"Ask away."

"Did you ever wonder why you and Buzz were, and I guess, are, best friends?"

"Might have something to do with the fact that we spent just about every day together from when we were five until we went to college."

"I know that. I'm looking for the reason. You two always were so different. It has been my experience that while opposites attract, they usually don't stay together too long."

"You make it sound like we're married."

"Your friendship has outlasted most marriages I know, two of my own included."

"I guess you are going to tell me in what ways we are different."

"I think you know, but in a lot of ways. Mainly, Buzz was always outgoing, popular, most comfortable in a group. Plus, you could always tell he wanted to be the person everybody looked up to. You have to admit you were never any of those things."

"Why don't you just say brooding, underachieving loner?"

"I didn't say that. Also, I wasn't trying to say, in any way, that Buzz was better person, just unlike you. That's why it seems to me so peculiar that you have stayed friends for so long. I hope it doesn't come out the wrong way, but it was almost like Buzz used you as his foil. To make his star shine even brighter, so to speak. Kind of like you were the Dr. Watson to his Sherlock Holmes, or the Spock to his Kirk, or …"

"…the Tonto to his Lone Ranger?"

She laughed. "You said that, not me."

"You are saying I wasn't good enough for Buzz to want to be friends with me?"

"I didn't say he was better than you. And certainly not in any moral sense, if that defines better. I'll drop a bombshell on you … I was never a big Buzz Wildrick fan."

"No kidding."

"I was just thinking that, in most situations where people interact, a concept I refer to as Social Darwinism takes over."

"Social Darwinism?"

"Survival of the fittest, or more accurately, survival of the coolest. If you ever worked in marketing or advertising, you would know what I'm talking about.

"I didn't and don't."

"There are three basic principles of Social Darwinism. You can apply them to just about every situation where people interact. Number one is that just about everyone wants to be perceived as 'cool'. Number two is that in order for some people to be cool, others must, by definition, be uncool. In other words, not everybody can be cool. Number three is that cool people usually want to associate only with other cool people."

"That sounds complicated, if not downright diabolical," I said.

"No. Think of American society as one big high school, with celebrities being our star quarterbacks and cheerleaders."

"I'm getting this now. Buzz was cool, so he should have wanted to hang out with other cool people, and not somebody uncool like me. He had to have an ulterior reason for having me around, which was actually to make himself look cooler."

"You aren't as dumb as you pretend."

"Thanks, but I'm not pretending. This is legitimate stupidity. Maybe it's not so much I'm not cool, as maybe I'm trying to leave a small karmic footprint. Ever think of that?"

"Small Karmic footprint?"

"No fame, no money, no friends, no nothing. That way I haven't put a dent in the karmic cycle."

"Hate to tell you this, but that's not cool."

"I think you inhaled too much smog out in California."

"Why do you think when somebody wants to sell a product, they find a celebrity to pitch it?" Kathy asked.

"I buy off on the advertising thing, but this is real life. In the Midwest, Middle America, not New York or California. People here are genuine, not fake wannabes waiting for somebody famous to tell them how they feel about everything. Plain old, ugly, boring schmoes, perhaps, but genuine nonetheless."

"Who are you kidding? There is no such thing as small-town life anymore. In a few years Prairie Stop will just be another suburb of Chicago. And, you may not want to acknowledge it, but there is elite, or want to be elite here, just like everywhere else. You described your life as sad, but what's really sad is the people here who called all the shots in high school still think they are in charge. Like Buzz."

"I may be rushing to judgment, but I'm beginning to sense some hostility toward Buzz."

Kathy laughed. "Picking up on that, are you? Let's just say, I could tell you a thing a two about Buzz that might radically alter your opinion of him."

"Like what?"

"You sure you want to know? I feel like I would be telling a child that there is no Santa Claus."

"Now you're really making my head spin."

"Ok, get ready to be disillusioned. Did you know Buzz used to cheat in school?"

"I remember he used to borrow my algebra homework from time to time. That wasn't a good idea, by the way. I was horrible at algebra. He should have stolen my brother's. He was a certified math genius."

"I'm not talking about that. I'm talking about knowing what the questions were on the tests before he took them."

"How could he do that?" I asked.

"Remember Mr. Zurnow's chemistry class, where there was one section that met in the morning and the other in the afternoon? He used to give the same test to both sections. Zurnow was either too trusting or dumb to consider somebody would use that as a way to cheat. Buzz apparently did. He would have somebody from the morning section tell him what the hard questions on the test were. And don't ask me how I know, but he did it."

"Ok, so he cheated in high school chemistry. This was the same guy who was at football or basketball or baseball practice over two hours a day and had the hopes and dreams of an entire small town sitting squarely on his shoulders."

"And, for that reason, he gets a license to cheat?"

"No, but Buzz had a lot of talent and corresponding pressure on him to succeed. Maybe he was entitled to some slack."

"I think you could equally make the case that since he was Prairie Stop's Mr. Everything, that he was a role model. Role models don't have the luxury of not playing by the rules. What do you think he would have happened to him if he had been caught cheating? Instead of going to Notre Dame, he'd be assistant manager at the local convenience store."

"I doubt that," I said. "I knew some of those guys Buzz played ball with at Notre Dame and, believe me, they weren't choir boys."

"More likely, if he had been caught cheating, I'm sure somebody would have found a way to cover it up or look the other way. But I've got another story for you about Buzz. And I've never told anybody this."

"It couldn't be any more shocking than the first one."

"Sarcasm comes naturally to you, but still, it doesn't suit you. And I think you need to hear this, even after all these years. Remember Becky Hall?"

"Sure," I said. "Her dad was an eye doctor. They had one of those big old houses near downtown."

"Well, I don't know if you recall, but Becky had a bit of a reputation. Her middle name was Jane, so her initials were BJ. Need I go into more detail?"

"I think I remember that too. She was very popular."

"I'll say. A girl with a good head on her shoulders is always very popular."

"Not sure what you mean. I heard she had a sweet personality and made all her own clothes."

"Right. Anyhow, she had a big party, two weeks after graduation. Her parents were out of town. You wouldn't go with me because you hated crowds and socializing."

"I don't like crowds, it's true. Maybe there's an inherent fear that when a bunch of white people get together, the village where I live is going to be trampled, the men massacred, and all the women and children taken prisoner."

"Like I said, you didn't like crowds. I went with Beth and Buzz."

"As memory serves, that was the one where the police showed up and total mayhem ensued. Boy, was I sorry then that I didn't go."

"What I'm going to tell you about happened before the police came. I spent most of the evening trying to avoid Larry Smith, one of Buzz's football buffoon pals. Unbeknownst to me, he had a crush on me. I finally got tired of him trying to paw me, so I went upstairs. The house had three stories, and I went all the way to the top floor. You had to open a door on the second floor hallway and then go up a skinny flight of stairs to get to the top. Becky's dad had a small office up there. The door was closed but I heard some noise behind it. The door had a keyhole in it. I don't know what prompted me to do it, just being a busy body, I guess, but I got down on my knees and looked through the keyhole." She paused to light a cigarette.

"And?"

"I wasn't the only one down on my knees. Your best friend was sitting on Dr. Hall's desk with his blue jeans down, with Becky Hall on her knees, between his legs, performing her specialty. In what seemed to be an enthusiastic and competent fashion. Not that I had much of a frame of reference, mind you."

"What did you do?"

"I stayed and watched, of course. I viewed it as a learning experience."

"This is getting interesting."

"It was very erotic. Perhaps I'm a bit of a voyeur. I must say, I have to give Buzz credit where it's due. When he finished, there was a most prodigious quantity. Considerable projection, too. It went everywhere."

"Point of clarification," I said. "She didn't swallow?"

"She apologized to him about that. She said she was worried her boyfriend would taste it later."

"Yuck. I must say your story, while very entertaining, seems to be somewhat fanciful."

Kathy backed away from me in mock anger.

"What, are you calling me a liar?"

"I'm not saying you are a liar. But Buzz wouldn't have done that. His girlfriend and future wife was the most beautiful and popular girl in town. It would be like passing up a five star restaurant to eat at Ed's Greasy Spoon. Even if it is a true story, I'm not sure what somebody did when they were young, foolish and with hormones raging should be held against them forever. What's the point in telling me this?"

"Because, my innocent friend, I don't think you know him. It's like you've always had tunnel vision when it comes to Buzz.

"Beth wouldn't put up with that," I said.

"You think so? I didn't really keep in close touch with her over the last couple years, but I'm sure she knew he was having an affair."

"She told you that?"

"More or less. I talked to her not long after her son died. She was very upset, needless to say. And she told me that she was tired of living a lie. I inferred from that that she knew Buzz was having an affair."

"She didn't happen to tell you who the other woman was, did she?"

"No, but I remember very clearly a remark she made right after that. She said 'she even looks like me'."

"You are figuring the other woman has to be Jackie Matthews."

"You're the one who said she looked like Beth."

"And the next step would be Buzz knocked off her husband?"

"It sounds crazy, I know," Kathy admitted.

"Ok, but why then would Buzz ask me to find said missing husband?"

"Maybe he wanted to see if he covered his tracks well enough, and he wanted somebody he could control doing it."

"It's all becoming clear to me now. You should have been a detective."

"All I'm telling you is not to take anything for granted when it comes to Buzz Wildrick. He's had people fawning all over him for too long."

"I'll take that under advisement," I said, "but don't look for me to have a change of heart anytime soon. Regarding Buzz, at least. Yeah, he can be egotistical, self-serving, and he's probably taken some short cuts along the way. Maybe he doesn't have a heart of gold. But I tell you, and this sounds corny, but if I was in the army, and I was in a battle, I'd sure as hell would want him as the general or in the foxhole next to me, or both."

"Like I said at the beginning, I know that. Just wondering why. Didn't mean to get you riled up."

"I haven't begun to get riled, but it's been a long day, and I think I'm going to have to hit the hay."

"I knew you were going to kick me out."

"I didn't say you had to leave. Do you want the top or bottom?"

"Beg your pardon?"

"The top or bottom bunk. You can have either one. I sleep in a queen bed in the main bedroom."

"That sounds tempting, but I need to get going. My sister is with my dad tonight and she will need some relief. Maybe we can have a sleepover another time. I'll bring some Ovaltine. What are you going to do tomorrow?"

"Probably try and talk to Matthew's alleged girlfriend. Name's Rosanne Parker."

"What about after that?" she asked.

"I'm not sure. Depends on what she has to say," I answered.

Chapter 10

I woke up the next morning with a slight headache, exacerbated when I sat up in bed. Although I hadn't felt close to being drunk the night before, the alcohol I had consumed in the last two days was more that I had in the prior six months combined. Course it might have been related to my accident. The doctors told me that I might have headaches, but that they would gradually subside in frequency and intensity. Generally, they had, so I attributed the headache to the cheap wine I had consumed with Kathy the night before. I laid back down until the headache subsided, then I gave Ivan Rich a call. When he picked up it sounded like he was chewing on something.

"Catch you at a good time, Ivan?" I asked politely.

"Just finishing up the crossword."

"On county time?"

"You ought to know that you have to pace yourself in this line of work. Give the brain time to recharge." There was a pause. "Hey, you're a smart guy. What English author wrote Turn of the Screw?" he asked.

"Al Goldstein," I said.

There was a snort.

"That was Screw Magazine."

"Try James, for Henry James. But I think he was born in America."

"Bingo," he said, after a pause. "Alright, back to work. How's it going Logan? Solve the mystery of the disappearing professor yet? You've been on the case a whole day. I would think you're about ready to crack it."

"Matter of fact, I think I just saw him going into a Doughnut World off of 52. Might want to send a squad car over there. Wait a second, save the call, there's probably already one over there."

"Funny. Pardon me for not laughing. In the meantime, what can I do for you? Not that I'm looking to do anything for you, by the way."

"What do you know about the new mall going up in Prairie Stop?" I asked.

"Just what I read in the paper. And it isn't going to be in Prairie Stop. It's going to be near Prairie Stop. And it's not a done deal."

"Then you know Professor Matthews thought there used to be an Indian village near the site. And he was trying to delay the mall project so he could go dig up whatever he thought was out there."

"I might have heard that."

"You wouldn't maybe see that as a motive for somebody wanting to get rid of him?"

"No. First of all, from what I understand, the professor only wanted to make sure that if there were some Indian stuff at the site, that whatever it was be properly removed before the construction started. He wasn't trying to stop anything."

"I don't know much about construction," I said, "but I'm not sure I would want to pay twenty guys with heavy equipment to stand around waiting while a guy sifted through a bunch of dirt with a pair of tweezers and a magnifying glass."

"They weren't close to starting anything. In fact, I'm not sure that site was final. The developer, a guy from Chicago, name's Coban, I think, was also looking at some land over by Miller Acres. From what I hear, they wanted to give him the land and were practically begging him to build."

I didn't say anything for a few seconds. Miller Acres was thirty miles southeast of Prairie Stop. Ivan asked me if I was still on the line.

"Yeah. Who told you that?" I asked.

"One of my cousins is retired from the county but works part time as a building inspector for the city of Miller Acres. He likes to talk."

"This is getting interesting. By the way, do you know exactly where they were going to build, if they build in Prairie County?"

"You know where Goose Creek Road is?"

"Near the country club, I take it?" I asked.

Goose Creek Golf Club was a country club built by one of the steel companies as a perk for its managers and executives, back when the demand for steel was insatiable and the domestic steel industry couldn't make enough to satisfy it. When the industry began its freefall from prosperity to distress, and tens of thousands of workers lost their jobs, the formerly exclusive club was opened up to anybody, provided they could afford the initiation fee. Buzz was a member there. He bitched constantly about how the monthly dues were constantly going up.

"Yeah. Make a right on County Road 7 from the bypass. You'll go about a mile to a stop sign. That's Goose Creek. If you go left, it takes you to the country club. If you go the other way, you'll eventually reach an old abandoned farm. Used to be owned by a family named the Porters. I think at one time the country club had thoughts of adding another eighteen holes there, but then the steel industry tanked."

"My sister and her husband are members," I said, remembering they took me to lunch there a couple times.

"Good for them," Ivan said. "That whole area is what they're aiming to develop."

"Does Coban own it?"

"From the little I know, he owns some of it outright, and has options on other parcels. There are still some Porters around. Maybe they own what's left. Why?"

"I'm thinking out loud here, Ivan, but let's say you're Coban and you have two choices of where to put your new mall. One place is your ideal site, close to a growing part of the county, close to the South Shore Line, close to Chicago. But you may not be able to break ground right away because of some crank. The other site isn't ideal, but you can go in and start digging tomorrow. You've borrowed a lot of money and every delay costs you. Big time. Plus, every day you delay, the people that are backing you are be getting worried that maybe you aren't going to finish the project. Where do you go?"

There was a pause.

"This is getting farfetched, but I'll play along. I would go where I could get started right away," Ivan said.

"I would do that too. Now let's say you are somebody in Prairie Stop who owns land near where the new mall is going. You're looking at property that may go up, who knows, twice, three times, ten times in value. The sky's the limit. Or maybe you're a guy who owns an asphalt company around here, and you're looking at one of the biggest jobs you've ever done. But all of sudden your golden goose flies away. The goose is ok. See, he can go somewhere else where people will love him. But what about you?"

Another pause.

"I guess I'm screwed," he replied. "According to your logic, anyhow."

"And because of some professor whose biggest decision up to now is deciding whether he should have the beef or fish at the faculty Christmas party. I think that might make me feel not too friendly toward said professor."

"Yeah, but not friendly enough to make me want to get rid of him? Come on, Logan, this is Prairie Stop, not New Jersey."

"Look, one thing I've learned is that where there's money involved people do stuff they wouldn't ordinarily do. Greed is a big motivator."

A sigh.

"What is it you want of me?" Ivan asked.

"Find out exactly who owns the land around and where the mall is supposed to go."

"I guess I could check with the County Assessor's Office."

"Great idea," I said. "How soon can you get back with me?"

"You know, Logan, it may come as a surprise to you, but I got other stuff to do. Aside from that, what makes you think the Assessor's Office is going to drop everything just for me?"

He had a point.

"Your cousin could tap somebody, right?"

"Oh, for crissakes."

"Ivan, it will take you a few minutes to make a call."

"Yeah, while I'm doing that, what exactly are you going to be doing?"

"I'm going to see if I can find out who locally has been working with Coban. I already got one name."

"Who?"

"I'll tell you later. Right now, I got to get going. There's somebody at the door."

Before I hung up, Ivan started to say something about holding back information from him, but I didn't give him a chance to finish.

I called the Video Warehouse and asked to speak to Rosanne. The guy who answered said she didn't come in until noon. Almost as soon as I put the phone down it rang. It was Buzz.

"Sorry I had to cut out so early last night," he said. "What's your plan for today?"

"I'm going to try and talk to Matthew's alleged girlfriend in a little while."

"Now that's a good idea. She probably knows something that Ivan Rich couldn't get out of her. Then what?"

"I was thinking about maybe taking a drive out to where you and Steve Coban are going to be building the new mall."

Buzz snorted.

"I'm not building anything."

"That's what I heard, if Coban decides to relocate the project to Miller Acres."

There was silence on the other end, then a click of the tongue.

"I should have known, when you mentioned the mall last night, that you were going latch onto it like a bulldog on mailman's leg. Coban or me had nothing to do with Matthews' disappearance."

"Maybe not everybody's so understanding as you or Coban."

"Alright. Do what you got to do. If you do go out there, be careful. I heard there's been trouble with kids out that way."

"What kind of trouble?" I asked.

"The usual trouble with teenagers with too much time on their hands. Kids on dirt bikes, tearing things up. Drinking beer. Having parties late at night. Man, I wish I had that much free time when I was that age. I understand Bill Hanlen has had to keep two squad cars out there some Friday nights."

"Thanks for the warning, but I think I can handle a couple of kids. I'll talk to you later."

CHAPTER 11

I threw on a sweatshirt and shorts and went out for a run. I thought it would help rid me of the vestige of the headache. In contrast to the day before, it was a bright fall morning with the temperature in the low fifties. Since my accident, it seemed like it took me forever to warm up, and when I started out, if often felt like my legs were solid oak planks. I mentioned this in one of my follow-up visits to the doctor. He looked at my chart and said, "Says here you had oblique fractures to both femurs, plus two dislocated kneecaps. Frankly, I'm surprised that you can run at all." After that I didn't feel too bad if it took me a couple miles of combined jogging and walking before I could move without numbing discomfort.

I plodded my way slowly through streets I had traveled hundreds if not thousands of times before. You would think that the familiarity of it all would be boring; quite the opposite. As I ran, I remembered things that had happened at different places in my growing up in Prairie Stop. The corner where Buzz and I had thrown some apples at a school bus and ran like crazy when the driver got out of the bus and started to chase us. The hollow tree in the park where some older kids had hidden some fireworks, which we confiscated, and which later got us into all kinds of trouble for setting off. The field where we had played endless games of two man to a team football and baseball. Buzz and Beth and I walking home from high school, them holding hands, me just happy to be in their company. My thoughts were interrupted by tires screeching on the pavement. A black Olds Cutlass came around the corner ahead at high speed and was now heading down the street I was on. I was on the road, but got up on the sidewalk as a precaution. As the vehicle approached me it veered slightly toward my side of the street. There was a long puddle on the street near me and it appeared they were aiming to splash me. They missed. The horn blared and someone yelled, "FAGGOT" through the open window. I assume it was meant for me. I heard loud laughter as the car sped off.

The car was familiar to me. I had seen it before in the driveway of a house a few doors down from mine. I was very sure it belonged to a friend of the two brothers who lived there, along with their mom. I didn't really know them, they had not been in the neighborhood very long, but I would give her neighborly hello when I saw her. She was divorced. I found out later her ex-husband had been in school with me. Since I didn't see her car much in the driveway during the day, I figured she worked full time. The sons had each graduated from high school within the last few years, but didn't go away to college, and if they worked, it wasn't a lot. I'd seen the mom cutting the grass, so it didn't look like they helped around the house much either. Mainly it seemed they sat in the garage with their friends, smoked cigarettes, drank beer and judging from the flickering light emitting from the garage at night, played video games. I didn't like to run by the house when the garage door was open, because I had a sense I was getting malevolent stares. In nice weather, they sometimes relocated over to the small park across the street from me. My next door neighbor, an eighty year old widow, used to walk her dog in the park. She told me once she asked them not to throw their cigarette butts on the ground. In reply, they told her to "fuck off". I offered to go talk to them about it, but she said she was afraid they would retaliate. She also told me when they were in high school, they had harassed the daughter of another neighbor to the point where she stopped taking the bus to school. I recalled their dad as being something of dipshit, so the apples didn't fall far from the tree.

I think if it had been some random kids yelling at me, I would have been annoyed, but let it go. Since I knew who it was, the further I ran the more I got worked up. When I got back to my street, I jogged up by where the brothers lived. The Buick was across the street. I went over to it, looked around to see if anyone was watching, and then kicked the left taillight out. Then the right one. Then I went over to the garage. The door was open, I assume to let the voluminous cigarette smoke out, and five guys were sitting on an old sofa and two beat up chairs. A big glowing electric heater mounted on the ceiling kept them warm. I'm sure the mother appreciated the resulting high electric bills. Two of the them had video controllers in their hands, and all were staring in rapt attention at a TV on a table in front of them. One of the brothers looked up when he saw me.

"Hey, how you fellas doing?" I said, nonchalantly.

A couple of them startled at my appearance. They looked at each other. It was obvious they recognized me from thirty minutes ago. Obvious too, the brothers knew I lived a few houses down. One of them, I think the older one, nodded.

"Good," he said, giving me kind of nervous smile.

"Say, excuse me for interrupting, but I was wondering, do you know whose Buick that is across the street?"

There was an awkward paused.

"Doesn't belong to anybody here, man," one of the kids said. A small skinny kid with long greasy black hair and wire-rimmed glasses. There was muffled laughter.

"Ok," I said. "Well, just wanted to let the owner know the taillights are busted out. He should get them fixed soon. It's dangerous without them working, plus you could get cited for it."

The small skinny kid jumped up and went to the door to look across the street.

After he saw the pieces of broken red glass on the ground he gave me an incredulous look. "Motherfucker! My car! What the fuck did you do that for?"

"Wait a second. I thought the car didn't belong to anybody here." I scratched my head in mock bewilderment.

"That's my car, asshole! I'm gonna call the cops!"

"I used to be a cop," I said, rubbing my beard stubble thoughtfully. "Let me give you some names."

That gave him pause.

"Motherfucker!" he said again.

"Watch your language. There are ladies present. You know, back in the day, kids wouldn't scream obscenities at people walking down the street. Or over in the park. Or standing in a shit-hole garage. Times have changed, I guess. Still, if I was you, I wouldn't yell stuff out a car window unless you want to get your taillights busted out."

He was enraged now but wasn't sure what to do. I was almost twice his size. He looked at his buddies for support, but none of them acted like anything was going on. There was a baseball bat leaning up against the wall in the garage, and the kid grabbed it. For a second, I thought he was going to take a swing at me. He paused, and then swung it hard against the metal garage door bracket. It made a big clang.

"Motherfucker!" he yelled a third time. It seemed like he had a limited vocabulary.

The older brother, who was the bigger one, jumped from the couch.

"Goddammit, Eddie, don't bust up the house!"

Eddie looked at the brother and then at me. It looked like he was going to start crying. Finally, he heaved the bat into the yard.

"Fuck you all!" he said and stalked off to his car.

We watched him go in silence.

"I don't know about you guys, but I miss him already," I said, shaking my head.

The older brother looked pissed and bewildered at the same time. I thought he was going to say something but thought better of it. I looked directly at him.

"Eddie was right not to try and hit me with the bat," I said. "Within an hour he'd be downtown looking at a felony assault charge. Or in the hospital. My bet is the hospital, even if all you little weenies jumped in."

Nobody even looked up at me.

"So, anybody else got anything?"

Nothing.

"That's what I figured. See you around the neighborhood."

CHAPTER 12

After I showered and dressed, I drove over to the Video Warehouse. No cars were parked in front of the store and no one was in sight when I walked in. I guess early afternoon on a weekday was probably the slow period for video rentals. A doorbell noise triggered by my opening the door announced my presence, and a young woman walked out from a rack of videotapes. As soon as I saw her I remembered seeing her in the store before. As she walked to the register she gave me a smile and a quick hi.

I said hello back.

"Help you find something?" she asked.

"Actually, I was looking for Rosanne Parker. You must be her."

The smile disappeared.

"Are you a cop? If you are here about Mike, I haven't seen or talked to him for over a week. That's God's truth."

"Who's Mike?" I asked.

She gave me a quizzical look.

"Mike's my ex. You look like a cop."

"Used to be. Name's Logan Wells. I'd like to talk to you about Jason Matthews."

"Jesus!" There was an exasperated tone to her voice, which then became defiant. "I already talked to a cop about Jason."

"Yes, that would have been Detective Ivan Rich. That's how I got your name. Mrs. Matthews hired me to see if I could find her husband."

"That's a good one," she said.

"How's that?"

"Nothing. Listen, I already talked to the police, so unless there's a law or something that says I got to talk to you, I'll pass. I got a lot of stuff to do. The guy who works before me is an idiot and lazy to boot." She picked up some videotape containers from behind the counter.

"I'm trying to find Professor Matthews. I thought you were close to him and would want to help."

She stopped and turned toward me.

"I just have a few questions," I added.

"Ok. I'll talk to you about Jason. But you're going to have to follow me around while I put these tapes back. And if the owner comes in, you got to pretend you don't know me. I don't need to lose this job."

When Ivan Rich told me Matthews was having an affair with one of his students, for some reason I pictured a sexy blonde knockout. Rosanne Parker wasn't blonde and wouldn't by most standards be considered a knockout, but she was attractive. That was probably the reason I remembered her from before. I would have guessed she was in her mid-twenties, but there was hardness to her dark brown eyes that made me wonder if she was older. She wore a pair of large dark framed glasses, perched halfway down her nose, which along with her hair, which was frizzy but pulled back neatly behind her head, gave her the look of a frazzled librarian.

She grabbed some more videotapes and started walking through the store with me trailing after her.

"How did you and Professor Matthews meet?" I asked.

"He used to come in here a lot, during the summer anyhow. He was polite and nice. Most people usually aren't. We talked a bit I told him I tended bar at night. He asked where and he showed up one night. I was surprised but didn't mind. He definitely didn't give off a creep vibe. We talked some more."

"About what?"

"Movies at first. Then other stuff."

"Like?"

"Things people talk about when they get to know each other. The weather, politics, our families, things we had going on."

"Did you ever talk to him besides here or the bar?"

"You probably already know, so, yes. We met a few times for lunch and dinner. There was nothing to it. I liked being with him, and he liked being with me."

"You've got a son, don't you Rosanne?"

She gave me a hard look.

"Yes, I've got a boy. He's six. Just started kindergarten."

"Mike's his father?"

"Yes, but I'm not sure I care to discuss that with you."

"I'm guessing from the way you acted when I came in that maybe Mike has been in trouble with the law before. Probably more than once."

"So what? He made some mistakes. He paid for them."

"What kind of mistakes? You know, back when I was in uniform, the young guys we had real trouble with had short fuses, if you know what I mean. Did Mike have a temper?"

"None of your business. You don't know him and you don't know me."

"I apologize."

"You don't know thing one about him, ex-cop. Mike had a hard life. He came from a broken home. His dad left before he was born. If that happened to you maybe you would have a temper too." I obviously had hit a nerve.

"Like I said, I'm sorry. You're right. I don't know Mike and I shouldn't have said that."

I followed her back into the room where the adult videos were kept. Box covers displaying all types of sexual acts inundated me.

"Rent a lot of these, do you?" I asked.

"What do you think? The tapes back here are about ten percent of our inventory, but over fifty percent of our receipts. You strike me as the kind who's into porn, right?"

"Big time. I got a garage at home stacked full of it. Can't even get my car inside anymore."

"I thought so. What I've found out working here is all guys like porn. I'm not being judgmental, it's just a fact. I can take it or leave it myself. I'd rather go out to an expensive restaurant and have a guy treat me nice. Then I would watch porn with him until he barked at the moon."

I thought about that for a second.

"How about Professor Matthews?" I asked.

"I was wondering when we would get back to him."

"Well?"

"Not sure how or why I should tell you this, but Jason was having problems at home."

"Of the marital kind?"

"After we got to know each other, he told me had some health problems. He tried to downplay it, but he implied that they were causing some issues, relationship wise, if you know what I mean."

"His wife is a lot younger than him."

"Right. He gave me the impression she wasn't too pleased with the situation. He thought maybe watching some of these would help put him, let's say, in the right frame of mind."

"He asked if you could recommend some?" I asked.

"Sure. He came in here out of the blue one day and said he was having troubles in the bedroom and asked what videos were the hottest. You got to be kidding me."

"He must have been worried."

"I think he thought his wife was unfaithful," she said.

"Did he actually say his wife was having an affair?"

"He suspected she was. But I don't think he was sure."

"How close did you and Professor Matthews get?"

"I told you we were friends.

"Just friends?" I asked.

"You mean did we have sex? You aren't paying attention. I already told you he was having problems in that area."

"Did that stop him from trying?"

"I liked him at lot, but we weren't that way. In fact, sometimes I got a little nervous when we were alone together. I knew he was attracted to me, and I liked him, so I was worried about what might happen. The last thing I need right now is to get involved with a married man. But I didn't want to lose his friendship either. He made me feel good about myself. Some notion, huh? He even talked me into going back to school. Plus, he was nice to my son."

"When did you start school?" I asked.

"Last spring. I signed up for a class with him. American History."

"That must have been difficult, working, and with a kid, going to school."

"It wasn't easy, but I don't plan on working in video stores and bars all my life."

That might have sounded pretentious coming from someone else, but not from Rosanne Parker. I could see what Jason Matthews saw in her.

"No to change the subject, but did Jason ever discuss his work with you?"

"Sure, we talked about a lot of stuff."

"Then you know he was writing a book about the life of the Shawnee Chief Tecumseh."

"Yeah. He was pretty obsessed with that, I think."

"Did he ever mention anything about a sword he was trying to find that belonged to Tecumseh?"

"A few times. One afternoon, after class, he took me and Tommy, my son, out to an abandoned farm out by the interstate. We tramped around for a while. He was pointing out to me where he thought an Indian village was. He said the sword was out there somewhere … it was just a matter of finding it. He seemed convinced. Sounded a little far-fetched to me."

"Rosanne, do you have any idea what happened to Jason or where he may have gone?" I asked.

"I wish I did. I hadn't seen him for a while before he disappeared. His wife gave him a hard time about me. Although I can't blame her for that. I'd probably feel the same way if it was my husband. But to answer your question, I think he was depressed about his marriage. I hate to think what he might have done."

"He was that despondent? Did he ever talk about suicide?"

"In kind of an abstract way. Mainly in relation to his wife."

"How?"

"Like I said, he was blaming himself for her not being happy. I think he thought she would be better off with a younger guy."

I heard the doorbell noise again.

"Look, I got to get back to the register," she said.

"I understand. Just a couple more questions. Parker is your married name, correct? Your ex-husband's name is Mike Parker?"

She didn't say anything but nodded slowly.

"What does Mike do?"

"He's a mechanic. When he's working that is. Which isn't a lot."

"Where he's working now?"

"His uncle's place. Phil's Auto. It's east of town."

"Did your ex know about you and Jason?"

She hesitated. "He saw us together a couple of times."

"Is Mike the jealous type?"

She didn't say anything for a minute, guessing where I was going.

"I think you need to leave now," she said, tersely.

"Look, if something happened between Mike and the professor, it's only a matter of time before the real cops find out. Once they do, and if Mike has been in trouble before, he's going to go immediately to the head of the suspect list. Trust me, that's just the way things work."

"I tell you and everything is hunky dory."

"All I'm trying to do is find Professor Matthews. You tell me what happened and more than likely it just stays with me."

"More than likely?"

"If he didn't have anything to do with Matthews disappearing, sure."

"He didn't," she said, but not emphatically.

"That didn't sound very convincing."

"They had words ok? Mike was hanging out in front of my place one night and saw Jason. He said some things to him."

"Like what?"

"Something to the effect that Jason should be ashamed of himself for going out with someone young enough to be his daughter. Except he didn't put it quite that nice."

"What did Professor Matthews do?"

"He didn't say anything, but later I could tell he was upset. I think in his life he hasn't run into too many people like Mike." She shook her head. "My life, that's all I run into."

"Was that the only time Mike spoke with Jason?" I asked.

"As far as I know. He tried to ask me some questions about him, but I told him Jason was none of his business."

"What kind of questions?"

"Who he was, what he did, if he had money, where he lived, stuff like that. Like I said, I told him to mind his own business."

"Did Jason ever say anything about Mike?"

"No. Just said at the time that he seemed like a hothead."

"Did he ever say that Mike had attempted to contact him?"

She hesitated then shook her head.

"No."

"You don't seem sure.

"I said no."

"I know you haven't seen Mike in a while, but when was the last time you spoke to him?"

"You know what? I'm not talking to you anymore. And if you don't leave right now, I'm running out of here screaming that there's a pervert back in the adult section."

CHAPTER 13

There was a message on the machine from Ivan when I got back. I called
him right away.

"That was quick," I said.

"I remembered one of my other cousins works in the Assessor's Office. He
was in a talkative mood. Takes after his mother. If that woman knew the plans
for D-Day we'd all be speaking German right now."

"What did you find out?"

"There are a lot of parcels out there. A group called the South Lake
Partnership has been buying it up. They haven't been able to buy it all at once
because different Porters own different parts of, and they don't get along too
good. By the way I heard some of the Porters weren't too happy on the price
they got for the land. I guess it didn't occur to them that if they had stuck
together they could have gotten a better deal."

"Divide and conquer is a tried and true strategy. Ask Julius Caesar. Is
South Lake Coban's group?"

"Yeah. I'll get to that in a second. But what's interesting is South Lake
doesn't own all of it. Some of what they've bought they've sold already."

"That is interesting. Why would buy it and then sell it right away?"

"Profit, for one. About a year ago South Lake bought some parcels from
one Eunice Porter. They paid fifty grand for it. Few months later, they sold it
to the Pipefitters Union Pension Plan, for twice what they paid."

I thought about that. "Let me ask you something, Ivan, you think
undeveloped land goes up in value that much in a few months?"

"I wouldn't think so, but your former boss apparently thought so. My
cousin tells me, confidentially, that he thought the county prosecutor was

looking into the sale. Apparently fleecing a pension plan is against the law. The story, off the record, is that maybe one or more of the pension plan trustees took some cash to vote for buying the property."

"The bribe I guess coming from South Lake?" I asked.

"My cousin didn't want come right out and say that. Spreading gossip like that would be good way to get yourself canned. But that would be the logical guess."

"So what else do we know about South Lake?"

"It's Coban's firm," he said. "One of several he apparently operates. Oh, and the general counsel for South Lake is listed as one James Buster Wildrick. He's also listed as a partner."

I didn't say anything.

"Wildrick tell you that?" Ivan asked.

"Not exactly. He mentioned his firm did work for Coban," I said.

"Probably just slipped his mind."

"I guess if that mall doesn't get built, some people are going to be stuck with a very expensive cow pasture," I said.

"That's one way to look at it. On the other hand, if the mall does get built, they might be sitting on a gold mine."

I pondered that for a few seconds.

"Say, Ivan, not to change the subject, but what kind of background did you do on Jackie Matthews?"

"Oh, you know the usual. Grade school report cards, name of childhood pets, how many pushups she could do in gym, that type of stuff. What is it with you? One-minute Matthews is missing cause he was wanted to keep a mall from being built, now we are back to the wife."

"Information on her family is what I'm interested in. I think her mother is dead. She has a father and brother. She is from Chicago, by the way."

"You can get that stuff yourself."

"Sure, I can. Drive over to Chicago. Spend a week hanging around the county courthouse, spinning my wheels. All you got to do it make a few phone calls. Use the power of your authority."

"Dammit , Logan. I'm not your errand boy."

"I need Jackie Matthews' maiden name. The names of the rest of her family and what happened to them or where they are now. That's bare minimum. Anything above that is a bonus."

"Yeah, well, I'll see what I can do." He didn't sound happy about it.

CHAPTER 14

I decided to call my former employer, the County Prosecutor's Office, to see if they had anything on Steve Coban or the South Lake Partnership. If there was an ongoing investigation, they probably wouldn't tell me anything, but it couldn't hurt to ask. There was one person there who I thought would be of help, an assistant DA by the name of Bill Reuter. He started in the office a year after I came back from South Bend. We used to run and work out together on occasion, including having a couple of post workout beers. A few times we skipped the workouts and went right to the beers. He had the odd habit, considering his job, and also that he was married, of frequenting the topless bars in the seedier towns just east of Chicago. Once he had talked me into going with him on one of his outings. I got home at three in the morning, drunk and broke, and smelling like I had taken a bath in cheap perfume. I declined future invitations, but his wife had called me a couple times after that, late at night, asking me if I knew where he was.

He didn't pick up. District attorneys, even assistants, are hard to get a hold of. The call went to one of the secretaries who I recalled I had been on good terms with. She sounded glad to hear from me and asked me how I was doing, but when I asked to speak to Bill, I thought her tone changed, becoming wary. Maybe it was just my imagination. After what seemed like ten minutes, he finally was on the line.

"Hey, Logan, how's it going?"

Come to think of it, he sounded wary too.

"Good, Bill, what's with you?"

"Same old, same old. Keeping the barbarians at the gates."

"How do you tell the barbarians from the decent folk?"

"Unfortunately, each day the line is becoming more and more blurred. Hey, Logan, I've been meaning to tell you, I'm sorry I didn't come to see you more in the hospital."

I didn't remember him coming to see me at all but decided not to mention that.

"Don't worry about it. I can't stand hospitals either."

"And I thought you got a really rough deal on the job and the pension. That was damned unfair."

"Bill, not to sound trite, but nothing's fair. You know that."

"Yeah, well I feel bad about it anyhow. You know you can apply for reinstatement, don't you? I'll tell you, the guys here would like to see you back,"

"Yeah. I'm not sure how I feel about that yet. I'll give it some thought."

"How are you doing?"

"Good, considering. Everything hurts. I still have occasional lapses in memory and headaches. I'll walk into a room sometimes and forget what I was looking for. Did I just say occasional memory lapses?

He laughed.

"Could just be early senility, I suppose." I said. "Other than that, the doctors think I made an amazing recovery. I think if there was a betting pool, I would have bet against myself to make it, let alone be walking around. Yet here I am, with just a few dents in the fender."

"Great. We ought to get together sometime."

"You still running?" I asked.

"No, and I've put on about twenty pounds. I think I'm heading for a coronary by the time I hit forty. If I make forty that is."

"We could try running some Saturday afternoon and then having a couple of beers, if you want. Got to tell you, I've been moving slow since I got out of the hospital."

"Let's do that." He didn't sound like he was looking forward to it. I don't know if it was the idea of seeing me or running.

"Sounds good. I'll call you. In the meantime, I was hoping maybe I could get some information from you."

"Regarding?"

"You ever hear of a group called South Lake Partnership?" I asked.

There was long pause.

"Bill? You still there?"

"Yeah, sorry, the boss just stuck his head in the office. I may have to get going in a minute."

"I understand. South Lake Partnership?"

"Oh, yeah, sure. That's the group that wants to put a new mall in up by the interstate."

"Principal is a guy from Chicago name of Steve Coban. Know anything about him?"

Another hesitation.

"I think we must have a bad connection, Bill. Either that or the accident affected my hearing. You keep fading out."

"Sorry. Can I ask what your interest is in Coban?"

"Not much. I'm doing some checking on the BHU professor who's gone missing," I said.

"I heard," he said.

"News travels fast in a small town."

"For sure it does. You think Coban had something to do with Matthews?"

"No, not really. The professor was on record as being opposed to the mall. I also heard a rumor some of South Lake's activities weren't kosher, and that you guys were looking into them."

"Where did you hear that?" There was a note of suspicion in his voice.

"Like we just agreed Bill, it's a small town."

"You know, if there was something, I couldn't talk about it."

"It would just be between you and me. All I'm trying to do is tie up some loose ends."

I could almost hear him deliberating on the other end.

"You think there's a connection?" he asked.

"Bill, you know how it works. You rule out all the possibilities and then see what's left."

"Yeah. I could be looking at some trouble for this, but what the hell."

"There is something?" I asked. Bill was being coy, and I was curious why.

"The office got a letter a while back. Unsigned, but the writer purports to be knowledgeable about some funny business going on in Pipefitter's Union. More specifically, the Pipefitter's Pension Trust. He alleges that at least several trustees of the pension plan were bribed to swing a questionable land deal with South Lake. We checked into it."

"And?"

"Well, first, you never know about that anonymous stuff. Could just be someone with an ax to grind. Somebody looking to stir up shit."

"Agreed, but what did your boss think?"

"Off the record, he thought there was something there, but decided we weren't the ones to go after it."

"Why?"

"Pension fraud is kind of obtuse for one thing. Not like a guy holding up a liquor store. We don't have the resources or expertise for something like that. Two, it's a little awkward since Buzz used to work in this office, and still is tight with a bunch of people here. We turned it over to the federal prosecutor."

"What did they do with it?"

"That I can't tell you because I don't know. But if I were Buzz or Steve Coban, I might be worried. Especially with Coban's background."

"What do you mean?"

"He's got a reputation for not playing by the Marquis of Queensbury rules. He also has some associates in Chicago of questionable repute "

"Mob?"

"Not exactly. As the saying goes, just guys who know guys."

"Anything specific?" I asked.

"A few years ago Coban bought a vacant school from the Chicago Board of Ed. He wanted to raze it and turn it into a shiny office building. Some of the neighbors didn't think it would fit into the character of the area and started a petition to stop him. Shortly after that the school burned down, thus ending the debate. Arson investigator said it was a professional job, but nobody was ever charged. Oh, seems a bum was in the place when it got torched. He ended up a smore."

"Chicago's a tough town. That kind of stuff is business as usual. I don't see the motivation for Buzz bribing anybody, though. He didn't need the money."

"You know him better than I do, but I heard he isn't as well fixed as everybody thinks. He's got kids in college, right?"

"Two."

"I heard one goes to someplace in Ohio where it's twenty-five grand a year."

"The other one is going to the same school," I said. "Buzz thought he could save on gas."

"Fifty grand a year? Holy shit, that's more than I make. That can eat up a lot of dough fast. I heard he spent a lot of money too when his wife got, well you know what happened, all the trouble she had. What a shame that was."

"Yeah."

"I know you're tight with them," he said.

"Since I was eight years old."

"Must have been rough, with their son and all."

"Yeah. You don't have any thoughts on what the Feds are doing with this?" I asked.

"No. My guess is that right now they are trying to spread the net as wide as they can. Catch as many of the smaller fish as they can and hope they lead to the bigger ones. That's the way they work. Listen, Logan, I'm starting to feel a little uncomfortable with this. If I jeopardize a federal investigation, my next career move will be to find another career."

"I understand, Bill. No one's going to find out. Say, changing the subject, I wonder if you could check someone's sheet for me."

"Why don't you ask Ivan Rich?"

"I like talking to you better."

"Thanks, that means a lot to me. What's the guy's name?"

"Mike Parker," I answered.

"Don't tell me this Parker had something to do with the disappearing professor too?"

"Like I said before, just crossing the T's and dotting the A's."

"You mean I."

"Sorry, was just remembering you liked T and A." Then I added, "By the way, how's the wife doing?"

There was a pause, then a disgruntled "give me a minute", then a long wait. I was about to hang up when he came back on.

"I've got two Michael Parkers with recent activity. One did a few months for possession of controlled substance. The other one has considerably more experience with the legal system. I'm guessing that's the one you're interested in."

"Probably. What do you have on him?"

"Where do I start? Drunk and disorderly. Charges dismissed. DUI. Six months probation. Petty theft. Fine and restitution. Possession of marijuana. A few more like that, and then he stepped it up bit."

"To what?"

"Felony assault. Got in a fight in a bar."

"Assault for a bar fight. Somebody must have got hurt bad."

"You could say that. Looks like he put a guy in a wheelchair. Could have been worse for Parker. They had trouble figuring out who started the fight. Anyhow, he ended it."

"What did he get for that?" I asked.

"Five years. Did fifteen months in Michigan City, and then got parole." He paused. "Say, this is interesting."

"What's that?"

"Looks like Parker was represented by Buzz Wildrick' firm."

"No kidding? That is interesting. Anything on Parker since he's been out?"

"Clean, according to what I've got here. Sometimes, a young guy like that, things happen to him in prison that make him not want to go back. If I had been used as a meat packing plant by the Muslim Brotherhood, I think I'd do my best to stay out of trouble, too."

"That's kind of racist, isn't it, Bill?"

"Ok. Maybe it was the Aryan Brotherhood. Either way, I get the willies just thinking about it. Anyhow, he hasn't been in trouble since he's been out."

"Or at least hasn't got caught."

"Yeah."

"Just one more question, Bill."

"It will have to be the last one," he said, a note of exasperation creeping into his voice.

"Did I tell you I really appreciate your help?

"What now?"

"Vince Tomasini died in a car accident a while back," I said.

"That's not a question," Bill said. "That's a statement of fact. Anyhow, I didn't know him that well. He was before my time."

"Mine too. When I got there, he just been voted out and started his own practice. I was just wondering about the accident."

"He hit a railroad bridge abutment at 90 mph. It was out in the middle of nowhere and the car burned for a while before anybody showed up. We had a forensic guy look at what was left, but there wasn't a whole lot to sift through."

"Any suspicion that it wasn't just an accident? As in, maybe somebody tampered with the car?"

"Sure, anytime an ex-DA dies of unnatural causes you wonder if maybe somebody he put away decided to get even. I understand Tomasini was a bit of an asshole, so there was additional motivation. On the other hand, I heard he drove like a maniac and drank like a fish, so maybe he was due."

"I heard that too. Did the forensic guy come up with anything?"

"As I remember, and it's been a while, our guy thought something didn't look quite right, I think with the brakes. But he didn't have enough to say for sure. Said if someone did do something, must have really known what they were doing. Like a car mechanic or engineer."

CHAPTER 15

I decided to go for a drive. I made my way over to Highway 35 and headed north, until I saw the sign for County Road 7. I exited and drove almost a mile. Goose Creek Road leading to the golf club looked to be newly paved and in good condition. The other direction was a different story. The road seemed to get progressively narrower the further I drove, as if the dense brush on either side was trying to reclaim what once belonged to it, and the asphalt was rutted and pot-holed. There were numerous battered and worn signs as I drove declaring "NO OUTLET", "NO HUNTING", and "DUMPING PROHIBITED." A little over a mile down Goose Creek, the woods cleared and I could see an old farmhouse. It was about a two-hundred yards off the road, up a small hill. A partially washed out gravel driveway led to it. Even from the road the house looked dilapidated. The drive had been blocked off with thick steel chain that was padlocked to five-foot metal posts sunk in concrete on each side of the drive. A large "PRIVATE PROPERTY, TRESPASSERS WILL BE PROSECUTED TO THE FULLEST EXTENT OF THE LAW" sign was posted. The metal posts were situated such that it would have been difficult to drive around them, at least in a car. Someone had gone to no little effort to keep vehicles off of the property. I decided to take a look around, menacing sign or not. I pulled my car in front of the chain and got out.

As hiked up the drive, I got a peculiar feeling that someone was watching me. I passed the feeling off as general paranoia and rebuffed the compulsion to look over my shoulder. The small farm house was in worse condition than it appeared from the road. All the windows had been broken out and the front door was off of its hinges and halfway open. The only thing I could see inside were piles of debris, including old cans, newspapers, pieces of broken furniture, and a few old tires. As I stuck my head in the front window, there was a noise from inside that I took for a small animal scurrying around. I walked slowly around the house, not sure what I was looking for. The gravel drive continued on to the top of hill. I guess maybe the barn had been up there. I wasn't sure what I was going to see, but I figured I had come this far, so went on up the hill.

From the top, I got a good view of the surrounding fields and woods. Although I couldn't see it, I could now clearly hear the traffic on the interstate, which was probably only a few miles away. Another few miles north of that was Lake Michigan and the National Lake Shore. I don't know about such things, but it did seem like the place had the potential for development. Close to the bypass, the interstates and Prairie Stop.

At the bottom of the other side of the hill was a small creek, which was lined by brush and a few short trees. If Tecumseh and his followers had wintered in this area, I could imagine that where I stood would have made a good place for an encampment. Close to water, and the vantage point proffered by the hill would have made it difficult for an enemy to sneak up.

It was then I heard the motorcycle. More specifically, more than one motorcycle, approaching from a distance to my location. I looked back toward Goose Creek Road. There were two of them, just emerging into view on the road down where I had left the Mazda. I figured they were probably kids out for some off-road riding, like Buzz had warned me about. As they got closer, they looked too big and solidly built to be teens. I briefly considered that they could be cops, but unless the county had ditched their Harleys for dirt bikes, they weren't police either. Both riders wore dark black visors, which along with their helmets, made it impossible to see their faces. Unusual, because while it had been clear earlier, clouds had rolled in off of the lake and it was now overcast. Plus, I knew a lot of kids liked to ride without helmets.

The riders slowed when they went by my car, then came to a complete stop about twenty yards past it. They revved their engines and looked back at the car, as if deciding if the Mazda posed a threat. Then they went back to it. I thought about going back down the hill but something told me to stay put.

When they got to my car they circled tentatively around it, peering intently in the interior. The circling went on for what seemed a long time. Out of habit, I had locked the car and the more they circled the Mazda the more nervous I got.

I wasn't expecting what happened next. One of the riders stopped circling and pulled his bike up by the driver's door. He unwrapped what looked to be a foot and a half section of chain from around the back of his bike seat. He swung it in the air once, and then he brought it down hard against my driver's side window.

"Sonuvabitch!" I yelled, loudly, more out of surprise than anger.

I must have yelled louder than I thought, since the rider who was on the other side of the car heard me and looked up. He yelled something to the window breaker. They didn't immediately pinpoint where I was. They moved away from the car and circled, heads turning in different directions. Then one of them pointed up the hill to where I was standing. I thought when they saw me they might bolt, but instead they gunned their engines and started to make their way around the chain barrier at the entrance to the drive. They were coming after me.

I got an immediate sinking feeling in my stomach and had an impulse to run. Back when I was in uniform, one of the questions we asked of suspects was, "If you didn't do anything, why did you run away?" The best answer I heard was, "it seemed like a good idea at the time." I tried to tell myself that whoever they were, I wasn't doing anything worse than trespassing. If they were just kids, or cops, I wouldn't have been worried at all. But they weren't kids, and weren't acting like cops, and there was something menacing about the way they had casually knocked out the window of my car. That they immediately turned toward me gave me the impression that they weren't going to give me a lecture on respecting property rights. At the very least, I needed put myself in a more defensible position. Standing where I was, out in the open, they could literally run me over if they were so inclined. If I could get down to the creek they would have trouble following me. They might even have to dismount. If they did, there was a chance I could work my way along the creek to the road and then outrun them back to my car.

I started down the hill, the angry sound of the motorcycles increasing behind me. Judging from the intensity of the noise, they would be up the hill in a couple minutes. I had about sixty yards to make it to the cover of the brush which lined the creek. There were about ten yards left of it to go when I hazarded a glance back over my shoulder. I was much relieved to see that the bikers hadn't crested the hill. Not only did I not see the motorcycles, I also didn't see the branch laying on the ground that my right foot, and then my left foot, caught in a scissors action. I went sprawling headfirst the last five yards into the brush and landed on the creek bank. The brush wasn't enough to stop my momentum, and as various forms of vegetation whipped across my face, neck and hands, I slid all the way down to the creek. I wound up with right side of my head in about an inch of cold water. Stunned, I could only lay there for a few seconds, until the water trickling in my ear gave me incentive to sit up.

Heart pounding, I took a quick physical inventory. My right ankle hurt but not enough to be broken. I wasn't as sure about my shoulder, as I seemed to have difficulty raising my right arm. I wondered if I had cracked my collar bone when I hit the ground. My hands and face were scratched and bleeding, plus my jacket was soaking wet.

I didn't have a lot of time to dwell on my condition. Judging from the sound, the motorcycles had reached the top of the hill. The engines suddenly quieted and I knew they would be wondering what happened to me. It would not take them long to figure out there was only one place I could have gone. On the other hand, they didn't know exactly where I had gone into the creek, and I was reasonably confident they couldn't see me in the heavy brush.

I righted myself and cautiously peeked out over the bank. I could see the bikes through an opening in the branches. Although I couldn't hear them, it looked like they were discussing something. Rider One pointed down the road, to where it continued on between the fields. He must have thought I was Jesse Owens in the old days to have made it far enough down the road to get out of their sight. Rider Two looked where his companion pointed, then whirled and pointed at the creek, almost directly where I was hiding. I instinctively ducked down further, fearing against logic that he might have seen me.

To my surprise and relief, they apparently were going to separate. Rider One began to head slowly down the road, away from me. Rider Two turned and started down the hill toward the creek. He was heading in a line which would intersect with the creek about forty yards south from my position, also good for me. Once he got a little further down the hill he would be far enough away and at such an angle it he wouldn't be able to see me when I started to move.

I watched Rider Two make his way down the hill until he was out of sight, and then listened as the engine noise faded slightly. I gave it another minute then got to my feet, painfully and slowly, and began to walk north along the edge of the creek. I moved as quietly and quickly as I could but wasn't doing a good job at either. My ankle hurt, limiting my already not so good mobility, and I was slipping on the wet rocks and leaves, splashing and generally making a racket. I must have sounded more like a platoon than one man.

I wasn't covering a lot of ground quickly and knew it would just be a matter of time before Rider Two would start to head back in my direction. I debated whether I could make it up the hill and down the gravel road to my car before I was seen, and seriously doubted it. Even if my ankle wasn't hindering me, there was just too much open space to cover. But if I kept sloshing along the way I was, by the time I got to my car, both Rider One and Two would probably realize what I was doing and cut me off before I could get even close to the Mazda.

I decided to take the chance and moved out of the creek. I could still hear the motorcycles but they didn't seem to be close. I took a quick peek through the brush and then I was on the hill and running toward the old farmhouse as fast as I could.

I wasn't seen immediately, but if I had the advantage of surprise, it didn't last long. I wasn't far up the hill when I heard the roar of a motorcycle behind me. I glanced over my shoulder and saw him. He was riding fast and hard, sitting up over the seat, his head bent over the handlebars, his rear wheel spinning and shooting dirt out high into the air.

I tried to run faster but it felt like I was standing still. If my legs normally felt like planks when I started out, now they felt like concrete pillars. I was running like a sixty-year old man with a piano on his back. I thought about trying to make it back to the relative shelter of the creek but realized there was no time. I turned to face Rider Number Two. He was now just fifteen yards away from me. It must have been the one who hit my car window, because the chain he did it with was now in his upraised left hand. I had a brief thought of how much it was going to hurt if I got hit full force by it.

I dove to my right just as he went by. The chain, which I believe was meant for my head, instead hit struck me a glancing blow in the rear of my upper right thigh. The pain had the intensity of a sharp electric shock but wasn't hard enough to break bone or skin. It still hurt and I cursed in response to it. I rolled over and got up on my knees again.

Rider Number Two had gone on up the hill well past me before he was able to slow enough to turn and face me. He only hesitated a split second before he started back downhill towards me. As he turned, the bike's rear wheel was spinning in the soft earth as the machine sought traction. I stayed in a crouch as he approached, figuring that would give him a smaller target, especially since he would be going faster downhill and wouldn't get a good shot at me lined up. Sure enough, when he went by me I was able to roll to my right and only took another glancing blow from the chain, this one hitting my left shoulder. It didn't hurt as bad as the first one.

I had managed to dodge serious harm twice, but I knew this contest was about to end soon, and not in my favor. Rider Two was going to either nail me with the chain or get tired of trying to do that and just ram me with the bike. Still on the ground, I looked and felt for something I could use as a weapon. I felt the tip of rock with the fingers of my right hand. It was mostly buried and I frantically dug the dirt around it to get it loose. I had a little more time since Rider Two's momentum was greater going downhill and he went well past me. The ground was damp from the rain yesterday, otherwise I'm not sure I would have been able to pry the rock loose, but I did. It was about the size and shape of a large squash, and probably weighed at least two pounds.

I could always throw with accuracy. Not far or fast, but accurately. Once, when we were ten, Buzz and I decided to take on the Meyers brothers, the neighborhood bullies. They lived on our way to school and liked to yell insults at us as we walked by. One fall afternoon, we hiked through the woods to the edge of their backyard and yelled at them to come out. The brothers came out of the back door like a bunch of angry wasps, the oldest brother first, followed by the other two. It was a mesmerizing and fearful sight. I turned to Buzz, waiting for the signal to throw the apples we had brought along. He was running away back down the path. I was somewhat surprised to notice I wasn't scared at all. I carefully took aim and discharged my first apple, which hit the oldest Meyers brother in the forehead and he went down as if shot. The two others tripped over him and also went down. Then I ran away too. I gave Buzz shit about it for years.

Right now, I was plenty scared. I didn't have time to get to my feet. Rider Two was less than twenty feet away and closing fast. I got out of my crouch, onto my knees, brought the rock back and released when he was less than ten feet away from me.

I think the fact that I had hurt my shoulder earlier might have actually helped my aim. If had been able to put more velocity on the throw I would have probably overthrown him. As it was, it was a perfectly thrown strike, heading directly for his head. He tried to duck under it at the last second, but the rock, almost like a Steve Carlton slider, ducked with him, and hit precisely in the middle of the dark black face shield. He went straight back off the motorcycle. The bike continued on toward me, almost hitting me as the engine cut out. Then it veered toward the right, and defying the laws of physics, stayed upright until it got to the brush surrounding the creek, where it went finally went down.

I got up and walked over to where Rider Number Two was lying on the ground. He was flat on his back, his hands spread and extended over his head As I approached he moved his right hand slowly to his now cracked face shield, as if it remove it. The movement became more frantic and I figured it was because he was having trouble breathing. I leaned over him and pulled the shield up. There was a lot of blood. I couldn't tell if the blood was coming from his nose, mouth or both. I wondered if he had bitten his tongue. I guess the shield wasn't meant as protection from being hit by a miniature boulder.

I knelt and turned his head toward the side thinking this would allow the blood to drain away and make it easier for him to breathe. That seemed to work, and he gagged then spat out some blood. He mumbled an obscenity as his right hand reached for my throat, so I figured he was going to be OK. I brushed his hand away, got up and kicked him in the ass as hard as I could.

"That's for the window," I said. He grunted and tried to grab my leg, I broke loose and delivered a much more forceful kick. I was aiming for his stomach but I slipped slightly as I was rearing back and it landed low. He cursed and curled up in a defensive position.

I thought about looking for some identification on him but changed my plans when I heard the second motorcycle. Rider Number One was about hundred yards away at the top of the hill. I don't know if he saw what happened to his partner but didn't feel like hanging around for him to find out. I started toward the farm house, which I now optimistically thought looked a lot closer.

It seemed like I was now able to run faster. My legs felt looser and the pain from my first fall had diminished. Maybe the fear boosted adrenaline was starting to kick in. I had no illusion that I could outrun the motorcycle all the way to my car but was hoping that if I could get to the house it would afford me temporary shelter.

I got lucky again. Instead of heading directly towards me, Rider One went for where his partner was lying on the ground. If he had come straight for me he would have been upon me in no time. I glanced over my shoulder and saw he had helped Rider Two to his knees. I wish I had kicked him harder. By the time Rider One headed after me I was almost at the house. I went in the front door just as he reached the back of the house. I tried to push the door closed, but it was heavy and half off the hinges and I didn't succeed in moving it much.

The interior was dark and I tripped and stumbled on something as I made my way into the front room. Thankfully, I didn't fall. I looked down and, squinting, saw what I had tripped on was a piece of metal pipe, about three feet in length, like what would be used for a gas line. It was half propped up on a cinder block. I picked it up.

I heard Rider Number One go once around the house, then around again, looking for a point of attack. Then the motorcycle engine abruptly cut off. It sounded like he was right by the front door.

"You, in the house." The voice sounded angry yet controlled, as if he was someone who was used to giving orders and having them carried out. I didn't say anything.

"Come out and you won't get hurt. I'm a police officer."

That one threw me.

"Toss your badge in the door and we'll talk," I said.

There was silence, then, "If I come in there, bad things are going to happen."

I didn't say anything this time. My silence was apparently irritating him, because when he spoke again the anger was more noticeable.

"Last chance."

At times, I find the oddest things go through my mind. Right now, I was remembering a short story I had read in college that was written by Herman

Melville. It was called Bartleby the Scrivener. I don't know why, but it stuck with me. The main character keeps repeating, when asked to do something, the line "I would prefer not."

I said in a loud but steady voice, "I would prefer not."

I don't know if he heard me or not, but the motorcycle roared to life and he was coming through the door. Whatever was left of the door hinge broke and it came crashing down, almost right on top of the motorcycle. Rider Number One raised his left arm to deflect it, but the door hitting him and his own momentum caused him to lose his balance and he, the bike and the door went down with a loud crash and a huge cloud of dust.

I watched him cautiously for a second, while I spit the dust from my mouth, then heard rather than saw him start to move. I stepped forward and swung the pipe down at the pile. I hit something, but I think it was probably the door. I swung it again and this time was rewarded with a grunt. I circled around the man and motorcycle on the floor, toward the door and the outside. Before I reached the doorway, I turned.

"Who are you?"

"Fuck off."

"You shouldn't have said that to a guy with a pipe in his hand."

I went back to where he was lying in a and swung the pipe one more time, this time as hard as I could, aiming it at mid-right leg. He screamed.

"Godamn it, my knee!"

"I can do it again, if you like."

This time, no reply. I went out the door and stumbled down the hill toward my Mazda. When I was a few yards away, I heard a motorcycle start up. It had to be Rider Number 2. My immediate thought was I should have kicked him harder and a few more times. My second thought was that he was going to check on his buddy before he came after me, and maybe after doing so, would decide enough was enough. My final thought was that my second thought was wishful thinking. Whoever these guys were, they were serious and now certainly pissed off. I was sure they were going to come after me, even if they could only crawl, and I didn't plan on hanging around to see what happened.

I bought my Mazda after Buzz negotiated a settlement for "pain and suffering" from the insurance company of the old man who had run me over. He didn't have much insurance, I didn't get much money, and it was probably unwise to buy a car with what I did get. It was a year-old Mazda 626 that one of the secretaries in the prosecutor's office needed to get rid of. She loved it, but it had rear wheel drive, wasn't good in the snow, and not suited for the winters in Northwest Indiana. I liked it because it had the turbo engine and could get to 60 mph in under seven seconds. For that reason, when I got in and fired it up, I wasn't too concerned about somebody on a dirt bike catching me.

I stomped on the gas pedal, the rear end spun around, and gravel flew out from under the rear wheels. In a few seconds, I was heading down Goose Creek Road at over 40 mph. As I was topping a small hill, I looked in the rearview mirror and didn't see anything except road and woods. I congratulated myself on my escape and relaxed a bit as I turned my attention back to the road. Unfortunately, at that very moment, I was aghast to see there were two Prairie County Sheriff's Department sedans coming straight at me, fast up the hill from the other direction. Their light bars were flashing, but the sirens weren't on. There was less than fifty yards separating our vehicles, the road was narrow, and because it was lined with trees and brush, there was no room for evasive maneuver.

I slammed on the brakes, at the same time jerking the steering wheel to the right. Normally the Mazda would stop on a dime, but not on a road in that condition. The rear of the car started to skid to the left, which I immediately tried to correct by turning the wheel back to the right, and tapping the accelerator, but, in the split second I was doing this, the terrifying thought flashed in my head that I was going to be t-boned at a combined impact of around 70 mph.

It didn't happen that way. That it didn't was due entirely to the deputy driving the first sheriff's car. Instead of slamming on the brakes, which would have been the instinctive reaction, he saw what was happening, and reacted instead by accelerating, at the same time veering his patrol car to the right, to where he was almost off the narrow road. In fact, I could hear branches clipping the side of his vehicle as he went by. But he went by me with inches to spare. I breathed a very short sigh of relief.

My luck was short-lived. The driver of the second sheriff's car did what the driver of the first didn't do. He slammed on the brakes, and there just wasn't enough room on the road for both of us. Only that the Mazda was traveling at somewhat oblique angle spared us from a head-on collision. I watched, almost as if it was in slow motion, as the big sedan roared inches by me. I thought for an elated, irrational second that he would miss me altogether, but then felt and heard his front bumper clip my left rear fender. Although the impact wasn't great, since my vehicle was moving, the force was enough to send me spinning uncontrollably off the road.

I was just a passenger now, watching, as the Mazda, in what seemed to be an instinctive will to survive, seemed to actively dodge a number of trees. Brush slapped against and sides of the car, and I bottomed out a couple times. But there were too many tree and the car was still going too fast. There was a tremendous collision, an almost simultaneous loud bang, and then nothing.

CHAPTER 16

When I came to, I smelled food. Fried food. Intermixed with the smell of disinfectant. The combination was nauseous. I opened my eyes slowly. I was lying in bed. Since it wasn't my bed, and there were vinyl white curtains enclosing the space I was in, I deduced that I was probably in the Prairie County Hospital. I had no idea how I got there.

I heard a noise. In a chair at the foot of the bed was Ivan Rich. He was trying to stuff an enormous hamburger into his mouth. A large order of fries was on a small cart next to him. I watched him for a few seconds.

"That from Burger House?" I asked, figuring the food was from the popular burger joint a block from the hospital.

Startled, a chunk of the burger flew out of his mouth and landed on his lap. Ivan cursed and quickly brushed it off.

"For crissakes, I just got these pants back from the cleaners."

"Sorry. Maybe they got a coupon this week."

"Don't worry about it. I'd rather crap in my pants than be in the trouble you're in." He had a smug look on his face after he said that.

"I'm in trouble? That's good. How about those two guys who tried to use me for a motocross course?"

"Those just weren't two guys, you moron," he said. "They were off-duty Chicago PD."

"Cops?"

"Two of Chicago's finest. Officers Wilson and Kaminski, by name. By the way, I saw them bring them in. The one guy's face looked like a pizza. What the heck did you hit him with?"

"A rock. A very large rock. What were two Chicago cops doing out at Porter's Farm?"

"The developer, Coban, hired them to keep an eye on the place. So, in addition to assault, they got you for trespassing."

"One of them tried to separate my head from my shoulders," I said. I tried to sit up further but felt a stab of pain from my right over my rib cage. I eased back down.

"Oh yeah," Ivan said, "the icing on the cake is you almost took out a couple of our guys when they were responding to the call."

"What call?"

"Maintenance guy at the country club heard motorcycles, and figured it was kids tearing the place up. He called."

"Are the deputies alright?"

"They're going to need some new underwear, but otherwise they're ok."

I processed the information Ivan had just given me. One thing I was still unsure about.

"How did I get here?" I asked Ivan.

"You hitchhiked. How do you think you got here? They brought you in an ambulance."

"I don't remember being in an ambulance," I said, truthfully. I remembered my car hitting the tree, but nothing else.

"Well, I wasn't there, but the paramedics said you weren't very cooperative when they tried to get you out of what's left of your car. They said you were throwing punches and cursing them. They had to give you something to calm you down." He gestured at my left arm, and I noticed a bandage.

I rubbed my chest.

"It feels like Joe Frazier slugged me wearing brass knuckles," I said. "How long have I been here?"

"An hour maybe."

"I thought I was just having a bad dream," I said. Another thought occurred to me. "How's my car?"

"Let's put it like this," Ivan said. "You'll need a dustpan and a magnet when you get it. It's totaled."

"Shit on rye," I said. I only had the Mazda for about six months.

"You got insurance, right?"

"Just liability coverage." That was all I could afford at the time.

Ivan laughed. "Look at it this way, Logan. If you didn't have bad luck, you wouldn't have any luck at all."

The curtain opened and a doctor I knew from my recent long hospital stay walked in. I could only remember his first name was Frank. I used to call him

Dr. Frank. He was the doctor in the emergency room when they brought me in after I got run over by the car. Even after he wasn't in charge of me anymore, he would come by on occasion to see how I was doing.

"Mr. Wells," he said, "if you wanted to visit, you could have just called."

"Dr. Frank. I agree, we need to stop meeting like this."

He looked over at Ivan, annoyed.

"There's no eating in here. It would be better if you waited out in the lounge," he said.

Ivan made no motion to move.

"No can do, doc. Chief says I'm not supposed to let Logan here out of my sight."

"Your chief isn't in charge here. The guys in white coats are. Did you happen to notice I'm wearing a white coat?"

"I don't care if you are wearing a pink tutu and pair of tights. My chief ordered me not to let this man out of my sight, and that's what I'm going to do."

I have to give it to Ivan, he didn't back down easy, although I knew who was going to win this one.

"This man isn't going anywhere in his condition. Wait outside," Dr. Frank said, sternly.

Ivan still wasn't budging. Dr. Frank looked around the room, then back at Ivan.

"I don't mean to alarm you, but do you have any idea how many germs are roaming around in a place like this?" He glanced down at Ivan's sandwich. Ivan looked down too and got a worried look on his face. After a pause, he wrapped the burger, got up, and started to walk out. Before he left, he muttered something like, "Goddamn doctors think they're God."

Dr. Frank watched him go, a bemused look on his face. Then he listened to my chest with his stethoscope. After he did this he spent a few minutes probing and palpating various parts of my body. Eventually he appeared to be satisfied, stood up and scrawled some notes down on a chart he had attached to a clipboard.

"What is it with you and cars?" he asked. "You seem to be either getting hit by one or crashing your own into a tree."

"I would consider this a walk in the park," he continued, "compared to the last time you were here. A lot of cuts and contusions, none too serious. We cleaned them up. Your ankle is swollen. Looks like it might be sprained." He paused. "Tell me, were you wearing your seat belt?"

"No." Dr. Frank's eyebrows raised. "I was in a hurry and didn't have time to put it on," I added, defensively.

"Is your car equipped with an airbag?" he asked.

"I bought the car used, but I think it had the airbag option."

"I would say you were lucky. Very lucky. I'm guessing the airbag deployed and saved your life, as it was intended to do. But, since you were you weren't wearing a seatbelt, the bag probably knocked the wind out of you. Maybe even knocked you senseless. You apparently fought with the paramedics who were trying to get you out of the car."

"That's what I was told. I don't remember."

"I understand that other two gentlemen brought in here were trying to harm you, so considering the circumstances, I might have thrown a punch or two myself," Dr. Frank said, then added, "and the not remembering might be partly my fault."

"How so?"

"We have an established protocol whereby paramedics can administer a drug called Ketamine to individuals whose behavior presents a danger to themselves or others. It's a fast-acting, usually safe anesthesia. You were given an injection of it. Sometimes it causes short-term memory loss."

"I don't feel like I was drugged."

"Another advantage is that it doesn't last long," he paused. "Unfortunately, your behavior and memory loss could be explained by another concussion. With your history, any type of head injury is problematic, especially with the second one coming so close on the heels of the first one."

"I'm fine, doctor," I immediately said. I didn't plan on being in the hospital for the next couple days.

"I'm not saying you aren't. By the way, can you tell me what date it is?"

"November 31st."

"I've missed your sense of humor," he said, but didn't laugh. "I need to check your pupils."

He took his penlight and looked into my left and right eyes. He asked me to keep my eyes on the light as he moved it above my head, then below, and to each side. Then somewhat unexpectedly, he reached over and tapped me on the knee. It was the leg with the bad ankle.

"Ouch," I said, as my leg jerked.

"Pupils not dilated, reflexes seem ok. That's good. I wouldn't be surprised if you had a couple bruised ribs from the impact of the airbag, but other than that and the ankle, you seem in surprisingly good condition. I would suggest trying to limit your movement for the next few days. The most important thing is if you have any severe headaches or vision disturbances, dizziness, you need to run, not walk, back here."

He sat down again, where Ivan had been sitting, and wrote for another minute, then stopped and looked at me.

"Whatever you did must have been big."

"How's that?"

"The county sheriff is outside. Along with Attorney Wildrick."

"You know him?"

"Sheriff Hanlen? He's been here a few times. Wildrick? Never met him, but I've heard of him. Kind of hard not to. He a friend of yours?"

"Yeah. Long time."

"Interesting. I understand he's something of a local legend," he said.

"I'm guessing you haven't lived here all your life."

"No, and I'll be the first to admit I live an insular life."

"You could say he's a legend. A guy leads the high school football team to a state championship, makes second team all-American at Notre Dame, marries the prom queen, opens a successful law practice and makes a ton of money, then coasts on his laurels."

Dr. Frank gave a half smile, which I think for him was probably as close as he got to raucous laughter.

"I'd really like to keep you here overnight, just to make sure you're OK," he said.

He must have read my mind, because he raised his hand and added, "I have a feeling you aren't going to do that, in which case my advice to you is to go home and lay in bed for a few days. We can't let you drive yourself home, either. That would be criminal negligence."

"No need to worry about that. My car is in pieces somewhere out by the interstate."

"Good. Ask whoever comes to get you to bring some clothes. The ones you came in with aren't wearable anymore."

"That was my lucky shirt, too."

There was a noise behind the curtain, then Buzz's head appeared between them.

"How's he doing, doc?" he asked.

Dr. Frank looked at Buzz.

"I must be a good doctor, or at least congenial. Your friend here keeps coming back to see me." He stood and looked at me. "I'll be back in a little while." He nodded to Buzz as he left.

Buzz had a worried look on his face, which was rare for him. "You OK?"

"I think so."

"Because I got to tell you, you don't look OK."

"I feel like I did after that game against Miller, when I had to return seven kickoffs and they beat the hell out of me on every one of them."

"You ran the last one back all the way, as I remember."

"Fear is a powerful motivator," I said.

"Listen, I don't want to cut the sympathy short, but Bill Hanlen is outside. He's hopping mad. He's got three men in the hospital, two of them Chicago PD, and two deputies that almost got clobbered. You better tell me real quick what happened out at the farm."

I sighed, and then I told him as concisely as I could about the events out at Porter's Farm.

"What the hell did you run away from them for?" Buzz asked.

"It seemed like the thing to do at the time." I was going to say more but just then the County Sheriff, William Hanlen walked in.

Bill Hanlen, Sheriff of Prairie County, called "Chief" by most of his subordinates and nicknamed "Big Bill" by the papers, was a large man, both literally and figuratively. He stood almost six and a half feet tall and most of it was muscle. In fact, if it weren't for the slight graying of his flattop, you wouldn't have known he was a couple years north of sixty. He was a powerful political figure in the county. It was said, only half-jokingly, that if you wanted to get elected to anything in the county the first step was to get a picture of yourself in the newspaper shaking hands with Hanlen.

Hanlen had a dour look on his face. It was a look I recognized from a few of the times our paths had crossed before. My recollection was that he didn't seem to think too much of the county prosecutor's investigative staff.

Hanlen was wearing a dark blue polo shirt, knit sweater and pants of an odd green color, which led me to think that he might have been summoned from the golf course. Hanlen was an avid golfer and would play all year round if he could, unless there was too much snow on the ground. I doubt if getting called off the golf course did much for his disposition.

"They tell me you're going to live," he said.

"You don't look very happy about it," I replied.

"I just spent twenty minutes trying to explain to a deputy chief in Chicago how we got two of his cops here with the crap knocked out of them. I got two deputies that are lucky they're alive. You could say I'm not in a good mood."

"In that case, it probably wouldn't go over well if I said they started it," I said.

"You're damn right, and you might not find any of this so funny after I haul you downtown."

"Now hold on there a minute, Bill," Buzz interjected. "What were you figuring on charging Logan with?"

His question apparently took Hanlen by surprise. He turned and looked at Buzz with first an angry, then puzzled expression, and didn't say anything for a second.

"Are you his lawyer, Buzz?" he asked, finally, in a quiet tone.

"Technically, Logan is working for me." Buzz responded softly, as if he was trying not to make Hanlen any madder. The chief and he were friends, but I knew that both men were used to getting things their own way.

"That means trespassing won't hold up," he continued, "since I represent the property owner, and I told Logan it was OK to go out to Porter's farm. And he tells me the Chicago cops never identified themselves, either as police officers or security guards. And even if they had identified themselves as law enforcement, they have no authority in Prairie County."

He pointed at me. "Come on, Bill, they broke into Logan's car, and then tried to run him over. Whatever he did to them sounds like self-defense to me."

Hanlen raised his hand to his head and scratched his flattop. From the vigorous way he was scratching, it looked like the only way he could maintain his composure. Then he gave a tight grin. Not a happy one, more the "you got me" type.

"Alright, Buzz. If those other fellas want to file charges, I'll just tell them that they will be going up against the best lawyer in the county. I'm sure that will send them scampering back to Chicago."

Buzz didn't say anything, wisely, I thought.

"But I am going to need to know, right now, and with no bullshit, what this has to do with Jason Matthews."

Buzz looked at me quickly, almost as if to say, "Keep your mouth shut." Then he looked back over at Hanlen.

"I'm not sure it has anything to do with Matthews at all, Bill. Logan went out to Porter's Farm on his own. He's heard Matthew's claim that there are Indian relics on the property. I told him it was bull, but I guess he thought he needed to go out there and take a look. While he's out there, he gets jumped by a couple of guys, who, for God knows what reason, decide to rough him up. He decides not to let them." He paused for a second. "You know, if anyone should be pressing charges maybe it should be us."

Again, the vigorous head scratching.

"Don't try and threaten me, Buzz. I'll decide who is getting charged with what. I'm wondering why you would let Logan here go out there. Especially if you knew two Chicago cops were keeping an eye on the place. Seems peculiar you forget to mention that to him."

"Couple things, Bill," Buzz replied. "One, like I said, I didn't send him out there and didn't know exactly when he was going. Plus, I didn't know for sure that Steve Coban had people out there. He told me he was thinking about hiring a couple of off-duty cops for security, but that's all."

Hanlen shook his head.

"You got more answers than I got questions, Buzz. By the way, I got the impression that these two were known for liking the rough stuff. The deputy chief almost sounded like he wasn't too sorry they got some of it back. That's what makes it more interesting. If I was Logan, I might be wondering if those two guys were out there waiting for me."

"Now, why would they be doing that, Bill?" Buzz said, an edge in his voice.

"You tell me. I told you I didn't want Logan getting into the Matthew's investigation. I only sat still for it as a special favor to you. Maybe somebody else didn't like the idea of him trying to find out what happened to the professor."

"Who, exactly?" Buzz asked.

"I'm still trying to figure that out. By the way, you never answered my question. Are you Logan's lawyer?"

"Not unless he needs one. You think he does?"

"I can take care of those Chicago cops, if that's what you mean. Since Logan doesn't need a lawyer, you won't mind if I talk to him without you here, will you?"

It looked like maybe Buzz did mind. For a second, I thought he was going to refuse to leave. Then he shrugged.

"Heck no. If Logan wants to talk to you that's up to him. I'm not his lawyer, just his friend. In fact, right now I got to get back down to the office," he said, looking at his watch. "You guys have a good chat. Try not and talk too much about me when I'm gone."

Buzz looked at me. "I understand you are without a vehicle. I'll get Beth's Volvo over to your house. Keys will be under the driver's floormat. I'll call you later."

After he left, Hanlen pulled a chair up close to the head of the bed and sat down. His bulk totally overwhelmed the small hard plastic chair. He fiddled with a knob on the side of the bed for a few seconds before he spoke.

"We don't know each other that well, do we, Logan? I mean, we've known each other for a long time, but not that well."

I just looked at him and nodded.

"My wife said she saw you up at the college. She said she asked how you were getting along, and you said good."

"Better than I was, anyhow."

"TV cop shows would have you think we always get hurt by the bad guys," he said. "You and I know different. More likely to get hit by a car or trip in a dark alley. And that was a shame about you getting fired. I wouldn't have allowed something like that to happen one of my men."

"Technically, I wasn't fired, or even laid off. They gave me a disability pension. Course they decided to only give me half of what I was supposed to get."

"Yeah …Did I tell you I bumped into your old boss a while back?"

"Shannon?" I figured he was talking about Bob Shannon, the Prairie County Prosecutor. I was confused when he said a "while back". He had to see or talk with Shannon several times a week.

"No."

"Which one?" I had a few different bosses in my stint in South Bend.

"Ed Lyons. I was at a conference with him in Indy."

Ed Lyons had been my unit commander and later chief of the detective bureau when I worked in South Bend. I had a rocky relationship with him.

"How's that fat, incompetent megalomaniac doing?"

Hanlen laughed. "Sounds like you aren't in Big Ed's fan club."

"Sorry. I'm not having particularly good day and you brought up a bad memory."

"Ed told me he's up for a chief's job, somewhere up in Michigan. Ann Arbor, I think. By the way, he's lost a bunch of weight."

"Good for him."

"We talked a little bit about you."

"The conversation must have been seriously lagging at that point."

"You know how it is. You talk about all sorts of things."

"I'm surprised he remembered me," I said, which I only half-believed. Lyons wasn't the type of guy to forget someone he had a problem with.

"Oh, he remembered you. Said you were one of the best detectives he ever had. He mentioned a couple of the cases you broke that they had given up on."

"That's odd, considering he promoted about half a dozen guys over me."

"He mentioned that too. Said he had a problem with you because you were something of a wise ass and not a team player."

"Yeah, I suppose we didn't see eye to eye on some things. I thought my job was to get felons off the street, not trade beers and bullshit with the boys after work."

"You know as well as I do police work isn't like a normal job. You need to bond with the men you work with. You might be putting your life in their hands someday. That's not the same as selling refrigerators."

"I think you're right," I said. "If I was selling refrigerators all that would matter would be how many I sold. Not who I went bowling with."

"You sound bitter. My old man told me never to trust a bitter man."

"My old man was part Indian, and he told me never to trust the white man, so I guess we're at an impasse."

I thought that would get a rebuke from Hanlen. He frowned, and his brow crinkled, but then it passed. "I almost forgot about that. What tribe?"

"Mohawk."

"I'm from Minnesota. We got some reservations up there. Chippewa and Sioux mostly."

"Dakota."

"I said Minnesota," Hanlen said.

"Most of the Sioux in Minnesota are from the Dakota branch of the tribe and refer to themselves as such. The Lakota Sioux are the ones that lived on the Great Plains. They were the ones the kicked the shit out of Custer."

Hanlen shook his head slightly and pushed himself further away from the bed. He looked like he was getting frustrated.

"How long have you lived in Prairie Stop, Logan?"

I think he knew the answer but figured I'd humor him.

"My family moved here when I was eight. I was gone fifteen years plus for college and when I worked in South Bend, but here I am again."

"I moved here right after I got out of the Marines. Back in the fifties," Hanlen said.

Another pause.

"Would you say the town has changed a lot since when you were a kid?"

"A lot more people, for sure."

"When I was first elected sheriff, we had fifty thousand people living in the whole county. Now we got over half that in Prairie Stop alone, and almost 130,000 in the county Do you have an idea how many people were in the sheriff's department when I first ran?"

"Forty?" I guessed.

"Close. We had thirty-five officers and another fifteen civilian employees. Now we got over a hundred and seventy."

"I guess you can you use them all."

"Sad but true. In fact, some days I'm not so sure we're even keeping up. When I started, we had a handful of armed robberies here a year. And it seemed most of those were done by guys from Chicago passing through. We had three just last month. Drug related of course. Might sound odd, coming from the county sheriff, but if it was me, I'd legalize just about everything and make people go to clinic to get it. That way it would be out of the hands of the thugs and we could get addicts treatment. Bet you would see crime cut by two thirds within six months."

"That's a progressive idea, chief, but not sure most would agree with you."

"You're right, but sometimes you got to do what makes sense. People here talk about how they used to never lock their doors when they went out. Now I wouldn't leave my door open if I was taking a walk around the block. There are a lot of folks out there who don't have anything. They do drugs to take their minds off their problems and got to steal to get more drugs."

A nurse popped her head through the curtain. She looked at the chief and then at me.

"I have the pain medication the doctor ordered, if you want it," she said.

I was in some pain, but because of Hanlen's spiel on drugs, thought I should decline.

"I'll pass on it for right now, thanks."

"Up to you. Just let me know if you want it. My name's Gina." She gave me a friendly smile before her head disappeared. Hanlen watched her go.

"She wasn't bad. If you're lucky, maybe she'll give you a rub down later."

"You've been reading Penthouse too much, Chief. And I don't plan on being here later."

"I'm no doctor, but you look like you need to be off your feet for a few days."

"Thanks for the concern. I'll be ok though. You were talking about the new Prairie Stop."

"Yeah. Then there's the other side of the coin. Ever seen any of those new places going up off Shawnee Road?" He asked.

"I got a sister who lives out that way."

"Yeah? I'm impressed. Who would have ever thought that people would be building million-dollar homes in Prairie County? Where does money like that come from?

"People from Chicago are moving in, I hear."

"I guess that's right," Hanlen agreed. "Twenty years ago, nobody in his right mind would make that commute. Now we got people in Chicago who figure if they are going to be in traffic for ninety minutes, they might as well drive east as opposed to the western suburbs. You got the South Shore Line too, if you don't want to sit on interstate. And they get a lot more for their money in Prairie Stop. Problem is, the more of them that come to the country, the less of the country there is."

My head was starting to hurt, and I was beginning to wish I had asked for one of the pills.

"Chief, I wasn't aware you were such a student of socio-economic trends," I said.

"Goes with the territory, I suppose. The way I look at it, on a basic level, and like it or not, my job consists of making sure the have-nots don't take what the haves got."

"Keeping the unwashed masses from peeing in the country club pool?"

"Something like that. Let me finish my thought. I've found that rich people have something in common with poor people. Not all of them, mind you, but a lot of them.

"What's that?"

"They don't give a shit about anybody except themselves. The rich people because they don't realize what a struggle it is to make ends meet, and the poor people because they are so wrapped up in making ends meet they can't think of anything else. When most folks make about the same amount of money, when everybody is part of the middle class, then people can relate to each other better, and they are less inclined to pick each other off. There is an implicit understanding that the sum is greater than the parts."

"Chief, you need to get some of this stuff down on paper."

Hanlen frowned. "Tell me, Logan, do you take me for some hick country sheriff?"

"No. I can assure you, chief, I never would underestimate you. I don't think many people do."

"I read the papers. Some people are saying its time I step down. Get a younger man in the job."

"Don't sell yourself short, Chief. You don't look a day over fifty, and you've forgotten more about law enforcement than most county sheriffs in this state know."

Hanlen snorted.

"No, I'd just like to hang in as sheriff for a couple more years. Then I think I'm moving to North Carolina. I can fish and golf there just about all year round. This missing professor isn't helping any with that plan. I'm starting to wonder if he took off just to make me look bad."

"He'll turn up, one way or the other," I said, stating the obvious.

"Yeah. Ivan says you got some theory that maybe somebody didn't like Matthews for trying to stop our new mall."

"It wasn't much of a theory really. There probably isn't much to it."

"It might be a good theory to keep to yourself, unless you got a real good reason to think it's true."

"Why would that be?"

"Kind of related to what I was talking about earlier. We got a lot of people in the county who aren't doing too good. The steel business is in the crapper. All kinds of stuff related to steel are being hit too. Days when a man could get out of high school and get a good job in the mill are gone. But you still got to pay the bills, right? Even if it means manning a cash register. Then you got the rich people that need somewhere nice to shop. Now, they're taking their money and tax dollars over to Chicago or Greenville. Seems like a new mall would help out a lot of people."

"You don't think one cranky professor was going to be able stop a mall from getting built, do you?" I asked.

'No, but there's people in the county, a small group I admit, that don't like change. They don't like outsiders coming in. They liked it when everybody knew everybody else. When everybody was the same color and everybody spoke the King's English. When the town shut down at 6 o'clock every night. To tell the truth, I kind of miss those days myself. You get enough of dissatisfied people signing petitions and calling their councilmen, and then all of sudden the guy who wants to build the mall is off looking for somewhere else to put it."

"You almost make it sound like someone did have reason to get rid of Matthews," I said.

"No. But if people start thinking that, then it casts a dark cloud over county. I don't think we need that, do you?"

I didn't say anything.

"What did you think of the wife?" Hanlen asked.

"I never met Matthews, but from what I know, I would say they were an odd pair."

"Think she could have got rid of him?"

"That would surprise me."

"She knew he was having an affair, apparently."

"Both Mrs. Matthews and the girlfriend says it wasn't an affair. Although the girlfriend wondered if the wife was the one having the affair."

"There's an old saying. A man has an affair with his dick … a woman has an affair with her heart."

"I think I heard that before, but not sure how relevant it is to the Matthews. In any case, Mrs. Matthews is a lawyer. That means she doesn't have a heart."

He laughed. "Too bad Buzz isn't around to hear you say that."

"Buzz practices law for a living. He's not a lawyer."

Hanlen grunted, then stood up, indicating our discussion was over.

"One other thing. You are off this case, effective immediately. You understand?"

I nodded.

"If by some chance you remember something else regarding the professor, like maybe something you forgot in our little chat here, I want you to let me know about, and I mean right away. When you call the office, tell them you need to speak to me personally and its urgent."

"What about Ivan?" I asked.

"I'll fill him in later. To be honest, the boy's been a bit of a disappointment to me on this one. But he's related by blood or marriage to half the people in the county, so there's nothing I can do about that. Nepotism is a bitch. By the way, I'll have him give you a ride home."

I can't imagine Ivan would be too pleased to act as my chauffeur.

"That's alright. I'll call somebody when I'm ready to go."

Hanlen stood.

"If I were you, I'd take it easy for a few days. You don't look so good."

CHAPTER 17

I watched Hanlen go and then pressed the call button for the nurse. She appeared in a few minutes.

"How are you feeling?" She asked.

"OK, but I think I could use a pain pill, only when you get a chance."

"Sure. Give me a minute."

When she came back, she handed me a couple of pills and a small cup of water.

"Off to happy land," she said as she watched me swallow the medicine.

"I feel better already."

"Good. Are you related to the Wells family that lived on Norwich Drive?" she asked.

"Matter of fact, I'm one of the Wells family and I still live on Norwich Drive."

"My maiden name was Moretti. I was friends with your sister."

I thought about that.

"Sure. Gina Morreti? 'Course I remember you. I think I went to one of your birthday parties when I was about nine or ten. There was a magician there, as I recall. I think he wanted to shoot a carrot out of my brother's mouth with a pistol, but my mom wouldn't let him."

"It's Linden now. The last name, I mean. And that was probably my twelfth birthday. My dad made a big deal out of it. What's your sister been up to? I seem to remember she went to Northwestern. That's where my kids are now."

"She graduated with honors. Got a good job and made a pile of money. She and her husband have a place off Shawnee Road."

"I might have heard that, but I never see her anymore. You'd think I would I bump into her at the grocery store or somewhere."

"Since she got rich, I'm not sure she has a need to eat anymore. Or go to the bathroom either."

She laughed.

"So that's how rich people are different," she said. "Well, as my aunty used to say, she's done very well for herself."

"How about you? How long you been working here?" I asked.

"I started right after I got out of nursing school. Then I took about fifteen years off while I raised my kids. I just started working again a few years ago."

"How many kids?"

"Two. Like I said, both at Northwestern. One's in pre-med and the other one is in a pre-law."

"You've done very well for yourself."

She laughed.

"Can you tell me something?" I asked.

"Sure."

"I came in with a couple of other guys. Do you know what happened to them?"

She gave me a look. "Why do you want to know?"

"We were in a car accident. I wanted to see how they're doing."

"Car accident? I've worked the ER for a while. I don't think the county sheriff usually shows up for a car accident, unless somebody dies."

"I just wanted to apologize to them, and make sure they're not hurt."

She gave me a wary look.

"I'll see what I can find out."

She came back about ten minutes with a puzzled look on her face.

"That's strange," she said. "They aren't here anymore."

"Not here anymore?

"I was told an SUV pulled up about an hour ago, and the two men you asked about got into it. We didn't even have a chance to treat them properly"

"They can just leave like that?"

"This isn't a prison. We can't treat people if they won't consent to being treated."

"Didn't Chief Hanlen try to keep them here?"

"No, from I what understand, he spoke to the doctor about letting them leave. It was almost like he didn't want them here."

"May sound like an odd question, but any chance anyone got a look at the license plates on the SUV?"

"What do you want the license number for?"

"Not the number really. I was curious about the state."

She shrugged. "I can ask. The unit secretary was outside catching a smoke when the car pulled up. She said it looked expensive."

She came back into the room a few minutes later.

"The doctor said you can leave whenever you're ready. He said to tell you he recommends against it." In a lowered voice, she added, "Oh, the secretary thinks the plates on the car were Illinois."

I asked Gina to look up the number for Kathy's dad. I called and lucky for me Kathy picked up. She sounded concerned when I told her where I was, but I cut her off when she asked what happened. I told her where my spare key could be found and asked her if she could bring some clothes over. She said it might be an hour or more before she could get to the hospital and I told her not to rush.

I remember signing some forms, and then I must have drifted off. When I woke up, Kathy was sitting in the chair next to me.

"Hi."

"You just get here?" I asked.

"A little while ago. You OK?"

"Yeah. A couple bumps and bruises."

"I can see that. The nurse was giving me the rundown. You sure you want to leave? Maybe it would be better if you stayed."

"I'll feel better at home. You got my clothes?"

She reached down and came up with a brown grocery bag.

"Your wardrobe is kind of limited. I found some jeans, a T-shirt and a sweatshirt. All of it looks like it's about twenty years old. Probably the same stuff you wore in high school. I don't know how many people who could say that."

I started to swing my legs off the bed, felt a stab of pain in my side, grimaced, and put my legs back where they were. I guess Doctor Frank was right about my ribs.

"Let me help you."

"I can do it."

"If you're worried about me seeing you, don't."

She watched me very tentatively get dressed.

"Does anything not hurt?" Kathy asked.

"No, and that includes my pride."

A nurse, not Gina Linden, came back and tried to put me in a wheelchair. I politely refused. She politely insisted, but when I continued to refuse, she eventually gave up and went away. Before she left, she handed me a bag that had what was left of the clothes I was wearing earlier, plus my wallet and care keys.

It had gotten quite a bit colder and a light rain was falling as I waited for

Kathy to bring the car around to the emergency room entrance. An ambulance was parked on the other side of the entranceway. One of the attendants and a nurse were leaning against the side of the van smoking cigarettes. During my last hospital stay, I noticed how many people in the health care profession smoked. Probably for the same reason a lot of cops smoked; periods of frenetic activity mixed with a lot of down time. Smoking was a great time-killer.

Kathy pulled into the drive in a huge Oldsmobile. She got out and came around to help me into the car.

"Nice ride." I said.

"It's my dad's. He loves big cars. I don't think they make them like this anymore."

I got in the front seat. It felt like that I was sitting on a living room sofa compared to my Mazda.

"I could go to sleep here," I said.

"Feel free. But I'll have to wake you up when I get to your house. I don't think I'm strong enough to drag you into it.

The ride from hospital to my home appeared to take seconds, yet the gentle click of the windshield wipers did almost make me fall asleep. Kathy assisted me into the house. Once in the house, I immediately collapsed into the recliner. Kathy walked into the kitchen and came back with two glasses of water. I looked at the clock to see if I could take another pain pill. I could so I did.

"Tell me what happened today." Kathy asked.

I gave her a quick version.

"These two guys, cops, just came after you? I would have been scared senseless."

"I was scared, but also confused. I was wondering what I did to get somebody so pissed off at me."

"Do you think they were trying to kill you?"

I thought about that. "No, I think they wanted to scare me. Rough me up maybe but not kill me. Technically, I was trespassing, so I guess they figured that would give them the excuse."

"And then they just disappeared from the hospital? Sounds like someone didn't want them talking to anyone."

"About anything," I added.

"Do you think Buzz had something to do with it?"

I didn't say anything. I was thinking about Buzz and Hanlen talking in the hospital. Unless somebody had been tailing me, Buzz could have been the only one who knew I was going out to Porter's farm.

"Well?" Kathy asked.

"I need to think about that. In the meantime, I think I'm going to hit the sack. It's been a rough day. Thanks for coming to get me. I owe you."

"You sure you will be alright?"

"Be good as new tomorrow. I'll call you first thing."

CHAPTER 18

I was dreaming. In the dream, I was a boy, sleeping out in the open, a coarse blanket my only cover. It was cold and my breath made a cloud that disappeared slowly under the full moon. I could see the breath and hear the snores of others around me. I felt a hand on my shoulder.

"Are you awake, my son?"

It sounded like my father's voice, but when I turned to see, it wasn't him, and not a face I recognized. I'm not exactly sure how I knew, but I knew it was Tecumseh.

I nodded slightly, as my hand went to the tomahawk beside me.

Tecumseh nodded approvingly.

"I approach you without warning in the middle of the night, but you do not cry out. Instead you reach for your weapon. This is what a warrior should do."

I was pleased by his words but made no sound.

"The Long Knives will be upon us soon. Their leader is a great hunter, and he has tracked us to this place. He plans to attack us while we sleep. But his men are few, and they will be scared."

"Should we wake the others?"

"Soon." He cast an eye around him and I could see in the moonlight that a look of contempt appeared on his face. He gestured around him.

"These are lazy dogs, not braves. If you and I were not here, their scalps would all be on the Long Knives belts before dawn."

"We traveled a long way today. They are tired."

He gave me an approving nod.

"You understand of other's weakness, yet you yourself are not weak. Rise and come with me."

I got up quickly and followed him out of the camp. He glided easily though the woods, on a path I could barely see. After going about fifty yards, he stopped suddenly, and raised his to signal me to stop. We were in a small clearing. Tecumseh motioned for me to crouch down.

"Listen to me my son. I must tell you something. You may not understand, but you need to hear."

He looked up at the sky and pointed at the moon.

"The moon is like the Shawnee. The brightest light in the night. The white men are like the stars. Although not as bright, they are many. Like the moon, the Shawnee will shrink and disappear so that only the stars will be left."

"We can fight the Long Knives."

"We will have to fight, because no matter where we run, the white man will follow us. But even if each of our warriors killed a thousand Long Knives, there would a thousand more to take their place."

A tremendous wave of sadness overwhelmed me.

"Then what will become of our people?"

"Our people's way of life is disappearing. The white man cuts down the forest and plows all the fields. He kills or frightens away all the game. Each man takes as much as he can without thought of his neighbor or what will happen to those who come after."

"Why do you tell me this?"

"You need to know these things. No matter how few of our people are left, you must never let them forget how great a people the Shawnee once were."

I turned my face away so Tecumseh would not see the tears forming in my eyes. I felt his hand on my shoulder.

"It is no shame to shed tears for your people. Now let us prepare to fight the Long Knives. They will be upon us before much longer."

As we walked back to the camp, there was a noise, which seemed not part of the dream. The noise continued and then Tecumseh and the forest were gone and I was reaching for the phone. I'm not sure how long it had been ringing. My alarm clock said 7 am.

"Did I wake you?" It was Buzz.

"Yeah."

"Sorry. I thought you were still in the hospital until I called over there and found out you left. I thought maybe something happened to you."

"Something did happen to me."

"Don't blame me for that. I didn't tell you to go poking around Porter's Farm. You may remember I discouraged you from doing same."

"Yes, you did. Although it's curious you were the only one who knew I was going out there."

There was silence on the other end.

"Just for saying that I ought to come over there and kick your ass."

"I'm full up on ass-kickings this morning, thanks."

"You should have stayed in the hospital."

"There are some things I have to ask you about, Buzz."

"What things?"

"Why didn't you tell me you and Coban were partners?"

"I've got an interest in one of his companies. I'm not sure you could say we are partners."

"Same difference. You didn't think you should mention that?"

"I didn't mention it for just the reason we're now having this conversation. I knew you'd get fixated on some conspiracy theory. Yes, Steve Coban is rich and powerful but despite your opinion, not everyone who is rich and powerful makes people disappear who get in his way."

"Tell me something, Buzz, what do you stand to lose if Coban's plans get derailed?"

He didn't answer right away, and when he did his voice was subdued.

"Don't be an idiot. This isn't just about me and Coban." He almost spat the words out and neither of said anything for a few seconds.

"I got to ask you a few more questions, Buzz. Now's a good time as any. Where were you the night Matthews disappeared?"

A short laugh. "You're kidding, right?"

"I wish I was."

"That would have been Thursday, right? I drove up to South Haven that afternoon. There were some things I wanted to do to the house before winter." The Wildricks had a vacation home near South Haven, Michigan, right on the lake.

"How long were you up there?"

"I left around noon and came back Friday afternoon. Satisfied?"

"Anybody see you up there?"

"How the hell should I know?"

"A neighbor, the mailman, anybody?"

"It's a summer place. Most of my neighbors only stay there in the summer. Hence there was no one to see me. Get it?"

I remembered the Wildrick lake home from the times I had been up there. It was out of South Haven proper and somewhat isolated. In the off-season you could easily be there a week and nobody would know you were there.

"I have to ask you something else, Buzz. Did you have something going on with Jackie Matthews?"

"You ask that like you already think I did."

"Tell me no and I'll believe you."

The voice was softer this time, barely discernible.

"I shouldn't have gotten you into this."

Before I could say anything in response, he hung up.

CHAPTER 19

I tried to go back to sleep but the phone was ringing again an hour later. I thought it was probably Buzz again and picked up with an abrupt "yeah?"

An authoritative voice I did not recognize, said "I wish to speak to Logan Wells."

I sat up and winced as I did do so.

"You got him."

"Mr. Wells, this is Doctor Richard Cook. Mrs. Jason Matthews asked me to call you. I have a few minutes now before rounds, if it isn't too early for you."

"Not at all, Doctor. Thanks for calling."

"First, I generally do not discuss my patient's confidential medical information. Although I understand the emergency nature of this situation, I'm still uncomfortable with doing so." I was about to say something, but he paused and continued.

"However, Jackie made it clear that Jason's welfare is at stake, so I will answer, within my discretion, the questions you have."

"Fair enough, Doctor." I said. "I understand Jason had some heart issues."

"He had atherosclerosis, which is a form of arteriosclerosis, colloquially referred to as hardening of the arteries. Basically, the disease occurs when there is a buildup of plaque in the arteries. Typically, the plaque buildup is asymptomatic until it reaches a point where there is actual arterial blockage, at which time the affected individual may suffer a catastrophic event, such as a heart attack or stroke."

"What causes it?" I asked.

"Both genetic and environmental causes. In Jason's case, his father suffered from coronary disease. Jason also has borderline hypertension. High blood pressure is known to cause atherosclerosis."

"How was it diagnosed in Jason's case?"

"He had a couple Transient Ischemic Attacks, or TIAs, colloquially known as 'mini-strokes'."

I was getting the feeling Dr. Cook didn't care for colloquialisms.

"You put him on some medications."

"A couple of high blood pressure meds. I don't have his file here, but I know one was Atenolol. I'm sure the other was a diuretic, but the name escapes me."

"Was he taking anything else?"

"Jason was very anxious and depressed after the TIAs. Frankly, I can't say as I blame him. I prescribed an antidepressant which has some sedative properties. Trimipramine, I believe. My intention was to have him take it for several months until he came to grips with his health issue, and then take him off of it."

"Doctor, don't mean to get off the track here, but as long we are talking medications, what would you prescribe Anafranil for?"

A pause, then, "I didn't prescribe that for Jason."

"Yeah, I know, I was just curious."

"Well, I probably wouldn't prescribe it. Its prescribed for severe cases of OCD. I would most likely defer that to a psychiatrist."

"What's OCD?"

"It's an abbreviation for Obsessive Compulsive Disorder, a potentially serious mental health issue."

I was glad he said abbreviation, instead of colloquialism.

"Ok. Thanks. I think I have an idea what that is. Back to Jason. Did his medications have side effects?"

"All medications have side effects, Mr. Wells. Not all people experience them to the same degree."

"I'll try and phrase this delicately, Doctor. Would loss of sexual function possibly be a side effect of the medications you prescribed for Jason?"

There was a pause.

"Yes, but if there was, I wasn't aware of it. If Jason told me there was a problem, we could have adjusted the dosage or tried another medication."

"You sound like you have been around the block a few times, Doctor. Is impotence something a male patient would typically open up to you about?"

"Since you asked, my observation is that women seem to treat their bodies with considerably more objectivity and rationality then men do. That is, a woman would be more inclined to discuss an issue that a man would not. I hope this doesn't sound chauvinistic, but I would suspect it has to do with the nature of childbirth. But, to directly answer your question, no."

"The reason I ask is that Jackie Matthews told they were going to start a family. I'm thinking that might have been a problem because of Jason's health issues."

"Perhaps, but there was a bigger problem in Jason's case. And I'm quite sure his wife was aware of it."

"Can you tell what it is?"

"Well, Jason contracted epidemic parotitis a few years ago."

"What's that?"

"The mumps. He never had them as a child. Men of his age who get the mumps typically experience a significant decline in fertility."

CHAPTER 20

After my conversation with Dr. Cook, I went back to sleep, only for an hour, and again the phone rang.

"How are you?" Kathy asked.

"I've been better. " I said., "But, all things considered, I don't feel too bad."

"It's good to look on the bright side. Should I come over again?"

"Much as I would like that, I've already wasted half the day."

"Maybe you should take it easy," Kathy said.

"There's an old Indian saying … it's better to strike when the anvil is hot."

"That's an Indian saying?"

"Stolen from us by the white man, just like everything else."

"I see. Where are you going first?"

"Downtown. Menlo's Men's Wear."

"What for?"

"I need a new suit."

"Getting married?" Kathy asked.

"Married or buried. My dad used to say those were the only reasons to buy a suit."

"One preferable to the other, hopefully. Where else?"

"Chicago," I replied. "To see Buzz's friend, the big shot real estate guy. If he's around that is."

"Then?"

"Professor Matthews had a relationship with a female student. Her ex-husband apparently didn't like the idea. He also happens to be an ex-con with a bad temper."

"Ex-con? What did he do?"

"Assault, among other things."

"So now he's your lead suspect?"

"Not necessarily. I just want to talk with him so I can cross him off the list."

"When will I see you?"

"I'll call you later."

"Please do. I guess it wouldn't do any good to tell you to be careful."

"It would, and I will."

I went into the bathroom and looked in the mirror. My face was discolored in a couple of places, and there were number of small scratches. Other than that, I looked better than I thought I would.

I got a number from information for South Lake Partnership. I called and asked to speak to Steve Coban. The woman who answered asked me my name and the purpose of my call. I gave her my name and told her it was personal. She asked me to hold for a minute. When she came back she told me that "Mr. Coban isn't available."

"Ok. When might he be available?"

"I'm sorry. Mr. Coban is extremely busy. He doesn't take unsolicited phone calls."

"Well, I feel like we know each other. We've got a mutual friend. He suggested I give Steve a call regarding a business opportunity."

"I'm sorry, but as I said, Mr. Coban doesn't take unsolicited calls."

"Why don't you tell him Buzz Wildrick said I should call? It's regarding a real estate investment."

"Please hold."

There was long pause. When she came back, she was more deferential.

"I'm sorry, Mr. Wells. Mr. Coban is not available right now, but he would like to talk to you. Is there a number where he can reach you?"

"I was just about to go out, but as it happens, I was planning on being in Chicago this afternoon. How about I drop by later?"

"Let me ask him."

"Mr. Coban says he can see you around 1:30. Tell me where you are coming from, and I'll give you directions to our offices."

After I hung up, I called the number Ivan Rich had given me for Liz Pirelli, the Chicago policewoman who verified that Jackie Matthews had been in Chicago when her husband disappeared. The number was for her precinct, and the person who answered told me she wasn't on duty. I told him I was Detective Rich calling from the Prairie County Sheriff's Department and that I needed to reach her as soon as possible. He wouldn't give me her home phone, but told me he would call her and ask her to get in touch with me.

I looked and felt slightly better after I had cleaned up a bit and popped a couple of the prescribed pain pills. The phone rang just as I was getting ready to go out to the car.

"Ivan?" A woman's voice asked.

"Officer Parilli?" I responded, deducing it was her.

"Who is this, please?" She asked, a note of irritation in her voice.

"I don't know if you remember me, Liz. This is Logan Wells. I was an investigator in the Prairie County Prosecutor's Office."

A pause.

"I remember you. I thought you got killed in a car accident."

"No, wasn't quite that bad. As the joke goes, the doctors did the best they could, but I pulled through anyhow."

"Huh. I'm confused. I was told Ivan Rich called and it was important."

"Sorry for the subterfuge. I thought you might be more inclined to get back to me if it was official."

"If what was official?"

"I needed to ask you a couple questions about Jackie Matthews."

Another pause.

"I don't know any Jackie Matthews."

"The professor's wife?"

"Yeah, OK. The wife of the professor that took a hike. Look, what's going on here?"

"I've been retained to help find Jason Matthews. Ivan gave me your name and said that you verified that Jackie Matthews was in Chicago at the time her husband was last seen."

"I'm not sure I should be talking to you. This is still an open case, right?"

"That's right, it is. But I've been given access to all details of the investigation. If you need verification, you can give Bill Hanlen a call and ask him." That wasn't true and I could almost hear her thinking that. There was a long silence.

"I tell you what, Liz, let me ask you a few questions, and if you are uncomfortable with answering them, just say so."

"Alright, I guess I can play it like that," she said.

"Thanks. You went over to the Drake?"

"Yeah. I talked to one of the assistant managers."

"What did he tell you?"

"He said that Jackie Matthews' car had been in the garage from when she checked in until she checked out. It's valet parking, so they have records of who comes and goes."

"She didn't leave in her own car. Is it possible she could have left with someone else?"

"Nobody said she didn't leave the hotel. Every day she was going to some function at DePaul."

"Right, sorry. What I meant was is there any proof that she spent each night at the hotel?"

"What kind of angle are you working on this?" She asked.

I didn't see any reason for pulling punches.

"Jackie Matthews is an attractive, relatively young woman in good-shape who had an older husband who wasn't. There may have been some needs that weren't being met in the relationship."

"I think I get the picture. But if she was looking for action, why not have the boyfriend come over to the hotel? Her husband wasn't with her, right?"

"Might have been too risky. She's ninety minutes or less away from home. Maybe the husband is a little suspicious, too. What if he decides to surprise her by driving into the city? Or maybe someone sees the boyfriend at the hotel and remembers it later."

"In the oft chance someone is asking about her later, like you are now."

"Exactly."

"Ok. Tuesday evening there was a call for room service. Plus, she made a couple of local calls."

"How about Wednesday?"

"She ordered some movies."

"I haven't stayed in a hotel for a while. Is it possible she could have ordered some movies but not been there to watch them?"

She didn't answer right away.

"I suppose so."

"Maybe Mrs. Matthews wasn't there Thursday night."

"Could be. There was something else. I was just thinking about something the maid said."

"The maid?"

"I spoke to the maid who took care of Mrs. Matthews' room. She said she made the bed Friday morning, but it didn't look like the bathroom had been used. No wet towels, used Kleenex, stuff like that."

"Liz, if you were at a conference, would you go out without taking a shower or putting on makeup?"

"No way."

"How about Friday?"

"More room service and local calls. Maid says the room was definitely occupied."

"The only night that sounds questionable is Thursday." The night Professor Matthews vanished.

CHAPTER 21

I looked out to my driveway and saw a newer model dark green Volvo station wagon, which I knew belonged to Beth Wildrick. Buzz had been true to his word. The keys were were where he said they would be. At least I would be traveling in style.

Menlo's Men's Wear was on the next block over from the Lincoln Tavern. I understood a number of the buildings downtown had been built during the period from 1900 to 1930 and were in the architectural style of that period. Three story brick or limestone structures, with business establishments on the first two floors and offices or possibly residences on the third floor. The buildings had been maintained with varying degrees of diligence, I assume depending on the prosperity of the occupants. Bloomfeld's, the large department store downtown, had closed its doors a couple years ago and was now a boarded-up eyesore. The former Farmer's First Bank looked like it could have been brand new. The Prairie Hotel, over a few blocks, and once acclaimed as one of the finest hotels in Indiana, had been shut for years and slated for the wrecking ball. Menlo's appeared a little worse for wear. Some of the mortar had worn away, the paint on the window frames was peeling, and a second-floor window was cracked.

When we were little, my dad and mom would drag us down to Menlo's at least once a year, so my dad could buy a new suit, a few dress shirts, and a couple ties. The suits were always either solid navy blue or charcoal black, the shirts white button-downs, and the ties conservative. He seemed to like to buy the new clothes, even though there were not many occasions he needed to get dressed up for. The funeral or wedding for a co-worker, or relative, or a trip into Chicago, at my mother's insistence, for a night on the town. For some reason, my father was always waited on by Ray Menlo himself, which made him feel important and no doubt spend a lot more money than he originally planned on.

I recalled racks of suits on the first floor, which had polished wood floors and mirrors lining the walls. Down in the basement they had the stuff that didn't move during the previous season, at a good discount off the original price. The first suit I ever had came from the basement. On the second floor were various accessories and shoes.

I hadn't been in the place for a while and noticed the former gleaming wood floors were dull and scuffed. There were still racks of suits, but not near as many as I remembered. And it seemed the whole operation was now on one floor. In one corner they had a sign advertising "25% off." A bell rang when I opened the door and a woman who looked to be a few years older than me approached from the rear of the store. She and I seemed to be the only ones in the place.

"Hello," she politely, although when she got close I could tell she was wondering how my face got beat up. "Can I help you with something?"

"I'd like to see Mr. Menlo, if I could. Is he here?"

"He's back in the office, getting an order ready. Can I tell him who is calling?" I had the impression she didn't want to interrupt him.

I handed her one of my old business cards. Her eyebrow rose when she read "County Prosecutor's Office."

"I'm his daughter, Cindy. Is there something wrong?"

"Not all. I would just like to ask him a couple questions."

I could see she wanted to find out why I was there, but instead just said, "I'll be right back."

A large, elderly man emerged from the doorway she had gone in. I hadn't seen him up close in a while, but Ray Menlo had aged well. I knew he had to be in his mid-seventies, but you wouldn't have guessed that looking at him. He was big man, well proportioned, although I noticed as he walked toward me he moved with a slight shuffle. He was wearing a white, crisp dress shirt, rep tie, and gray slacks, all of which they could have been brand new or close. His face was large featured, with what seemed to be a permanent bemused expression etched on it. He had genial blue eyes which were highlighted by rimless glasses, and a thick shock of grey hair which he combed straight back. I remember for years he used to dress up as Santa Claus for the annual downtown Christmas parade, and it was a role which he was well suited for.

"Logan Wells? Ben Wells' son?" he asked, extending his hand.

"Yes."

Before I could say more, he enthusiastically pumped my hand.

"Your dad was good customer of mine for many, many years. And you played football in high school, did you not?"

I knew Ray Menlo was a big booster of all the local sports teams, from the high school to BHU. He had an encyclopedic memory for all Prairie Stop sports history.

"That's me."

"You returned three punts for touchdowns against Rosewood one season, correct?"

I probably blushed but grinned at the same time.

"You got a good memory, sir, but two of them were called back for clipping. Of course, that was the game Buzz Wildrick had over 400 yards in total offense and scored three touchdowns."

"He was the best all round athlete this town ever produced," he said.

"Well, you don't need to tell me that. He does, constantly."

He laughed.

"Were you on the state championship team?"

"No, unfortunately. My dad thought I needed to pay more attention to my grades so I could get into college."

"Your father was a good man. A solid man. I would have gone to the funeral, but the paper said the services were private."

"He didn't like a fuss, especially over himself."

"I remember that about him. I sold your father a lot of suits over the years. Good repeat customer, even if he only bought one or two suits at a time. He and a lot of others like him kept me in business for so many years. It's different now. Men don't wear suits all the time like they did twenty years ago."

"General lowering of standards, I suppose."

"You may say that in jest, but there is some truth to it."

"I guess business has suffered."

"Is it that obvious?" He smiled. "Believe it or not, this was once the finest men's clothier between Chicago and South Bend. In fact, I even sold a couple suits to Ara Parseghian. I have his picture back in the office. Why don't we go back there and you can see it."

His office was a cramped little room at the back of the store, with a small desk and a few chairs. I seem to recall in the store's heyday he had a big office upstairs, with a large window which overlooked the main floor. There were samples of fabric and catalogs everywhere. The walls were covered with pictures, many of area sports teams, high school or college, or Menlo with various local dignitaries. He pointed out an autographed picture of the legendary Notre Dame coach. He even had a picture of Buzz in a Notre Dame uniform, sans helmet, giving a stiff arm to an imaginary tackler. Menlo moved some stuff off one of the chairs and motioned for me to sit down.

"What does the other guy look like?"

His question took me off guard, and then I realized he was asking about my appearance.

"It was a door. It emerged unscathed."

He laughed. "I've run into a few doors myself over the years."

"Now, how can I help you? I don't think you came here to discuss the better days of my establishment or Prairie Stop sports. Candidly, those are my only two areas of expertise. I was intrigued, and a trifle concerned by your card."

"I apologize for a bit of subterfuge. I'm an investigator for the County Prosecutor's Office, but on leave now. I'm trying to find out what happened to Professor Jason Matthews."

"Ah, Jason." He sat back in his chair. "That's just incredible isn't it? That a prominent man like that could simply disappear? I've been following the story closely, such as it is, in the papers. How could he just vanish? Has there been any progress in finding him?"

"Officially, not that I am aware of. Professor Matthews' wife retained me to assist in the investigation."

"Interesting." His forehead crinkled. "That would seem to imply she has lost confidence in Bill Hanlen."

"Not sure I would put it like that," I said. "Sometimes looking at the picture with a different set of eyes helps."

"I've known Bill for a long time. I can honestly say he has been one of the greatest public servants in Prairie Stop's history. When he ever steps down, they should name a building after him. Or put up a statute of him. Yet, I wonder if his time has come and gone. He not the good old boy sheriff of a small rural county anymore. Like some of my merchandise, his style is no longer in vogue."

Not sure I agreed with him, but I didn't want to get sidetracked on a discussion of Bill Hanlen's competency.

"You and Professor Matthews were friends, I understand," I said.

"Yes. We happened to share a mutual interest."

"Such as?"

"Well, I have to be careful how I say it, but for lack of a better term, historical preservation."

"Historical preservation doesn't sound too risqué."

"Well, unfortunately, you use say it nowadays and it conjures up an image of a bunch of old farts trying to save every tarpaper shack that's over 30 years old. All we really want to do is not black-top over the county's heritage. Do you recall a few years back when the county commission entertained a notion to tear down the courthouse and build a two-story shiny glass and stucco 'justice center'"?

"I do, but in fairness, I spent a fair amount of time in the place and it was in sad shape. You couldn't flush a toilet without getting your shoes drenched."

He laughed. "Yes, I remember. I had pair of alligator loafers ruined in there myself. But that courthouse was built almost a hundred years ago out of Indiana limestone. It's the focal point of downtown. You do the right thing and fix it. Sure, it was inconvenient, took forever, and cost a lot of money. There were those who thought it foolish at the time, but nobody questions the decision now. We preserved the character of the town square. Not sure the fellows on the present county commission, excluding myself, would have done the same thing. Progress now always means something new. My point is you don't have to destroy the past to build the future."

"I believe you and Professor Matthews were opposed to the plan to build a mall up by the interstate."

"I am not opposed to a development per se. I am opposed to that location. It will cannibalize from our existing retail establishments closer to the city, and encourage more sprawl, to the detriment of our neighborhoods. I also question the long-term success of such a project. Ever been by the outlet mall over in Lake City on a weekday? You could roll a bowling ball across the parking lot and not hit a car."

"I understand Matthews had his own reason for not wanting the mall."

"Jason thought there had been a sizable Indian village located in that area. In fact, he claimed Chief Tecumseh himself spent time in the vicinity. Had several discussions with him about it and he was very animated on the subject. Native American history isn't an avocation of mine, but nonetheless I found it fascinating. He wanted to do some excavation out at the proposed mall site, which I suppose could have delayed the project. That apparently concerned the mall proponents."

"This may sound peculiar, but did he ever mention anything about a British generals' sword that belonged to Tecumseh?"

He gave me an odd smile and paused before answering.

"You obviously know that was something of an obsession of his."

"Sounds a little fanciful," I said.

Menlo leaned back in his chair and put his hands behind his head and gave me an odd smile.

"Why do you say that?"

"From the little I know, Brock giving his sword to Tecumseh is at best a legend. Even if he did, there is nothing to prove Tecumseh was in this area after he got it. Plus, there's a lot of land out there. If there is a sword, it's been hidden for almost two hundred years. Seems unlikely it is going to be found now."

"I agree with all you say. But, what if it isn't a legend? And what if Tecumseh actually spent some time in this area after he was given it? Well, then, it's no longer a fanciful myth, but a possibility that the sword can be found."

"It sounds like Professor Matthews convinced you, anyhow," I said.

Menlo put his chair back on the floor and gave me a broad smile.

"Well, my dear boy, he didn't have to convince me of the sword's existence. He found it and showed it to me."

If I had been chewing gum, I would have either swallowed it or spat it across the room.

"I'm sorry. What did you just say?"

"I said, Professor Jason Matthews found the sword of Tecumseh. I saw it."

"When?"

"Several days before he vanished. Might have been Tuesday. I got a call from him right before the store closed. He sounded very excited and told me he had made a momentous finding out at Porter's Farm. I knew he was in the habit of searching around out there with a metal detector, and just assumed he had found some more artifacts. He asked me to wait at the store for him. Showed up about an hour later, lugging a big trash bag. He was out of breath and red in the face. I was a little worried about him and asked him to sit down and got him a drink of water. Put a splash of bourbon in it."

"What was he so excited about?"

"Well, after he calmed down, he told me had found something remarkable that afternoon. Something that was going to, as he put it, "change everything" for him. As you can imagine, by that point, I was quite curious. But he said before he could show me, he had to swear me to secrecy. He said he wasn't quite ready to announce his discovery publicly yet."

"Why let you in on it, then?" I asked.

"He said someone else had to see it. I suppose to prove he wasn't imagining the whole thing. I don't know … the articles in the papers said his wife was out of town. Maybe he couldn't wait until she got back."

"What did he have?'

"The bag was tightly closed, and when he opened it the first thing I noticed was a god-awful smell. Mildew and rot. I was concerned for a second he may had some human remains in there. Whatever it was, it was wrapped in an oilskin. Know what that is?"

"What a sailor wears?" I asked.

"What is known as oilskin today is actually something different than a couple hundred years ago. Back then oilskin was a waterproof material made by coating heavy cotton with linseed oil. This was well before vinyl and rubber of course. I mention that because while oil skin performed well, it obviously is not as durable as the modern materials we have now, including, by the way, the rubber material which is called oilskin."

"I understand," I said. "And what was underneath the oilskin?"

He smiled. "Sorry. You want the time, and I'm telling you how to build a watch. That's a symptom of old age. Jason unwrapped the oil skin, several layers of it. The outer covering was, as I alluded to, not in particularly good condition, but underneath it was surprisingly well preserved. When unwrapped, there was a sword in a leather scabbard. Along with a small silver breastplate, which I believe is referred to a gorget. The scabbard showed some dry rot, but the sword had obviously been highly polished before it had been stored. Jason withdrew it from the scabbard, and other than a few spots of rust, and tarnish on the handle and the gorget, the items appeared to be in remarkably in good shape."

"You sure it was Brock's sword?"

He laughed.

"There wasn't a name tag on it," he replied, "if that's what you're asking."

"That would have been nice. No, I mean why couldn't he have gotten an old sword from a pawn shop and made it look like he just found it?"

"Yes, I did consider that. Not that I distrusted Jason, but the thought occurred to me that due to his strong feelings about the mall site, he might concoct some elaborate fraud to get the project delayed."

"That makes more sense that finding the real sword," I observed.

"Perhaps, but Jason informed me that Isaac Brock served with the British 49th Infantry Regiment, which was sent to Canada before the war broke out. There was '49th Regiment' inscribed on the guard, plus '1807', which I understand was the year when Brock was made a general. Would you say that was proof?"

"I would, but I'm not an expert on stuff like that. Did he say how he came to find it?"

"He literally stumbled upon it. He said he was on a hill overlooking a creek and started to make his way down. He tripped and fell. He told me had he fallen all the way to the creek, he would have been seriously injured. But he managed to grab onto a sapling. When he pulled himself back up, he found a hollow under a small rock overhang. He told me you could look at the overhang from 10 feet away and not see it. At the back of the hollow was a pile of rocks. He said he wasn't sure why, but he knew something was under them. He had to go retrieve some digging tools from his car, but after a couple hours of moving rock and digging, he found the sword."

"Have you told anyone else about this?"

"You are the first. Like I said, I was pledged to secrecy."

"Didn't you find it peculiar that Matthews disappeared right after he found the sword?

"I find Jason's disappearance peculiar and disturbing. Whether the sword has anything to do with it, I couldn't say."

"Maybe Chief Hanlen should decide that."

"It did cross my mind to go to the authorities, I admit. But let me tell you this, Mr. Wells. I have the reputation among some elements of this community as being a tiresome crank. In the last election, my opponent pretty much accused me of being senile. This will be my final term as a commissioner. If I went to the police and claimed I had seen a 200 year old mythical sword that belonged to a legendary Indian chief, and implied that it was the reason Jason Matthews went missing, well, I wouldn't blame them if they locked me up."

CHAPTER 22

Traffic on the interstate was relatively light where I got on, but by the time as I got close to the Illinois border it worsened considerably. There might be more trafficked urban interstates than those leading to and from Chicago, but if so, I wouldn't care to drive them. A mix of agitated commuters, psychotic truck drivers, hapless cross-country travelers, continual road maintenance, and frequent lousy weather combined to make the Chicago freeways a true nightmare to travel on. When I finally got off on Lake Shore Drive I breathed a sigh of relief.

Lake Michigan looked gray and menacing to my right as I headed north, while the skyscrapers to my left appeared stark and foreboding. Maybe it was my frame of mind that caused me to see them that way.

Steve Coban's office was in what was built as and officially known as the Palmolive Building. For many people, the art deco structure was and would always be known as the Playboy Building. The magazine company had its headquarters there for many years, until Hugh Hefner decided he preferred the warmth of California to the bone chilling Chicago winters. I found a garage nearby where they charged twenty dollars for the first two hours, which seemed like it might be a bargain. As I walked into the lobby, storm clouds were forming over the lake. If I caught rain, or worse, leaving Chicago, it would certainly double the travel time going home.

The person I had talked to earlier told me to go to the 25th floor and make a right after I got off the elevator. I opened a door that had no identification other than the number 2507 on it. Inside was a spacious seating area with a leather couch and a matching love seat with a glass table between them. A couple golf magazines lay on the table. A young woman sat behind a large desk on the other side of the room. She watched without expression as I approached. When I got over to where she was, I gave her a bright hello and how are you.

"You must be Logan Wells," she said. The stone face didn't change.

"I'm a little early. Traffic was lighter than I thought."

"Mr. Coban will be with you in a few minutes. Why don't you have a seat, Mr. Wells?"

"That's ok. I'll just hover over here by you. By the way, do you validate parking?"

"No."

"Ok. In that case, could you see your way clear to lending me twenty bucks?"

"Can I get you a cup of coffee, while you wait?" she asked.

"Only if it's not any trouble."

Just as she handed to it me there was a buzz. She picked the phone up and looked at me.

"You can go in now."

"I don't think this will take long. Don't go anywhere." That got a half smile.

The room I walked into had been decorated to convey success, with a capital S. It was three times the size of the Prairie County Prosecutor's Office. The carpet was thick enough to make half of your shoe disappear with each step. A dark-brown, very expensive looking leather couch and two matching chairs flanked a glass coffee table on one side of the room. Adjacent to the wall on the other side was a bar, lit by recessed lighting. Straight back, between the bar and seating group was a huge half circle desk that looked to be made of mahogany. The desk sat in front of windows that overlooked Lake Michigan. I didn't know much about Chicago real estate, but I knew a view like that didn't come cheap.

Two men were in the room. One was behind the desk, the other sitting in front of it, slightly to the side. Neither one of them got up as I approached, but they had been engaged in conversation which stopped when I entered the room. When I got in front of the desk, I saw the one sitting to the side had a large white bandage covering his entire nose. He was wearing dark glasses, but even so I could tell he had two black eyes.

Finally, the man behind the desk got up slowly and extended his hand.

"Logan Wells, I'm Steve Coban."

Coban was a big man, six two or three, and looked to be a solid two hundred pounds. He had coal black hair, wavy and on the long side, and flecked with gray at the temples. He had large features and dark piercing eyes. When I shook his hand, his grip was like a vice.

He gestured at the man sitting to the side of me.

"I think you already know Jack Wilson. He's with the Chicago PD. He also does some work for me from time to time."

I glanced over at Wilson. He gave me a vitriolic look in return.

"How's your face?" I asked.

Wilson almost came out of the chair, but Coban raised his hand and he eased back down.

"No rough stuff here, Jack," Coban said sternly.

Wilson looked at me.

"Like I should talk," I said, shrugging my shoulders.

"You get so much as a parking ticket in this town, and your ass will be mine," Wilson spat out.

"Now you tell me. I'm double-parked in front of a fire hydrant."

"I think I can handle this from here, Jack," said Coban. "Give me a call tomorrow."

I watched Wilson turn and walk slowly to the door. He was limping noticeably. I didn't feel a bit sorry for him.

"Sit down, please," Coban said. He did likewise.

"Jack happened to be coming by this afternoon. I told him you and I had an appointment and he insisted on staying and meeting you. I guess you and he really didn't get a chance to be introduced formally."

"It's difficult to strike up a decent conversation with someone who's trying to run you over with a motorcycle."

"I apologize for the incident yesterday. Jack was filling me in on it. Seems like some errors in judgment were made." He smiled. "You aren't going to sue me, are you?"

"From what I hear, I would have to stand in line."

The smile disappeared.

"Buzz told me you have a dry sense of humor. Now exactly what can I do for you? Danielle said you mentioned something about real estate."

"I'm interested in the property I looked at yesterday," I said.

"Really. I can see why. It's an area poised for development."

"I agree, but what would happen if it ended up not being developed?"

"Oh, it will get developed. Most certainly. I always complete my projects."

"Professor Matthews of Prairie Stop University seemed like he wanted to stop, or at least delay you. Maybe there were some other folks too who didn't think the county needed more sprawl."

"Oh yes, the professor who disappeared. I heard about that. A shame. But he was a harmless crank. I doubt if anyone paid any attention to him."

"Kind of lucky for you he got lost."

"You are implying something. Pardon me if I'm being a bit thick and am not picking up on it."

"Ok, let me be clear. Maybe Matthews had more clout than you give him credit for. Maybe that worried you. I understand you don't like people getting in your way."

"That's a lot of maybes. I've run into Matthews' type before. They make a lot of noise for a while, then go away."

"I guess if the mall didn't work out, you could always hedge your bets and unload the land on some unsuspecting pension fund."

Coban frowned. "I really don't have any idea what you are talking about. One minute you are mentioning a missing college professor, now we are talking about a pension fund."

"There's talk that the trustees of the Pipefitter's Pension bought some land at the mall site from you at overly inflated prices."

"And who's doing the talking?"

"A confidential source."

"I see. Well, I can tell you, your source is inaccurate and the information possibly libelous. You're a former police officer, aren't you, Wells?"

I nodded.

"Then you should know the importance of getting your facts straight and not making vague accusations."

"Generally, I would agree with that. But I've found out that sometimes making vague accusations leads to getting the facts straight."

Rage came over his face, and I thought I was going to get an expletive as a response, but the look passed.

"No offense," he said, "but you appear to be a drinking man."

"On occasion. But I've been trying to cut back."

"You also look like a bourbon man. Am I right?" Coban got up from behind the desk and started over to the bar. "Rocks or straight?"

"Straight up."

"I've got some sour mash that I guarantee will make your tongue melt. Costs fifty a bottle, but worth every cent."

When he walked back over he handed me a half-filled tumbler.

"Confusion to our enemies," he said, and clinked his glass on mine. He was right, I only took a small sip but the whisky melted on my tongue.

Instead of going behind the desk he pulled a chair up near where I was and sat facing me.

"Were you involved any sports when you were in school, Logan? I think Buzz told me you were on the football team with him in high school."

"Matter of fact, I did a few different sports."

"Ah, yes. The days of youth and glory, when everything seemed possible. I did three sports when I was in high school. Made all-city in basketball, second string, one year. Of course, I was nothing like our mutual friend, right?"

"There weren't many like him."

"Exactly. You know I went to Notre Dame, too?"

"Buzz told me."

"A boyhood dream I had was to play football or basketball at Notre Dame. I had no illusions that I would be the next Paul Hornung or Austin Carr. I just wanted to be able to say I had played, even if it was one minute of one game. I wrote off football as soon as I walked over to the football field and saw the size of some of the players. Instead, I tried out for the freshman basketball team."

He took a sip of the bourbon.

"It came down to me and another for the last spot on the team. We were fairly even in terms of ability, but when it came down to it, I knew he was better than me. There was really no way I could convince myself otherwise. Can you imagine that, so close to my dream, yet having it pulled away at the last minute?"

"What did you do?"

"Two nights before the final cut, I told the other fellow that I knew he was going to make the team and said we should celebrate. We had beers to start, then shots and beers, then just shots. By the time he got back to his room, he couldn't remember his own name. What he didn't notice was that I was having one for every three he was having. Guess what happened?"

"You made the team, and he didn't."

"He was so sick the next day he didn't even make it to class, let alone practice."

"And you went on to star at Notre Dame?"

He laughed. "I think I played a total of ten minutes that year for the freshman team. The next year I got cut. But I can honestly say I played basketball for Notre Dame. Very few people can make that statement. It's actually opened a few doors for me."

"Now I'm being thick. Is there a moral there?"

"I think it illustrates something about me, for good or for bad. Making the basketball team was important goal in my life at that time. There are those who would say what I did was unethical to obtain it, but I was facing a problem and came up with a way of resolving it in my favor."

"That's an intriguing value system you've got there. I wonder how the guy who didn't make the team would feel about it."

"I don't wish to sound simplistic, but I've found out that people are of two types. Those who get pushed around and those who do the pushing. I have never been one to like getting pushed around."

"Why does anyone need to push at all?"

"You've have a naïve view of life if you think that."

Coban looked at his watch.

"I've enjoyed our conversation, but I need to get going. I've meeting a group of people later. The mayor will be there." He got up and moved back behind the desk.

"Let me be candid with you about a couple of things," he said. "When Buzz told me he had hired you, I briefly wondered why. I have no ill-will towards Professor Matthews, but frankly, I'm not too concerned about what's happened to him. Now, you've apparently come up with some peculiar theories about the propriety of my business practices. And you've implied, albeit in an indirect way, that maybe I had something to do with Professor Matthews' disappearance."

He paused and took a pull on the bourbon.

"I'm not at all interested in what you think. Still, I've found that if someone screams lies long enough and loud enough, someone will believe them. I wouldn't care to have any of my potential business associates scared off by some false rumors."

"Or even true ones."

"You might have missed the point I was trying to make earlier. I usually get what I want. Some people have qualms about doing what it takes to attain their objectives. I don't. You should take that under advisement. Now, good day."

A light drizzle was falling as I headed out of Chicago back to Prairie Stop. As I expected the rain and afternoon traffic delayed my trip home, but not by as much as I expected. By the time I got over the other side of the city, to Route 6, it was only a little after three.

Chapter 23

The area to the south and east of the Prairie Stop along Route 6 hadn't shared in the prosperity of other parts of the county. I assume it had something to do with its distance from the interstate and Chicago. I also had been reading about how many of the small family owned farms in the area were being taken over by large farming conglomerates. I passed a few closed gas stations and diners, and number of dilapidated barns and trailers.

Phil's Auto too looked like it was on its last legs. Obviously, a former gas station, the pumps were gone. I recall hearing something about a federal law mandating that all gas stations older than a certain number of years had to replace their underground fuel tanks. The law effectively forced many older independently owned stations out of business, as the cost of replacing the tanks was prohibitively high.

Behind the station buildings, in all directions, were decrepit vehicles of every conceivable type and make. Most of them were eaten with rust and scavenged of parts and hardware. Some were piled on top of each other, awaiting the final trip to the crusher. The station office itself was in bad shape, needing at least a coat of paint and couple of new windows. Although there was a vehicle on one of the lifts in the service bay, no one was in sight.

When I opened the front door, a bell rang, its cheery tinkling in stark contrast to the end of the road atmosphere the premises conveyed. A balding, bearded man with an immense belly sat behind a metal desk directly facing the door. He was eating a sandwich and reading a newspaper. He looked up briefly from the paper when I walked in, gave me a non-committal look, and then resumed his reading. I walked over to the desk and he reluctantly looked up at me.

"Help you?" he asked.

"I'm looking for a transmission for a '72 Pinto. Think you got one?"

That brought a guffaw.

"A car ahead of its time. Ford made it so it would burst into flames when collided with. That way you wouldn't have to worry if the insurance company was going to total it or not."

"My dad always bought American, but after he owned a Pinto, he switched to Toyota."

"I always thought of the Pinto as the nadir of the American car industry. Either that or the Chevy Vega. But in hindsight, the Pinto wasn't that bad a car. Really, a better car than the Vega. The Vega was a piece of shit on wheels." He shook his head.

"But if you were serious, I'm not sure where you could get a transmission," he said. "For one, we don't have one." He gave me a closer look. "You aren't from around here, are you?"

"I'm from Prairie Stop. Actually, I was looking for someone who I was told works here … Mike Parker."

The face that a few moments before had been genial now clouded over.

"You a cop?"

"Used to be." I didn't see any advantage to clarifying my status. If I said I was with the prosecutor's office he might clam up, and if I said I was private he might decide he didn't need to talk to me.

"Huh. Is Mike in trouble?"

"To my knowledge, no."

"What's your business with him?"

"I just want to talk to him."

"Hold on a second."

He got up slowly from the desk and walked into the service area. When he came back he had another man with him. This one was short, clean shaven, and with pitch black hair that he combed straight back, obviously with the assistance of a lot of hair cream. Although he wasn't big, he had a bull neck and the short sleeve shirt he wore was tight at the biceps. On his right bicep was the tattoo of a battleship. He had a long thin scar that ran just outside his right eye to below his eye socket. His eyes were dark and hard. He hands were big and the right one was holding a large crescent wrench. The fat guy I originally talked to gestured at me.

"That's him, Phil," he said, rather unnecessarily, since I was the only other person in the room. The man with the hard eyes looked at me without expression for a good thirty seconds.

"Phil Parker. You lookin' for my nephew?" he asked, finally. The tone was flat, but I could feel the tension behind it.

"If your nephew is Mike Parker, the answer is yes."

"Are you law?"

"Nope. Used to be."

"Friend of his? Cause I don't know remember seeing you before, and I know most of Mike's friends."

"Not a friend either," I said, evenly. "Just somebody who wants to speak to him."

"About what?"

"Would you believe me if I told you somebody died and left him a lot of money?"

The fat man laughed at that. Phil glanced over at him and the laughter immediately ceased.

"I'll ask again. What's your business with him?"

"I'd prefer to take that up with Mike."

Phil gave a tight smile.

"What do you think of that, Carl? He would prefer to take that up with Mike."

Carl didn't say anything but smiled nervously back. I guess he had seen Phil in action before and knew what might be coming next.

"Mister, you're out of luck. Mike ain't here."

"Perhaps you could tell me how I can reach him."

"Perhaps I could tell you to mind your own business. Or go to hell."

"I'm not looking for any trouble, my friend. Your nephew is connected with a missing person investigation. He would probably be better off talking to me than the police."

"Is that right? If you're not looking for trouble, you better leave, because nobody's talking to anybody, not you, not the police, not the FBI if they show up."

I smiled. "The FBI? Now you went and spoiled the surprise."

"You making fun of me?"

"Not at all." I said. "Why don't you let your nephew decide for himself who he wants to talk to? Maybe he's got something he wants to get off his chest."

"You're starting to piss me off. I think you better get going. And I mean now."

"Be glad to. As soon as you tell me where I can reach Mike."

Phil moved closer to me. Without warning he brought the wrench down hard on the desk. There was a loud bang. Carl flinched. Somewhat to my surprise, I didn't.

I think Phil thought banging the wrench on the desk would send me scurrying to my car. When I didn't, he looked somewhat wary.

"You ought to be more careful," I said. "You almost knocked Carl's dinner off the desk."

That was enough to tip him over the edge.

"You sunvabitch," he muttered as he raised the wrench and came at me.

I was ready and ducked under the blow. I lowered my good side, the right one, took a couple steps and hit him with my best shoulder block. I considered it one of my specialties when I played ball, and this time I delivered it perfectly. I slammed into his gut and drove him hard into the wall. I could feel the air go out of him like a punctured tire. He slumped to the floor with me on top of him. The wrench clanged somewhere to my right. I pulled off quickly, but he wasn't through, and I could feel his powerful arms reaching up to grab me. I broke free, turned, and found the wrench. It was solid and heavier than it looked. I drew it back and hit him about six times. He managed to block the first few with his arms, but I got through with the others. The two last ones I hit him hard right around where his shoulder met his neck. After the last one he gasped and lay still.

I looked over at Carl. He had picked up a can of motor oil and was apparently considering if he should throw it at me.

"I wouldn't do that if I were you," I said, breathing heavy from my exertion with Phil.

Carl lowered the oil can.

"That's better. Now find me some duct tape," I ordered.

Carl reached on shelf behind him and pulled off a roll of tape.

"Phil and I seem to have gotten off on the wrong foot. I'd appreciate it if you would tape his wrists together, so as to forestall any more outbursts."

Carl walked around the desk, bent over with considerable effort due to his girth, and did as I asked. Phil was moving a little bit and mumbling as he was being restrained.

"He doesn't look too good. Maybe we should get help," Carl said.

"Don't worry, he'll be fine. I've been professionally trained in how to hit a man with a wrench."

I saw a few tires inside the service bay and I went out and picked up two.

"Ok, Carl, let's get him upright."

We propped him up and I pulled the tires over Phil's head and shoulders so that his upper body was encased in them. He was starting to move a little more.

"If you don't mind Carl, tape his ankles too. I'd do it myself, but I've got a bad arm. Use a little more tape than you did for his wrists, please."

"He's going to be really pissed. I wouldn't want to be you when he gets out of there."

"No need to worry. By the time he gets out, I'll be long gone."

When he was done, I went over and checked the tautness of the tape. It wouldn't hold him long but he wouldn't be getting himself out in ten minutes either.

"That should do for a while. What do you say you and I step outside, Carl?"

"You're not going to hit me with a wrench, are you?" he asked, giving me a cautious look. I was holding the tool with which I had incapacitated Phil.

"I wouldn't overlook the possibility."

We stepped out of the office.

"I could be rushing to judgment, Carl, but Phil seems like he's got a short fuse."

He shook his head.

"The whole damn family is like that. Hotheads every one of them. I'll give you one thing though, I've never seen anyone handle him the way you did."

"Quick impression I got is that Phil's a bully who thinks he a tough guy. I've found out that there's a difference. Still, if he had connected with the wrench, I'd be the one dressed in Firestones. Let's stop here." We had walked about twenty feet out of the office.

"Do you know where Mike Parker is?" I asked.

"No, and that's the God's truth. And I don't think Phil knows either."

"Let's not get God mixed up in this," I said. "I thought Mike worked here."

"He did, at least up until a couple weeks ago. After he got out of prison, Phil put him on. More of a favor to his brother than anything. You might be able to tell that business isn't exactly booming."

"What happened a couple weeks ago?"

"He didn't show up for work."

"Did he call?"

"He called and told Phil he was taking some time off. Phil seemed to think it was because he had come into some money."

"Did he say how?"

"I don't know. Phil was kind of pissed about not showing up, so maybe he didn't get the full story."

"Do you know where he lives?"

"When he got out of jail, he was living with his mom, but I think he's moved out."

"How well did you know Mike?"

"I've known him a long time, but we've never had any heart to heart conversations, if that's what you mean."

"Did he ever talk about his wife or family?"

"His ex? Some. Mainly about his son. He was the one thing in his life that seemed like it brought the good out of him."

"Did he ever talk about anyone his ex was dating?"

"He might have. I don't remember."

"I'm guessing that Mike was the jealous type and had a hot temper. Based on the family history and all."

"I wouldn't know about that."

"You read the papers right, Carl?"

He nodded his head.

"Then you heard of that professor out at the university who's disappeared," I said.

"Yeah."

"You know he was friends with Mike's ex- wife, don't you?"

He didn't say anything.

"I'll take that as a yes."

"Alright. He mentioned it."

"I'm thinking Mike wasn't too happy about it. That'd make me mad, too. Some old guy with a pile of dough going out with the ex. The mother of my son. And the old guy's married to boot."

"That was Mike's business, not mine."

I looked around.

"You guys sure got a lot of old cars here," I observed.

"Price of scrap is low right now. Can hardly give the stuff away."

"Yeah, times are tough. What with the steel business in the toilet and all. I was just thinking … let's say somebody wanted to get rid of a car. He could bring it here, right?"

He seemed piqued by the question.

"That's our business. We buy old and wrecked cars for parts and scrap."

"Sure, that's your business. I'm just saying, if I wanted to get rid of a car, maybe so nobody would ever find it, this would be the place to do it."

"I don't know what you're getting at."

"Nobody ever brought a car in here and asked you to make it disappear?"

"What for?"

"How about insurance money?"

"That would be illegal."

"Yeah, you're right. You wouldn't want to do anything illegal. Still, you have to admit this would be a heckuva place to hide a car. All the wrecks you got here. I bet you guys are good at tearing a car apart, too. I was just thinking that because this professor whose gone missing, well, his car seems to have disappeared too."

"Is that right?"

"Yep. He and his car both disappeared. Late model Mercedes. Probably worth a small fortune."

"We got nothin' but old pieces of crap here."

"Yeah, I noticed. See, Carl, a dead body is a nuisance, but when you think about it, it's easier to get rid of a body than a car. You can toss a body in an incinerator, tie some weights to it and sink it in a lake, drop it in a well, bury it, etc. You get the picture. There's all kind of options. Plus, a body decomposes."

"I don't know what the hell you are talking about."

"See if you can stay with me on this, Carl. Unlike a body, a car has value. So maybe you need to get rid of the body, but do you throw away something of value? How easy is it to get rid of car, anyhow? You drive it into a lake, some pain in the ass fisherman is eventually is going to snag his line on it. And they make cars nowadays, so they don't even rust. So, what do you do with it?"

"I wouldn't know, but I've heard a lot of stolen cars are stripped for parts. Some are taken to Mexico."

"I've heard that too," I said. "But you got to think those are pros doing stuff like that. A team of guys with the right kind of equipment, either to strip a car fast or a flatbed to haul it. But I'm talking about one guy. I'm thinking he might bring a car to a place like this. Heck, if nothing else, you could just hide it here until you found someone to take it off your hands."

"Think whatever you want. We don't do stuff like that."

"I wonder, Carl, if the highway patrol and the county sheriff showed up and went through this place with a fine-toothed comb, what do you think they'd find?"

"They'd find a bunch of old cars."

"You ever been in trouble with the law, Carl?"

"No." He hesitated before he said it.

"You didn't sound real sure."

"I'm telling you no."

"Ok. But the thing is, if the sheriff was to find a stolen car, or worse, a car that used to belong to a dead person, you would be looking at some trouble yourself. No matter if it was Phil or Mike who actually broke the law. The legal term is accessory after the fact."

"I still don't know what you're talking about."

"You said you haven't been in trouble, Carl, and I believe you. But if you've ever been locked up, then you'd know what it's like when they slam the bars behind you. When I was a cop, sometimes that's all it took to get a guy to start talking. Once he was locked up, he'd do or saying anything to get out. You don't strike me as the type of guy who could handle jail."

There was a spark of anger in his eyes, quickly replaced by a resigned look, but he didn't say anything.

"Tell you what. I'm going to go call the county sheriff. He's got a personal interest in this missing professor. I bet he's out here in twenty minutes with a dozen men. Hate to do it to you, Carl, you seem like an ok guy, but I'm going to have to tell him you weren't very cooperative."

I shook my head.

"On the other hand, you give me what I'm looking for, and I'm going to tell him what a swell joe you are. He may even invite you to his house for dinner. Your choice."

He stared at the ground.

"Ok, got it." I started to head back toward the office.

"Wait a second," Carl said, hurrying to catch up with me.

I stopped and looked at him.

"Listen," he said. "There may be a few cars out there we might not have the right paperwork on. But I don't know anything about any professor or his car, I swear."

"See, self-disclosure does wonders for a relationship. Now you can tell me something else."

"What?" he asked, in a reluctant tone.

"Let's say Mike or Phil had a car he wanted to make extra sure nobody found. Where would they hide it?"

The look on Carl's face told me there was such a place.

"Carl, I should mention again the gravity of the situation you are in," I admonished him.

"There's no place like you're talking about."

"You know what? I worked long enough as a cop so I can always tell when a man is lying to me. And right now, I think you're lying to me."

"If I told you that, Phil would kill me."

"At this point, Phil should be the least of your worries."

"OK, OK. There's a barn at the back of the property."

"Now we're getting somewhere. What do you say we go take a look at it?"

"Alright," he said resignedly, "we should drive back there, though. It's kind of far."

"Ok. You drive. And be careful with it. It's a loaner."

A muddy road starting right behind the office ran through the middle of the junkyard. There were a couple of places to turn off, but Carl followed it straight back about half a mile until we came to a big barn. It was old, but unlike the rest of the place, appeared to be well maintained. It looked to have been painted recently and there were no sagging or missing boards. We got out of the Volvo.

"This was a farm at one time, just like about every other place around here," Carl said.

"No offense, but this would be about the first place I would look for something."

Carl gave me a look.

"Yeah."

He walked over to the double doors and unlocked the padlock and chain that secured them. We walked inside. In the middle of one side of the barn was an older model Ford pickup truck. It had no tires and was up on blocks. The engine had been pulled out of it and was held by a hoist about four feet above the engine hood. On each side of the Ford were some auto parts of various sizes and shapes, but other than that most of the space was empty. Given that Parker's business was auto salvage that seemed curious.

"Whose truck?" I asked.

"Phil's. He's only been rebuilding it for the last five years."

Carl went over to the far side of the truck and bent over to reach something on the floor. I heard a loud click, followed by a whirring noise, and then the truck started to move slowly away from me. It took me a second to realize the entire floor was moving sideways. It slowly traversed into the empty area about thirty feet then stopped. Where the truck and a concrete floor had been was now a large underground room. I looked down and could see at least two cars.

"Ingenious," I said, meaning it. "Don't tell me you guys did this yourself."

"The guy who built the barn dug a deep cellar under part of it. Big one too. He must have used it for cold storage, or a storm cellar."

"Who did the floor?"

"Phil built a wood and steel frame, and then poured an inch of concrete over it to make it look like the rest of the floor. It's not that complicated of a setup really. It basically works like a garage door, except horizontal instead of vertical."

"What's down there now?"

"I don't know," Carl said, shrugging.

"Carl, we already had this talk."

"Look I really don't know. Some guys bought a Honda in here about a month back. Phil was going to hang onto it for a while, then either sell it or strip it for parts. I haven't been back here since then."

"How do you get down there?"

Carl went off and came back with a metal extension ladder.

"There's ramps we use to get the vehicles up and down, but we can use this."

"Did Mike know about this space?"

"What do you think?"

"Ok. Carl, not that I don't trust you, but would you mind going down first? And then step back from the ladder."

He braced the ladder then somewhat awkwardly got on it and descended into the space.

I followed him, being careful to look behind me to make sure Carl didn't decide to take a whack at me with a crowbar. There had been two vehicles visible when he opened the floor and only two when I got into the cellar. One was a late model Honda Accord. The other was car was a Mercedes Benz sedan, new and in very good condition.

"Where did the Mercedes come from?" I asked.

"I've never seen it before. They must have brought it down sometime in the last couple weeks."

"You guys don't strike me at the types to move a car like this. Hondas or Fords maybe, but this one seems out of your league."

"You got to believe me. I've never seen it before."

I walked around the Mercedes.

"Did I mention the professor drove a late model Mercedes? Could be leaping to conclusions here, but seeing as how this one's got a BHU parking sticker in the windshield, I'm thinking this could be his car. What do you think?"

"I don't know anything about it," he said, his voice rising.

"You keep saying that."

"You got to believe me."

"I believe you, Carl. The bigger issue for you is whether you can sell it to the county sheriff. Get me a rag, would you? Something that's relatively clean."

He rummaged around and tossed me what looked to be an old diaper. It wasn't spotless but not filthy either. I wrapped it around my hand to open the driver's door.

My nose was hit with a combination of feint new car smell and leather, but not the stench of decaying flesh, which my imagination suggested would be there. I took a quick look through the car. There was nothing on the seats, either front or back. No bloodstains or bullet holes. I bent down to look under the front seats but there was nothing there either. I popped the middle console compartment cover. There were a couple gas receipts. One was from a Speedway in Prairie Stop dated almost a month ago. The other was from Coloma, Michigan, and dated almost a couple weeks ago. I had been in Coloma myself couple times. It was off I-196, which ran along Lake Michigan before curving inwards at Holland toward Grand Rapids. It is the way you would go to South Haven. I stuck the receipt in my pocket.

In my preoccupation with the car, I had neglected to keep an eye on Carl. When I looked up after pocketing the gas receipt, he was about halfway up the ladder. I cursed and pushed myself out of the car, banging my head in the process. He was almost at the top of the ladder when I got to it. I grabbed a rung and pulled back hard. He was a heavy man, but I had the leverage and momentum once I got the ladder moving. He held on for a good few seconds as the ladder came back, then let go. I jumped to the side to get out of the way and gave the ladder a shove in the opposite direction, so it wouldn't hit me. Carl's upper body came down hard on the left side of the Honda's hood, bounced slightly, and then started to slide slowly to the ground. The ladder fell on him.

I went over to him and got the ladder off. His eyes were half closed, and it looked like he was mumbling something. His arm was twisted at a funny angle.

"I'd say I'm sorry, Carl, but you brought that on yourself."

I didn't think he was hurt bad, but there wasn't anything I could do for him, except to call for help. I went back to the Mercedes, got the rag, found the trunk release and popped it. No body and no blood, although there was a peculiar smell. Mildew like. There was a compartment for a full-size spare. I unscrewed the wing nuts holding the top down and opened it. The spare was gone. In its place was a large plastic garbage bag. I lifted it out of the trunk carefully, trying to not touch anything except the bag.

It probably would have been a good idea to leave right away, but I felt compelled to open the bag. It was exactly as Ray Menlo said. Some foul smelling old fabric wrapped around a sword scabbard and the gorget. I thought about taking the sword out but decided against it. It seemed dishonorable. I put it back in the bag and left the barn with the plastic bag.

When I got back to the garage office, Phil had vanished. I was surprised that he got out of the tape and tires so quickly and wondered why he didn't come after me. Maybe he figured once I found what was in the barn, there was nothing else to do but leave and quickly.

I called Bill Hanlen's office. When I identified myself, I was put right through to him.

"What you got, Logan?" he asked, with no pretense of a greeting.

"I found Professor Matthew's car."

"Where?"

"A place called Phil's Auto. I'm here now. You know where it is?"

"Yep. Was Matthews with the car?"

"No."

"Have any idea how it got there, or where he might be?"

"To the second question, no. To the first, Professor Matthew's girlfriend used to be married to a guy named Mike Parker. He works at Phil's. You'll find that he's been in trouble before. Apparently, he wasn't too happy with the professor seeing his ex."

"Where is he now?"

"Don't know," I answered. "Not here. He disappeared right around the time Matthews did, although I suppose that could be a coincidence. Phil

Parker, who owns the garage, is his uncle. Unfortunately, the older Parker took off after I talked with him. I think if you can find him, you might get a line on his nephew. Just so you know, he's got a short fuse."

Hanlen snorted.

"I don't believe in coincidences. Tell me, did Ivan know about the ex?"

"If he did, he didn't mention it to me."

"I'm going to kick his ass. I don't care how many of his relatives he got to vote for me. Ok. That's good work, Logan. I'm going to be out there in twenty minutes. You stay put until I get there."

"Sorry, Chief, I got a previous engagement."

"You stay put, or I'll have every cop in the county looking for you."

"Oh, yeah, you should bring an ambulance with you. There's a guy out here who's hurt."

"Mike Parker?"

"Pay attention, would you? No Parkers are here. It's somebody who worked for them."

"Did you have anything to do with it?"

"Accident. He fell off a ladder. He'll probably be OK, but he could use some attention."

"Logan, if you leave that garage, you're going to be in big trouble. I'll have you brought in as a material witness."

"There's a junkyard behind Phil's. Follow the road behind the office all the way until you see a barn. Matthews' car is in a cellar in the barn. I didn't touch anything, so your evidence guys may be able to turn something up. The guy whose hurt is named Carl. He'll be there too. Like I said, you might want find Phil Parker, the owner, before he skips town. And now Chief, I got to get going."

"Goddammit Logan, I'm warning you."

CHAPTER 24

I took Hanlen for his word when he said he would have me apprehended, so I headed east on Route Six until I came to 421. A left would have taken me back to Prairie Stop. Without really thinking about, I took a right instead and headed south toward Lafayette, eighty miles away.

That part of state was flat as a pancake, but I always found the endless repetition of farm fields and the same looking small towns calming rather than monotonous. 421 changed into 43 south of Reynolds, and then I was going by the wolf sanctuary, where at certain times of the year you could go and howl with the wolves. I wonder what the wolves made of that.

I finally turned off at the town of Battleground and made my way through some residential neighborhoods until I got to the Tippecanoe Battlefield site. Without fail, my father would take us to the battle site at least once every summer. He said it was important for us to know our heritage.

The museum had closed at five, and there was no one in the parking lot except me. I got out and walked over to the 85 foot high marble obelisk which commemorated William Henry Harrison's victory. A statute of Harrison looked out attentively from the base of the statue. My father used to complain that there was nothing at the battlefield to acknowledge the struggle of our ancestors to retain their land and way of life.

A light rain was falling, and the temperature was in the forties. The conditions were probably very similar to the night in November 1811 when a confederation of tribes, incited by Tecumseh's brother, the Prophet, launched a surprise attack on Harrison's army. The plan was to kill Harrison immediately, and then capitalize on the panic and lack of leadership in the U.S. army. Instead, when the attack first started, another officer jumped on Harrison's distinctive large white horse. He was instantly shot. Having inadvertently thwarted the assassination attempt, Harrison rallied his troops. They were able held off the Indians until daylight, when the Indians, discouraged, greatly outnumbered, and with no more ammunition, fled. It was not a clear-cut victory for the whites, but Harrison was eventually proclaimed a hero and any hope the Midwestern tribes had of preserving their way of life was dashed.

The place had an eerie feel about it. I could almost see the Indian braves, half naked and their faces adorned with garish war paint, stealthily advancing through the trees toward the American positions. The U.S. troops would have been tired and shivering around their campfires, the fear of the savages palpable in the air. The battle would have started with a single shot, but within minutes the air would have been rent with bloodcurdling war cries and the crash of musket fire. Then to the mix would have been added the screams of the wounded and dying men, and the death chants of the mortally wounded braves. The chaos would have been overwhelming, with men fighting in darkness with no idea where their enemies were. I took a good look around and headed back to my car.

I had passed a Wal-Mart shortly before I got to Battleground. I drove back there and bought a pair of overalls and rubber boots, some large thick trash bags, a small spade and a flat shovel. When I got back to the battlefield the parking lot was still empty. I didn't think I had much to worry about company because of the rain and darkness. I put the overalls and boots on, and got the garbage bag containing the sword and gorget out of my trunk.

When I was there earlier, I had scoped out a ravine on the north side of the park. The ravine was not part of the park proper and was covered in overgrowth. I made my way across it, the brush and brambles hindering my progress. There was a stand of bushes on a small rise that from which you could see the upper part of the monument. I hiked over there, and using the spade, dug out around one of the larger bushes. Then, with the square shovel, I pried it up, roots and all. Then I took the spade again and began to dig. It was messy, but because the ground was damp it made it easier to dig. In short order, I had a decent hole dug. I made sure the garbage bag was tightly sealed, put it inside one of the new ones I bought, and then dropped it into the hole. I piled the dirt back on and put the bush back into position. I scattered the extra dirt and covered the area around the bush with fallen leaves and small branches, of which there were plenty in the vicinity.

I got back to the car, removed the boots and overalls and put them in a garbage bag. I looked up at the obelisk. Harrison faced confidently forward, but I imagined out of the corner of his eye he could see where I had buried

Tecumseh's sword. Some guy walking a dog would probably find the thing in a few weeks, and God knows what they would make of that, but it was there for now.

"Something to remember both you and Tecumseh, General," I said to Harrison.

CHAPTER 25

I got back on the highway, but after driving for a while in the rain, decided I didn't want to drive all the way back to Prairie Stop. There was also the matter of Hanlen's men looking for me. I found a small older hotel near Rensselaer. When Buzz tried out for the Bears, their summer camp was at St. Joseph's College in Rensselaer. I remembered going there a couple times to watch them scrimmage.

The hotel looked to be empty except for me. I asked the proprietor about someplace to eat and he mentioned a diner down the road. I noticed a large dumpster behind it. After eating some bad meatloaf, I drove behind the place and tossed the boots and overalls in the dumpster. I then went back to the hotel. I took a couple pills and started watching TV. In what was evidently a precursor of the holiday season, one channel was showing *It's A Wonderful Life*. I came in on the part where Jimmy Stewart as George Bailey went nuts after Uncle Billy lost all the bank's cash. I watched it until I drifted off.

I was in the midst of the forest, crouched behind a fallen log. A battle was raging around me. There was the crack of gunfire and men yelling and screaming. Shadowy figures ran by me, made indistinguishable by the heavy brush and smoke. I was frightened and wanted to run, but my legs were heavy and weak, and I wasn't sure in which direction safety lay. Every time I stood, bullets shrieked by my head. Eventually I gave up trying to move and cowered behind the log, in my panic even trying to burrow into the dirt beneath it.

"This way, my son!" a loud voice proclaimed. I looked in the direction of the voice and in a small clearing behind me was Tecumseh. He was wearing buckskin leggings, his torso naked, except for the silver British officer's gorget.

His face was painted with red war paint and he wore a single dark eagle feather in his hair, held by a beaded red headband. He had Brock's sword in his right hand and motioned to me with it.

My legs were no longer rubbery, and I was no longer afraid. I got up and started to run to where he was. As I approached the clearing, from another direction a man on a large white horse emerged. He was wearing a dark greatcoat with officer's epaulets and holding a large saber. He galloped toward Tecumseh who turned in a crouch to face him. The officer swung his saber in a high arc at the war chief, who straightened and struck the saber with his own sword. The saber flew out of the officer's hand as his horse reared. Tecumseh struck again at the officer with his sword, but the horse turned. The blade narrowly missed the rider but struck the officer's saddle. The officer turned again, this time with a pistol in his hand. The flint in the pistol snapped and Tecumseh dropped his sword and collapsed to the ground. The officer turned his horse and rode out of the clearing.

I went to where Tecumseh lay. His chest was covered in blood, and he was coughing up a red froth. When he saw me, he nodded.

"The white chief has killed me," he said.

I started to sob.

"Do not be sad for me, my son, I will soon see my father and brothers."

He was breathing very heavily now.

"Help me out of this place. It the whites find me, they will cut me into little pieces."

With difficulty, I got him to his feet. He seemed to recover slightly and was able to walk slowly, with his arm around my shoulder. Before we had gone ten paces, he told me to go back and get his sword. We made our way out of the clearing and then some way into the woods, always alert to the sounds of approaching soldiers. Eventually, it seemed like the sound of the gunfire faded into the distance, and Tecumseh asked to be propped up at the base of a large tree.

"Thank you, my son. My people will look for me and find me here. They will make sure the whites will not take my scalp and chop off my fingers and toes," he said. "It is almost finished now. You will take the sword of the British chief and bury it."

"I wish to go with you, my father."

"It is not your time for that journey. Listen carefully to me. I see danger ahead for you. You must walk like the panther through the forest, so that your enemies may not surprise you".

I woke up with a start. My heart was pounding in my chest and my T-shirt was wet with sweat. On the television, *It's A Wonderful Life* was still on. Now

Jimmy Stewart was getting ready to jump off the bridge. For a couple of minutes, I wasn't sure where I was. I looked over at the clock and it showed 7:30. I was still tired and tried to go back to sleep but for some reason couldn't, so I got dressed and tossed my stuff in the car. On my way out, I noticed the diner where I had dinner was open, so I stopped and had breakfast and a few cups of coffee.

I didn't go right back to Prairie Stop. I figured if the county sheriff's department was looking for me, it would be better if I arrived back in town under cover of darkness, so I had some time to kill. I drove east, then south to Monticello, the home of the small amusement park known as Indiana Beach. A cut rate midwest knockoff of a Jersey shore town, it was another place we used to go to occasionally when I was younger. I walked around the mostly deserted resort for about a couple hours then headed northeast to towards Plymouth.

Near Plymouth, at Twin Lakes, I stopped to see the Chief Menominee Monument, another spot of historical significance for my dad. The Potawatomi Chief, as a young man, was a follower of Tecumseh. Like Tecumseh, he refused to put his name on the treaties which ceded Indian lands to the whites. His intransigence and even conversion to Christianity didn't do him much good. Ultimately his tribe's land was taken anyway, and he was forced to emigrate to Kansas, dying not too long after he got there. In gratitude, the State of Indiana had erected a monument to him, the first such monument to a Native America erected in the state.

South Bend was an hour away, so I figured I would complete the circuit and stop there. In addition to living and working there for many years, I would on occasion go watch Buzz play football at Notre Dame. He was on the undefeated team in 1973 that beat Alabama in the Sugar Bowl to win the national championship. That year, he got me a seat for the last home game versus Air Force, then invited me to the big post-game party, where I rubbed elbows with a host of luminaries, including the Golden Boy himself, Paul Hornung, who had been my favorite football player growing up. Buzz even introduced me to him and told him I played football for Wallace College. Somewhat to my surprise, instead of laughing, or saying, "Where's that", the Golden Boy said he was familiar with Wallace and knew they had some good teams, including the only team that beat Notre Dame in South Bend from 1900 to 1928. He asked me about what position I played and generally seemed interested. I was ten feet off the ground. I found out years later, from Beth, that Buzz had just met the former Heisman Award winner and NFL MVP himself that night, and told him I was a huge fan, and gave him the tidbit about Wallace. That was the kind of thing Buzz would do.

I drove to the campus and walked around a bit. The Irish were away, in Florida, playing Miami, so the campus, which would normally have been a scene of bedlam on a fall Saturday, was subdued. I went by the stadium and even sat in silence in the chapel for a few minutes. I thought maybe some divine guidance could come in handy when I returned home.

CHAPTER 26

I got in the car and drove to Highway 30 west and headed back to Prairie Stop. It had been dark for an hour when I got into my neighborhood. I took the precaution of parking several blocks away from the house and cut through the yards to a spot where I knew I could see the front of my house. There was a car there that I was sure was an unmarked police vehicle. Hanlen hadn't been kidding when he said he would have me taken in.

The police car was going to be a problem. I needed things in the house and wasn't sure I could find them in the dark. I figured there was only one officer in the car, but I still needed to arrange some distraction so I could get in the house for at least fifteen minutes.

I looked down the street and noticed a flickering light coming from the garage of the juvenile delinquent brothers. I went back the way I came, crossed the street quickly and made my way over to their house. The light had been coming from their video game monitor. Thin tendrils of smoke wafted out into the luminosity of a flood lamp mounted on the roof of the garage.

"You guys really need some new hobbies," I said as I stood in the doorway. It looked like the same crew as before, with the omission of Eddie.

"What the hell you want, man?" came from the older brother.

"First, I want to apologize for the other day. I said things I now regret. That's what happens when you don't count to ten before you speak. Second, I would like to offer you fellows an opportunity to make some money."

"Fuck off." This time from the younger brother.

"I mean it. Fifty bucks."

"What do we got to do?" asked one of the other ones.

"Shut up," said the older brother.

"Real simple. There is a guy parked in front of my house. He wants to talk to me, bad. I don't want to talk to him, equally as bad. But I need to get in my house for a few minutes. So therein lies the dilemma. I'd like you guys to maybe distract him for me."

They exchanged glances.

"Why don't you just kick his ass?"

"I like your thinking. Direct and to the point. Unfortunately, he's a cop. Kicking his ass could be problematic."

"You want to give us a few bucks to get arrested? You got to be kidding."

"Who said anything about getting arrested? Toss some eggs at the car. When he gets out, yell an obscenity of your choice. I wouldn't use 'pig', though."

"Yeah, so he gets out of the car and we get arrested."

"No, that won't happen. He'll figure he can handle a few kids and won't call it in. You run in different directions. And, chances are, he's a forty-year old guy with a paunch. No way can he catch any of you. Just keep yelling. When he gives up, come back here, and go to sleep."

I could see them looking at each other.

"Make it hundred bucks and we'll do it."

They had me over a barrel.

"You got a deal," I said. "I'll give you $60 now. When you get back, there will be another $40 under the welcome mat on the front porch. If you keep him away from my house for twenty minutes, or more, there will be another $20 when I see you next. Don't worry, I'm good for it."

It wasn't a well thought out plan, but it worked. I worked my way over near my house and waited until I heard the splat of raw eggs hitting the police car. It seemed a couple minutes before there was a reaction, and I took the opportunity to edge closer to the back door. Then I heard the slam of the car door and saw a beam of a flashlight flitting in different directions. I heard yelling from several different directions. I wasn't sure what they were saying, but I did hear an adult voice in a commanding tone shout, "You goddam kids, get back here!"

There were a slew of messages on my answering machine. Several from Kathy and Ivan Rich, and even one from Bill Hanlen. I was surprised that there weren't any from Buzz.

I hurried down into the basement where I kept my .38 locked in a cabinet. I tossed some clothes into a bag and was out of the house in under twenty minutes. There was still yelling in the streets when I got to my car and drove off.

CHAPTER 27

South of downtown, in a not particularly nice area, there was a small, cheap motel which was used mainly be those desiring a short romantic getaway. They rented rooms by the hour, with a discount for cash. They were not too particular about getting your license plate number, and the TV had free adult movies, twenty- our hours a day, whether you wanted them or not. I got a room there. After I checked in called Ivan Rich at his home.

"Where the hell have you been?" he asked. "I've been trying to reach you for the last twenty-four hours."

"Nice to hear from you, too," I said.

"Well?"

"I was taking a trip down memory lane."

"I hope it was a good one. Hanlen is looking for you, and you are in deep shit if you don't come in. There have been some big developments in the Matthews' case while you were out traipsing around."

"I figured as much."

"By the way, thanks for your help making me look bad for the chief."

"You don't need my help to look bad, Ivan."

"Screw you."

"Are you going to tell me what's been going on? Did you find Matthews?" I asked.

"No, in fact we may never him turn up, seeing as how the guy who killed him is dead too."

"What are you talking about?"

"We tracked Phil Parker down a few hours after you found Matthews' car at his garage. After a little persuasion, he gave us a place where he thought his nephew might be hiding. It's an old cabin up in the woods by Hickory Pond, about ten miles off Route 6."

"And he was there?"

"Yeah, he was there alright. Only problem was, he wasn't breathing anymore."

"Somebody killed him?"

"In a manner of speaking, he killed himself. There was a kerosene stove that he used for the heat. Apparently, the vent pipe was fouled. He died of carbon monoxide poisoning. Looked like he's been dead for a few days at least, although the coroner can't say for sure yet."

"That's damn convenient, don't you think, Ivan?"

"Yeah, well, sometimes accidents happen. Everybody knows those old stoves are dangerous. Anyhow, Matthews' wallet was in the cabin. We figured he might have lured Matthews somewhere, killed him, got rid of the body, and then hid the car at his uncle's garage."

Then his voice got sheepish.

"I got to hand it to you, Logan," he said. "If you hadn't found out about Parker we'd still be at square one."

"I can't see Mike Parker killing Matthews. I don't think the motivation is there. He didn't want to go back to jail."

"Matthews was seeing his wife."

"That's another thing. They had broken it off."

"Look, the guy was an ex-con with a bad temper." Ivan was sounding annoyed.

"That doesn't mean he killed anybody," I said.

"Dammit, Logan, we—I mean, you—found this guy. Now you're saying he isn't the guy?"

"I'm not sure what I'm saying."

"Well, as far as the chief is concerned, this case is over. But he still wants your ass downtown. Oh yeah, one other thing."

"What's that?"

"I found out what you wanted. You know, the background on Jackie Matthews."

CHAPTER 28

I found a number for an R. Parker in the phone book. A voice I didn't recognize answered.

"May I speak to Roseanne Parker, please?"

"I'm sorry, she can't come to the phone right now."

"I know now is not a good time, and I apologize, but it's very important that I speak with her. I'm calling from the County Prosecutor's Office."

"Haven't you people done enough?"

I heard a voice in the background say, "Mother, wait", then Roseanne was on the line.

"Who is this?"

"Roseanne, this is Logan Wells. From the store the other day."

A pause. "You got balls calling me."

"I'm sorry about what happened," I said. "Believe me, I am."

"Mike didn't kill anybody. I don't care what anybody says."

"I don't think he did either, if it means anything."

There was a pause.

"And you might be able to help me clear his name. I know that doesn't seem like much, but maybe it will someday, to your son."

There was no response.

"How do I do that?" Roseanne asked quietly.

"When we talked the other day, I had the feeling you were leaving something out. This is very important. Did you talk with Mike at all anytime in the last two weeks?"

I could sense the hesitation.

"I can't do anything unless you help me," I said.

"Alright. He called around ten days ago and said he had come into some money. Said he was going to be getting some more. He said he would have enough that we could all go away together."

"Did he say how he got the money?"

"A big favor for a friend was all he said. I didn't want to hear talk like that, because usually when Mike talks about doing favors, it means doing something against the law."

CHAPTER 29

I called over to Buzz's house and his mother answered. She seemed glad to hear from me. We chatted for a few minutes, then I asked her where Buzz was.

"He said he still had a few things to do up at the lake house, so he drove up this morning. I'm over here with the dog."

"When did he say he was coming back?" I asked.

"He said tomorrow was supposed to be nice, so he was going to stay until evening. Is it important that you need to reach him, Logan?"

"Nope, not at all. Please don't tell him I called. I'll catch up with him when he gets back."

The next morning, I was up early. We finally got another nice fall day, probably one of the last ones for the year. There were some clouds, but the sun was out and the temperature was supposed to be in the high 50's.

The interstates weren't crowded on Sunday morning and I made good time getting to South Haven. The Wildrick family summer home, which formerly belonged to Beth's dad, was located outside of South Haven proper. Some upscale vacation communities had been built recently closer to the city, but Buzz's place was still in an area that had not been developed. The homes out his way were older and each property owner had several acres, so the homes were not sitting right on top of each other.

There was a private drive off the main road that led up to the Wildrick house. It was several hundred yards long and wove its way through some dense woods. I pulled the car off about halfway to the house, and then walked the rest of the way in.

When I finally caught sight of Lake Michigan, I paused for a second to take in its enormous expanse. The lake always looked cleaner and bluer the further north you went. The clouds earlier had melted away, which magnified the intensity and vastness of the lake.

Buzz's home sat up high on a promontory and the view of the lake and surrounding woods was stunning. A light breeze kicked up a few small whitecaps and there were a few small sailboats far out, but other than that, nothing disturbed the lake's tranquility.

The house had been just a big cottage when it was built, but Beth's dad as well as Buzz had added on to it a number of times, so it could accommodate more guests. Now it was more of a compound than a house, additions to the house spreading out in all directions. The front door was unlocked, and I walked in. I heard music playing faintly somewhere towards the lake side of the house, so I walked back in that direction.

One of the additions had been an enclosed glass porch which extended well out from the side of the house, supported by steel piers from the main house. Even on a cool day, if the sun was out, the porch would be more than comfortable, and it was a favorite place to view sunsets. I figured that's where the music was coming from. When I walked out onto the porch I saw someone lying on chaise reading a magazine. When I got closer, I saw it was Jackie Matthews. She was wearing a very short pair of cutoff grey sweat bottoms and nothing else.

I looked down at her. She made no move to cover herself.

"Why, Logan, how nice to see you."

"Likewise, I'm sure."

"What a lovely day, don't you think? Hard to believe its November." She put the magazine down and languidly stretched her arms over her head.

"I love the view from here, don't you?"

"Absolutely."

"Buzz didn't tell me you were coming up."

"I wanted to surprise him."

"How nice. I hope you can you stay for lunch. I've got some fresh shrimp and linguine. And a nice bottle of chardonnay chilling."

"Sounds good. We should check with Buzz on that first. When he hears what I got to say, he may not be in the mood for company. It's about your husband."

Now she reached to the floor by the chaise and picked up a BHU sweatshirt and put it on.

"My husband? You have some news, then?"

"Not good, I'm afraid."

She didn't change expression.

"You don't seem too broken up," I observed.

"Jason wasn't a well man, physically or mentally. I told you that. I had a feeling something bad might happen. I guess I have been preparing myself for it over the last days."

"Yeah. It had to have been a difficult situation for you. All those years together."

"I'm not sure what you are implying."

"Tell me, do you think he knew about you and Buzz?"

"I really don't care to talk to you anymore."

"Fair enough. Where's Buzz?"

"Maybe you should go."

"I know this house like the back of my hand. If you don't tell me, it will just take me a little longer to find him."

She hesitated.

"Down on the dock," she said reluctantly.

"I'll just run along down there then."

I turned back before I got to the door.

"Oh, by the way, congratulations," I said.

"On what?"

"You're expecting, aren't you?"

"How did you know that?"

"Just a lucky guess."

CHAPTER 30

You had to go down about thirty steep concrete steps to get to the dock and small beach. I went down slowly, leaning heavily on the railing, my ankle still feeling the aftermath of my excursion at Porter's Farm the other day. Buzz was below on his knees with his back turned toward me, applying some sealer to the dock. There was a can of Hamm's and a radio beside him. Dave Mason was singing "All Along the Watchtower".

"You missed a spot," I said.

He didn't startle when I spoke. He stopped what he was doing, got up slowly and wiped his hands on his workpants. He didn't say anything.

"I kind of like Dylan's version better," I said. "More elemental. How about you?"

"Me? I always liked Hendrix," he said, reaching for the beer. "Somebody told me once the only way to understand that song was to get high and listen to Hendricks doing it."

"I'll have to try that sometime," I said. "Not sure where I could get any grass, though."

"Hang around a school, I guess," Buzz said. "I didn't know you were coming up. I would have got some more beer."

"That's ok, I can't stay long."

Buzz looked up at the house.

"You saw I've got company."

"Yeah. You heard what's been going on?"

"I talked with Bill last night. He said they figured out what happened. Thanks to you."

"What did Hanlen say?"

"That the girlfriend's ex killed Matthews."

"I don't think he did, Buzz."

"Hanlen seems to think so."

"He's a fit, but not a good fit."

"Who's a better one?"

"You."

Buzz rubbed the stubble of his beard.

"You're kidding, right?" he asked.

"Wish I was. Him and maybe Parker too."

"Now, that is something. I like Hanlen's idea better."

"I can see why."

"Tell me how it happened, then," he said.

"Alright. I'm sketchy on the details, but here goes. You were having an affair with Jackie Matthews. Her husband knows about it but isn't sure what to do. He probably figures if he demands she end it, she is just going to leave him. Then he decides to confront the both of you. That was the night you picked her up at her hotel in Chicago and drove up here. I'm not exactly sure how, well, I think I know, but Matthews finds out you are here and shows up. Gives you an ultimatum. Leave my wife alone or else. The or else being him tossing a big wrench in the plans for the new mall. You can't afford that. Not just the plans falling through, but any delay increases the chance that some questionable finances related to the deal are going to be exposed."

"Questionable finances?"

"You and Coban were buying property, and then flipping it at greatly inflated prices."

"Most people refer to that as land speculation, and last I heard, it wasn't against the law."

"If you were bribing somebody, maybe it is. I heard the Feds are looking into it."

"I heard that too. Doesn't mean it's true. Anyhow, go on."

"For the record, I don't think you meant to hurt Matthews. Who knows? Maybe he took a swing at you. Or maybe the excitement got to him and he had a heart attack. You probably know he wasn't in real good shape. Anyhow, he's dead and you panic. You get rid of the body, probably out there," I said, pointing out at Lake Michigan.

"You call your former client, Mike Parker, and get him to dispose of Matthews' car," I continued. "I'm guessing Parker figured out what was going and tried to shake you down. So you arrange an accident for him. Then I find the rather obvious link between Parker and the professor. So now Matthews is out of the picture, and Hanlen has a suspect, who conveniently happens to be dead. A few more months go by, you divorce Beth, Jackie Matthews gets her insurance money, and everybody lives happily ever after."

I looked at him.

"Was I close?"

He shrugged his shoulders.

"Like I tell people, you were the best detective the county had," he said.

I didn't say anything, feeling he wanted to tell me what happened. He did.

"We were careful, but he found out about Jackie and me. It wasn't anything at first, just sex really, but then Beth left. There wasn't a whole lot left in her marriage either."

"That's why they invented divorce."

"Matthews wasn't going to go for that. Aside from that, Jackie had a lot to lose, financially, if she got divorced. A lot of his assets were tied up in trust that wouldn't go to her as long as he was alive. He wasn't in good shape. I know it sounds bad, but we thought we could wait him out."

"That was considerate of you."

"Yeah. Then I guess he gets the idea that the mall development was the hammer he could use to get rid of me. He seemed to have the idea if he stopped that, it would be my downfall. I wasn't the one he had to worry about … it was Coban. He didn't like people getting in his way."

"What happened?"

"You're right, Matthews shows up here. How he knew we were here, I got no idea. He was pretty worked up. I thought maybe he was going to blow an artery. Tells me to stay away from his wife, and he is never going for a divorce. Says he's got something now that will delay the mall development until the next century."

"What did you say?"

"Not much. I told him Jackie didn't want to be married to him anymore, and nothing was going to change that. When I said that, he lost it."

"How so?"

"He was lugging this big plastic garbage bag with him. You aren't going to believe this, but he reaches into it pulls out a sword. I thought he was going to try and cut my head off."

"You know that was the sword he had been trying to find. The one the British general gave Tecumseh."

"I figured as much. I have to give the old bastard credit. I thought that story was hokum."

"Then what happened?"

"He came at me. What the hell was I supposed to do? I grabbed his arms, but he was stronger than I thought, so I gave him a shove. He went back against the wall but came at me again. I tried to take his legs out, so I went low and hit him around the knees. He fell but he was still holding the sword. Went right through his middle. When I turned him over, I could see he was in bad shape."

"It was self-defense at the point, Buzz."

"There was enough lawyer in me to know. But then Jackie came into the room. I told her what happened and that we needed to get help. She looked over at Matthews, then got me up and sat me on the couch. She kneeled in front of me and said, very calmly, 'We aren't going to do that.' She said that there were no witnesses and there wasn't going to be anyone who would believe me."

"And you went along with her?"

"She said that even if no charges were filed, I would be ruined. I didn't doubt that. If someone shone a spotlight on me, some of that stuff I was doing with Coban was going to come out. It would have all worked out if the mall was built. But Coban was starting to have second thoughts. He was worried about what Matthews was doing."

"You two let him die."

"For what it's worth, not sure he would have made it anyhow."

"So you say. Go on."

"We took his wallet and keys and rolled him up in the rug. Dragged it down to the boat. Went out a few miles and weighed it down with an old anchor." He looked out at the lake. "I suppose I should sell this place."

"What about Mike Parker?"

"I knew he could get rid of a car. For some reason, probably because I defended him before, he thought we were pals. I told him ditching the car was part of an insurance scam for a client. I gave him a couple grand to take it and told him he could keep everything he got from selling it."

"But then he got greedy?" I asked.

"Yeah. I guess he reads the papers and put two and two together. Said he wasn't sure how easy it would be to ditch the car. He asked for more money. I told him I would bring it to him. Have a few drinks. He was hiding out in some shithouse out in the middle of nowhere. He had been drinking heavy before I got there, and we had a few more together. When he wasn't looking, I slipped something in his. We had a lot of drugs in the house on account of Beth. After he passed out, I tossed more wood on the stove, climbed up on the roof and wrapped my jacket around the stove pipe. It didn't take long. I left Matthew's wallet there."

"Did Coban have anything to do with any of this?"

"No, except sending those two Chicago cops out to rough you up. He didn't exactly appreciate me hiring you."

"I don't understand why you did that, Buzz. Ivan Rich is no Sherlock Holmes, but he would have eventually stumbled on the link between Matthews and Parker on his own. So why me?"

"Good question." We both looked up to see Jackie Matthews on the concrete steps. She was holding a gun up in both hands, pointed in my general direction. I recognized it as a .45 Colt which had been Beth's father's service weapon in the war. He used it scare off the coyotes which sometimes stalked the family poodle. Once Buzz and I borrowed it for target practice, and when her dad found out he really gave us hell.

"I don't think you are going to use that, even if you know how," I said. I wasn't as confident as I sounded.

"She knows how, Logan. Showed her myself. Did I tell you a couple months ago a hunter claimed he saw a black bear over at the Allegan game area? Who would have figured bears this far south?"

"It was my idea, actually," Jackie said. "Hiring you, I mean. I thought it would help convince the authorities I didn't know what happened to my husband and wanted him back. I admit, now it seems to have backfired."

Buzz stepped away from me.

"Aim that somewhere else, honey. Don't want anyone to get hurt by mistake."

She lowered the weapon slightly.

"Say, Logan, speaking of guns, I'm thinking you wouldn't have come up here unarmed. You always were the type to be prepared for anything. I'd appreciate if you would take off your jacket and drop it on the ground. Slow, if you don't mind."

I took off my jacket and tossed it on the ground. Buzz reached down and found the .38 in the jacket pocket. He looked to make sure the safety was on and tucked it in his waist band.

"That's better. Now we can discuss this like adults."

Jackie Matthews came down another step, still holding the gun in firing position, but the muzzle pointing downward.

She spoke slowly and deliberately. "Buzz, I want you to listen carefully to what I'm going to say. Logan didn't come up here just to satisfy his curiosity. He's going to go back and tell Hanlen everything."

"I guess there's that, then," Buzz said. "I've given it a lot of thought, Logan. I'm in bad way here, but I can't go to jail. How would you feel about forgetting the whole thing?"

"You're kidding, right?" Jackie asked incredulously.

"He's my best friend, Jackie. We can trust him."

"You think this is sixth grade and he saw you throw an eraser?"

"Tell her how we are, Logan. All the stuff we've been through together."

"Can't do it, Buzz. Even for old-times sake."

"I'm not proud of what I've done, Logan, but way I look at it, I figured I answered for all past and future transgressions when my son dropped dead on a football field."

"It doesn't work like that. One doesn't cancel out the other."

"In my book, it does," Buzz said.

"Ok. But you don't think if something happens to me, Hanlen is going to suspect something?"

"Nothing is going to happen to you. We can work something out."

Jackie Matthews moved down two steps.

"Do you want to tell him or should I?" I asked, looking at her.

Very slowly, a small smile appeared on her face. "Why don't you tell him? It would be more interesting that way. For me, anyhow."

"Tell me what?" Buzz looked both puzzled and annoyed. I looked at her again.

"I may be sketchy on the details."

"Oh, you'll do fine. Buzz was right. You are good at what you do," she said, almost grinning now.

"For Christ's sake! Find out what?" Buzz exclaimed. "Somebody better start doing some explaining to me, and I mean now."

"Sure, Buzz," I said. "You remember Ted Franz? One of your first cases, I believe. We talked about it the other day, albeit briefly. Remember the details? A sad outcome ... the young man killed himself rather than go to prison."

"I remember. What does that have to do with any of this?"

"A lot, really. You see, your friend Jackie here is Ted's little sister."

"That's not possible."

"It's not just possible, it's fact. She was going by her mother's surname when she started at BHU, so nobody knew the connection. But she is his sister. The rest of this I can't prove, at least right now, but I'm reasonably sure Jackie is responsible for the recent demises of your ex -boss, Tomansini, along with old Judge Garrison. She got you to get rid of her husband for her. Those three, along with you, were the four individuals who were primarily responsible for her brother being convicted. So that just leaves you. And probably me. But I'm just collateral damage."

"You're nuts. What the hell is the motive?"

"If I had to guess, I'd say to get even."

"I didn't think I would ever say this, Logan, but you're paranoid. The car that hit you must have scrambled your brain. You got conspiracy theories coming out the wazoo."

"Do you think it's just a coincidence that she was married to Jason Matthews and having an affair with you? By the way, how do you figure Matthews shows up here out of the blue?"

Buzz looked at Jackie.

"Tell him he's crazy. You didn't kill anybody," he said to her.

"I didn't kill anybody," she responded, then smiled.

"That didn't sound real sincere to me. How about you, Buzz?"

"But why now, all after almost fifteen years?" Buzz was looking at her in astonishment.

"I wasn't in any hurry. Ever hear the expression that revenge is a dish best served cold?" Her voice had a distinctly different tone than when I interviewed her at her house, or even when I just talked to her a few minute ago. A harsh, cruel, tone.

"I think they used that line in Star Trek. Not sure if it was the TV series or one of the movies," I said.

"Always with the wisecracks," Jackie said. "It's good you can be true to form, even to the end."

"That one had me puzzled too, Buzz," I said. "I think I know now. She's pregnant. I assume by you ... her husband had some problems along those lines. She couldn't keep putting off the dénouement to her long-term plan to settle the score for her brother. Be a little hard tampering with someone's brakes or hitting an old man over the head with oar when you are lugging a kid with you. It's not like daddy is going to be around to help out."

Jackie Matthews gave a cold laugh. "Funny, I had been considering letting Buzz live, for a while, to help out with the baby. Unfortunately, Logan, you have forced my hand. Anyway, my brother would have been out of prison this year, if he had lived. Perhaps the timing is right."

"You're a psychopath, lady," I said.

"Oh, no, definitely not a psychopath, at least from a legal standpoint. I understand clearly the difference between right and wrong. What those four men did to my brother was wrong. You see, my brother took care of me when I was little, when my father disappeared, and my mother was forever passed out on the couch. He looked out for me when no one else did. He didn't do anything except protest a senseless act of violence and they were going to lock him up for fifteen years. And he was so scared by that he ended his own life. You seriously don't think that was justice, do you?"

"No, but how does killing five men make it right?" I asked.

"Don't be naïve. Justice isn't about making things right. Justice is when those who have committed a wrong are made to suffer the consequences of their actions. That's the essence of justice, Logan. Wrong is punished. Those who would take a life lose their own lives. I believe I owe my brother that much, don't you?"

I couldn't think of anything to say.

"I will take your silence as a yes. Now, Buzz, if you wouldn't mind, please put Logan's pistol onto the dock. Don't want to use a cliché, but if you try anything funny, I'll shoot you."

Buzz slowly took my .38 from his waistband and dropped it to the deck at his feet.

"You know, Buzz," she said, "I was just thinking. Everybody knows Logan has been despondent lately. The accident, health problems, losing his job, has really brought him down. You shouldn't have piled more stress on him by asking him to get involved with Jason's disappearance. Probably pushed him over the edge. That's when he came up here."

"Even Hanlen is going to see through that," I said. "Especially after what happened to Parker."

"Don't do this, Jackie," Buzz pleaded.

"The question is who first. Your thoughts on that, Logan?"

"In your scenario, I think it would have to be me," I said.

She nodded approvingly. "That's what I thought too. I heard yelling, came down to the dock and saw you and Buzz fighting. As, I just said, you have been acting irrationally. You had some crazy notion that Buzz killed my husband. I had the foresight to bring Buzz's pistol with me and was able to shoot you. Unfortunately, you discharged your own weapon right after I shot you, and hit Buzz. A regrettable tragedy, certainly, but a most believable one, don't you think?"

She abruptly brought the gun up and pulled the trigger. Out of the corner of my eye, I saw Buzz move at the instant before she fired. He always had super quick reflexes. He hit me with enough force to knock me off my feet.

Buzz was between me and Jackie. He was holding his right hand over his chest.

"So that's what that feels like." He slowly began to sink to his knees.

"Goddamit!" Jackie cried out.

She fired again, but since Buzz was partially blocking me, the shot went over me. I did a crablike shuffle for my .38, which was less than four feet away. She got off another shot, this one hitting the dock right next to my head. Some splinters from the dock burned into my forehead. Immediately blood began to drip down into my eyes. I felt a searing pain as her third shot hit me in the left shoulder. I had the .38 now, but I could barely see.

They tell you to always aim low because there is a natural tendency to shoot higher than the target. I over-compensated, because I was having trouble seeing but it was a lucky shot and I hit her just above the left knee. She staggered and stayed up for a second, but then her leg buckled and she fell down the last few steps of the landing and hit the dock hard. The .45 went off as she fell but it was aimed skyward. I quickly got up and got her gun. She was dazed from the fall and the leg was already bleeding bad, but I figured if she got medical attention soon she would survive.

I went to Buzz. He was now on his side and a trickle of blood was running out of the corner of his mouth. He seemed to be struggling for breath.

"Always the goddam hero," I admonished him.

"What can I say? It goes with the territory." He was having trouble talking.

"How is she?"

"She'll make it. Need to get her to a hospital"

"Closest hospital is in South Haven."

"Yeah." I tried to raise him up to make it easier to breath.

"How about you? She get you?"

"Yeah, but I'll live."

"I wouldn't hurt you."

"Quit talking."

"I should have known something bad was going to happen when Notre Dame got their ass kicked by Miami yesterday," he said, now with half smile.

"I told you to quit talking. I'm going up to the house and call for help."

"Listen. I want you to get me close to the end of the dock. I'll take care of it from there."

"No."

"Don't make me kick your ass."

He was almost pleading now.

"Do this last thing for me, Logan."

I looked up at the cloudless sky, and then out over the lake. I thought of a similar fall day years ago when Buzz and I were walking home from high school and two small boys in the distance saw Buzz. They shouted out his name, in spontaneous burst of recognition and adulation. And the way Buzz turned, smiled, and slowly raised his arm in acknowledgment of the greeting.

Then I reached under Buzz's shoulders and started to pull him toward the end of the dock.

CHAPTER 31

A light snow was falling as I walked into the Lincoln. They had Christmas lights up behind the bar, and a small plastic Christmas tree was perched on top of the cash register. Rather than cheery, it seemed to make the place more depressing. I was running late, but a quick look told me that Ivan hadn't arrived yet. The place was empty except for an elderly couple in one of the booths.

I didn't recognize the bartender, a short plump brunette who looked about fifty. She gave me a tired smile when she approached.

"Hi, I'm Shirley. What can I get you?"

"A draft is fine. You pick."

"We have two for one on Old Style until seven." I looked at my watch and noted with satisfaction I had almost forty-five minutes in which to get completely sloshed.

"Old Style it is. Throw in a shot of chilled Bushmills. Better make it a double since I'm getting two beers. I don't like to be out of balance. Besides, I'm in celebratory mood."

"Sure. What's the occasion?"

"It's snowin' out."

"Good as reason as any."

When she brought the beer, I asked her if Pam had the night off. Her face clouded.

"Pam quit a couple weeks ago. A good friend of hers died. She really took it hard. She thinks she is going to move back to Florida." She shrugged her shoulders. " At least the weather is nice there."

I felt the blood rush to my head and felt dizzy.

"You OK?" Shirley asked.

"Yeah. I was just thinking of the last time I was here."

I raised the shot glass. "A toast to Pam, then. Good luck to her."

The door swung open and Ivan walked in. He sat down heavily on the stool next to me, and very uncharacteristic of him, put his arm around me then awkwardly patted me on the back.

"How are you doing, Logan?"

"I'm OK. Thanks for asking." I looked at him closer. "You looked like you dropped some pounds."

"Yeah. Me and the wife decided we need to lose some weight. Well, actually is was the doctor's idea. He said I wouldn't reach fifty if I didn't lose fifty pounds."

"Catchy advice. How's that going?"

"Hardest thing I've ever done. I like to eat."

I choked back a "You don't say". Shirley came over and Ivan asked for a light beer. When it arrived, Ivan took a sip, then looked at me.

"You sure stirred up a shit storm," Ivan said.

"Yeah, I've been reading the papers."

Logan raised his right hand and began ticking off a list with his fingers.

"Coban and six union officials indicted for fraud and misappropriation." A finger down.

"The new mall project shot down in flames." Another finger down.

"Two members of the county council, who were the biggest proponents of the mall, resigning. No evidence to suggest they did anything improper, just embarrassed all to hell." Another finger down.

"Investigations opened into the deaths of former prosecutor Tomansini and old Judge Garrison." Another finger down.

"It's good to shake the tree once in a while see what falls out," I observed, with what I hoped was a sage tone in my voice.

He gave me a look. "Who are you kidding? You didn't just shake the tree, you chopped it down."

"Good thing Jackie Matthews confessed," he continued, "cause we probably still don't have much in the way of physical evidence. Not for Buzz of course, but for the others. That's one diabolical lady."

"Why did she confess, you figure?"

"I dunno. Maybe she was proud of what she did and wanted everybody to know about it."

"What do you think will happen to her?"

"Hard to say. She's on the hook for three murders and accessory to two others, but I think the story of her brother is going get her enough sympathy to dodge the needle. Plus, she's going to have a baby. No way they are going to send a pregnant woman to death row. Why do you figure a psycho like that got pregnant in the first place?"

"Maybe that was part of her plan."

"How so?"

"For the reason you just mentioned. It's going to buy her some sympathy. She gets a few women on the jury and who knows? She's an attorney and pretty smart. They may let her out after twenty years. She waited almost that long to get even for brother. I could see a jury letting her off easy."

Ivan grinned after I said that.

"What's so funny?"

"I got a joke about a goat, a lawyer and jury that will make you laugh your ass off, but its not for mixed company," he said, nodding at Shirley, who had her back to us. "Of course, Mrs. Matthews did knock off a former judge and prosecutor, which may not count much in her favor."

"Buzz always liked intelligent women." I don't know why I blurted that out.

"Well, I know he was your best friend and all, but have to tell you, it was lucky for him he didn't make it. The coroner said he must have had the strength of an ox to drag himself off that end of that dock like that, being shot like he was and all. You don't know anything about that, do you?"

"I'd gone up to the house to call for help."

"Yeah, whatever. Anyhow, the life of an ex-cop or prosecutor in prison isn't a pleasant one, I hear.

"Buzz wouldn't have been afraid of prison," I said. "In six months he would have been running the place. He was afraid of the fall from grace."

"Fall from grace, huh? It that how you refer to somebody who kills two guys?"

"You're right, maybe he was more like Achilles. Shot in the heel with a poisoned arrow made of lust and greed."

"You're acting kind of weird, Logan, you know that?"

We sat in silence for a minute.

"Feel bad for his girls, though," Ivan said. "He had two girls, right? I heard the mother is selling the house and taking the girls to Florida. They weren't even able to have a proper funeral for him because of the scandal."

"Yeah, two girls," I said.

"Speaking of girls, it's all of over town that you're hanging around with your high school flame."

I laughed in spite of myself. "All over town? You sound like Old Man Potter."

"Who's Old Man Potter?"

"Don't tell my you've never seen '*It's a Wonderful Life*'."

"I've seen it. I just didn't memorize it."

"I doubt if anyone in town knows or cares that I'm seeing Kathy Plemmons. Now if it was Gloria Grahame, that would be a story. Talk about scandal. Did you know she married her own step-son?"

Ivan shook his head. "I have no idea what the hell you are talking about."

"See, actress Gloria Grahame played Violet Bick in the movie. That's who Potter was talking about it being all over town. George Bailey and Violet Bick."

"You're losing it, Logan. I know you've been through a lot lately. Maybe you should seek counseling."

"Sorry, I think the booze must be going to my head."

"Yeah? Here's a tip for you. Don't drive down Campbell tonight after 10. There's going to be a sobriety checkpoint at the old high school. Although they might cancel if it keeps snowing."

"Thanks. Can I mention your name if I get pulled over?"

"Go ahead, but I'm going to deny I ever heard of you. Oh, the last thing. Keep this under your hat, but word is Hanlen is going to step down."

"I could see that coming," I said.

He gave me a sly look. "And double secret, hope to die, but I'm thinking I might toss my hat into the ring."

The words "you got to be kidding me" were just about to leave my mouth, but I managed to keep them there.

"Gee, that's great Ivan. I wish you a lot of luck. You got my vote. I can't think of anyone more qualified than you." I've found that once you tell one lie to someone and they believe you, they are probably going to believe subsequent ones, so you might as well pile it on.

"I appreciate that, Logan. By the way, once I get in, if you want to come back, let me know. We can probably work something out. I could use a guy like you."

"Thanks. I'll keep that in mind."

"No problem." He slapped me on the back.

"Got to get home and eat my lean chicken breast and carrot sticks and all the other healthy crap. Good to see you. Stay in touch." He sounded like he was already running for office.

We shook hands and I watched him go out the door. I took my time finishing my drinks. Eventually, the other couple in the place left and it was just me and Shirley. She had put on a country station and Willie Nelson was singing "White Christmas". That reminded me that I had plans to meet Kathy for a late dinner, but she had called to cancel because her dad was a little out of sorts. I'm not sure I would have been good company anyhow.

The beer had gone through me quickly and I had to use the men's room before I left. In the back of the Lincoln, on one of the walls across from the booths, they had newspaper clippings and pictures of successful local athletes and teams. The BHU basketball team was prominently featured, several of the teams having reached the semi-finals of the NCAA small college basketball tournament back in the sixties. Beneath one of the basketball pictures, there was a picture of the high school football team which had won the state championship my senior year, when Buzz was team captain, most valuable player, and made all-state. I bent down and squinted in the dark o I could locate Buzz in the picture. Most of the team had intense or somber looks on their faces, apparently to convey the idea that playing football and winning a state championship was serious business. The coach, who bore a slight resemblance to Bela Lugosi, and who I never got along when I played, looked like he was pissed off about something. In contrast, Buzz, who was standing right next to him, had his usual irrepressible grin on his face. If you looked closely, his right hand was gripping the football in such a way that his middle finger was extended slightly. I laughed out loud. Buzz, at his zenith, giving the finger in team picture. His way of saying, you guys may take this stuff seriously, but I sure as hell don't. As I stared at him, I could have sworn I saw him wink at me.

ABOUT THE AUTHOR

After an overly long career in public finance, Mark took early retirement to pursue his lifelong dream of performing Barber's Adagio for Strings at Carnegie Hall. Mark soon realized that since he could not play violin, in fact, had never taken a lesson, this dream was probably not attainable. Not to be discouraged, he instead wrote a mystery novel. *The Sword of Tecumseh* is his first book.

Mark grew up in the Midwest and graduated from Franklin & Marshall College in Lancaster PA, where he was on the Dean's List and set a couple of school records while running on the track and cross-country teams. Mark lives in St. Louis MO with his wife Carol (yes, Carol Carroll) and dog Lucy. He still competes competitively in area road races as he works to finish the second Logan Wells mystery.